# PRAISE FOR MARK

MW01519531

"'Accidents' are intentional and the incidents are piling up… danger, murder, secrecy, a bit of romance, and down-to-the-wire, hold-your-breath anticipation."

> LINDA MARSHEELLS, LIBRARYTHING TOP
> 1% REVIEWER

*"Death in Nostalgia City* is a blast! It's a fascinating mystery set in a highly authentic world of '70s nostalgia – and the story works compellingly on both levels. It's an excellent read that's loaded with iconic touchstones of '60s-'70s pop culture."

> DICK BARTLEY, HOST OF RADIO'S THE
> CLASSIC COUNTDOWN AND ROCK & ROLL'S
> GREATEST HITS, MEMBER OF THE RADIO
> HALL OF FAME

"Bacon handles a complicated story well, giving us realistic characters in bad trouble. By the end of the book, he ties it all up in a satisfying conclusion. *Death in Nostalgia City* has good characters, a fast-moving story, complicated twists and a great climax."

> TODD BORG, BEST-SELLING AUTHOR OF
> THE *OWEN MCKENNA TAHOE MYSTERY
> SERIES*

"There is so much to love about this book. The characters are well developed, well rounded, and three dimensional. Both Lyle and Kate come into each other's lives and into the investigation with baggage. Kate has problems with commitments, Lyle with anxiety. They're realistic and easy to start caring and worrying about. The book pulled me in from the very beginning and never let me go."

OPEN BOOK SOCIETY

"A rollicking good read! It's a page turner, a fast-paced mystery... a winning collage of baby boomer fantasies and reminiscences."

ANN RONALD, BOOKIN' WITH SUNNY
REVIEWS

"Just as baby boomers love nostalgia and trivia, they will love *Death in Nostalgia City*. It's a twisty mystery set in a retro theme park in the Arizona desert. The fast-paced story travels to Boston and back as we meet a diverse blend of intriguing characters, all with something to hide. Reading this theme park thriller is more fun than winning a trivia contest and riding your favorite wooden coaster on the same day!"

WILSON CASEY, SYNDICATED COLUMNIST
AND GUINNESS WORLD RECORD
TRIVIA GUY

"Bacon is an excellent storyteller...readers won't be able to put this book down."

KAREN HANCOCK, SUSPENSE/THRILLER
EDITOR, *BELLA ONLINE*

"There isn't an ounce of fat in this novel. Bacon's prose is clean, crisp, and lightning fast. The plot moves like a theme park ride. *Death in Nostalgia City* is a spectacular read. The function of nostalgia—re-framing stressful times through a sepia lens—serves as the novel's clever subtext. Should conflicts of the past be reconciled, or simply glossed over with a comfortable, sanitized version of what never really was?"

*BRIAN KAUFMAN,* RABBIT HOLE REVIEWS

"How is the deliberate sabotage of a theme park connected to corporate blackmail, an Indian reservation, and murder? Mark S. Bacon takes us on a suspense-filled ride full of surprising discoveries. A read worth the ride!"

*SUSAN WHITFIELD,* AUTHOR OF *THE LOGAN HUNTER MYSTERIES*

"Bacon has written an entertaining crime novel full of action, intrigue and heart. With a pair of likable protagonists and a unique setting, this is one fast, fun ride. I want to visit Nostalgia City!"

*WENDY TYSON,* AUTHOR OF THE *ALLISON CAMPBELL MYSTERY SERIES*

### Desert Kill Switch

"…straight out of classical detective fiction…told at a fun, engine-revving pace."

*ELLERY QUEEN MYSTERY MAGAZINE*

"This is the kind of book where you keep saying 'just one more chapter.'"

"Bacon's prose is slick, his dialogue taut, and he makes great use of short chapters to tempt the reader to keep turning those pages. His creation of Nostalgia City, a retro theme park in which nothing older than 1975 is allowed, is a stroke of genius."

"This novel reaches out and grabs the reader from the beginning – from the car and bullet-riddled body disappearing to the non-stop action in Reno and Vegas. Lyle and Kate are both very likable people with whom readers can empathize… I highly recommend this delightful high-desert novel!"

"*Desert Kill Switch* weaves a fascinating mystery around murder, a missing body and a beautiful woman racing against time to clear her name. Antique cars and the threat of death in the desert combine to give readers a thrilling ride."

"If you like fast-paced mysteries, nasty characters, and enough twists and turns to keep you guessing to the end, this is a must read!"

LINDA TOWNSDIN, AUTHOR OF THE *SPIRIT LAKE MYSTERIES*

"This book is a gritty, fast-paced, and quick read; especially quick because it's difficult to put the book aside after reading the first few pages. The characters are engaging. The plot has plenty of twists and turns, lots of suspects and motives, and…a missing corpse."

*CHERIE JUNG*, OVERMYDEADBODY.COM

"[Bacon continues] his philosophical investigation of our relationship to the past, the roles, both positive and negative, that nostalgia plays in our emotional landscape. All of that is wrapped up in a rollicking murder mystery with two complex and appealing amateur sleuths and a frisson of romance."

*ALISON MCMAHAN*, AUTHOR OF *THE SAFFRON CROCUS*

"Mark. S. Bacon serves us a compelling second helping of mystery and mayhem in and around the fictional 1970's theme park, Nostalgia City. Readers will find themselves smiling and nodding in appreciation as twists and turns are revealed in the multi-layered mystery. The fast-paced plot-line is both creative and timely. I'm looking forward to the next installment!"

*CARRIE C. WOLFGANG*, NOVEL DESTINATION BOOK STORE, JAMESTOWN, NY

### The Marijuana Murders

"A death at the garage complex of Nostalgia City, an Arizona theme park that simulates an American town in the year 1975, propels Bacon's charming third Nostalgia City mystery (after *Desert Kill Switch*)...readers looking for escapist reading will be satisfied."

*PUBLISHERS WEEKLY*

"Bacon deftly blends nostalgia and crime. If you're looking for a mystery that touches on today's issues while harking back to earlier eras, *The Marijuana Murders* does so in a fast pace with humor and style."

*DEBBI MACK*, NEW YORK TIMES
BESTSELLING AUTHOR OF THE *SAM MCRAE MYSTERY SERIES*

"Through it all, Bacon keeps the pace fast-moving, the descriptions vivid, the setting unusual, the lead players interesting, the plot intriguing, and the surprises coming. You want more in a murder mystery?"

*DR. WESLEY BRITTON*, AUTHOR OF
*THE BETA-EARTH CHRONICLES*,
BOOKPLEASURES.COM

"Through finely developed characters and interesting plot twists, this murder mystery, set at Nostalgia City, thoroughly entertains!"

*BARRY SCOTT*, NATIONALLY SYNDICATED
OLDIES DJ

"Visit the Nostalgia City theme park where the 1970s are live and well and the murders are dope. Suspects are as plentiful as bellbottoms at the disco and the mystery as twisty as a vintage roller coaster."

*BECKY CLARK*, AUTHOR OF THE *MYSTERY WRITER'S MYSTERIES*

"I really enjoyed this delightful and well-done mystery. The characters are alive and sparkling and bring you right into the action. The murder and drug plots have twists and turns that will keep you guessing right into the final reveals.

*DOWARD WILSON*, KINGS RIVER LIFE

"An intriguing mystery that kept me engaged throughout. The investigation takes multiple turns, with red herrings and twists along the way."

CASSIDY'S BOOKSHELVES

"*The Marijuana Murders* is riddled with action and suspense. With mystery and secrets, it will keep you hooked trying to figure out whodunit. It's a fast paced read that will make you want more. I highly recommend *The Marijuana Murders*."

*NANCY ALLEN*, THE AVID READER.COM

# Dark Ride Deception

"A good mystery can always draw me in and completely captivate me. On top of an expertly crafted mystery, Bacon explores deep into many characters lives which adds multiple layers to the story."

*NOVEL NEWS NETWORK*

"Two mystery plots tantalize and interweave as chapters and sections alternate: Lyle sneaking his way to an answer, Kate finding her answers while she works to protect Nostalgia City's reputation. Of course, they are comparing notes, since they do have a relationship.

"Bacon's history of working with a Southern California amusement park (rhymes with "Dots Merry Charm") gives him an understanding of working in the park industry, and he provides realistic details for background. His previous books in the series give a confidence to the characters and pacing. *Dark Ride Deception* is a mystery thrill ride that, when I went to Disneyland in the Sixties, would have deserved an E-ticket."

*KINGS RIVER LIFE*

"Bacon's well-told mystery is clever, smooth, and intriguing, with a reluctant detective who has just the right touch of self-deprecating humor. The author's wry wit and engaging voice will keep you turning the pages of *Dark Ride Deception* until the very last satisfying twist."

*MARY ADLER*, AUTHOR OF THE *OLIVER WRIGHT WWII MYSTERY SERIES*

"What an ultimate thrill ride. It's so well put together, ingenious, and original. A unique premise that was very well executed makes for a great mystery read. Don't miss this one!"

"I don't think I was quite prepared to become so addicted and consumed by this story… I found the plot to be filled with mystery, drama, and much more."

"Theme park called Nostalgia City is almost as much of a unique character as the human characters. [It] adds a lot of out-of-the-ordinary places, people, and situations to this story…multiple threads keep things moving along at a fast pace."

"A thrilling mystery with plenty of twists and turns. I can definitely recommend this read."

"The characters were perfect for the story and I enjoyed the dual points of view… I will be going back to the beginning of the series to experience it.

# DARK RIDE DECEPTION

A **NOSTALGIA CITY**
MYSTERY #4

# MARK S. BACON

ARCHER & CLARK PUBLISHING

Genre: Mystery / Thriller

This is a work of fiction. Names, places, characters and incidents are either the product of the author's imagination or are used fictitiously, and any resemblance to any actual persons, living or dead, businesses, organizations, events or locales is entirely coincidental. All trademarks, service marks, registered trademarks, and registered service marks are the property of their respective owners and are used herein for identification purposes only. The publisher does not have any control over or assume any responsibility for third-party websites or their contents.

**DARK RIDE DECEPTION**

DARK RIDE (noun) /därk rīd/ An indoor amusement ride in which passengers travel in controlled vehicles and are typically entertained with music, vibrations, sounds, animation, and special effects.

# CHAPTER 1

The slender woman with the sad, blue-green eyes gasped, gagged, then threw up all over the back seat of Lyle's taxi. He took his foot off the gas and glanced in the back. All he could see was a mass of red hair as the woman bent down, head between legs. He rolled down his window, but not before the odor hit his nostrils like a sour tsunami. He breathed through his mouth as he hit the brakes at a red light.

Other cab drivers had warned him about nights like this. But he thought operating a taxi in a theme park would be fun, not at all like being the stereotyped big-city hack driver. Visiting Nostalgia City, a full-size re-creation of an entire small town from the 1970s, would put people in a vacation mood. They'd be happy. And the cab was an ideal escape from the grinding stress of his previous occupation.

"You okay?" he asked his passenger automatically, knowing she wasn't. He grabbed a handful of tissues from a box next to him and handed them back over his shoulder. The young redhead had looked a little unsteady when she got in the cab by herself in front of the Centerville Tavern and asked to be taken to the Desert Sunrise Hotel.

"S-sorry," she sputtered as she tried to sit up.

"Keep your head down. Breathe deep, slowly." Not unfamiliar with her condition, Lyle was certainly well beyond such excess now. Certainly.

He breathed through his mouth and wondered if the fragrance reached the tourists in the crosswalk in front of him. They took their time crossing the street, slowing to snap pictures of a Woolworth's store and a street-corner phone booth, their faces colored by the glow of neon-tube signs. Centerville, the park's '70s retro town, made you feel like you traveled back in time.

The stoplight changed and the driver behind Lyle honked. Maybe the park *wasn't* so far removed from real city life. The evening had been full of surprises.

Earlier, he'd picked up a middle-aged couple from the Fun Zone, the park's themed ride area, almost the size of a theme park itself. Both probably had been imbibing but not to the extent of his sick redhead. Lyle opened the trunk and offered to store the man's case, a cross between a doctor's bag and an oversized camera case, but he'd insisted he keep it with him. "Way too sensitive—I mean expensive," the man said. He clutched the case on his lap.

The couple—Lyle couldn't tell if they were married—had filled the few-minute ride with vituperation worthy of a baseball umpire and an irate manager. They argued about their choice of rides. The man had insisted they go on the Night of the Living Dead Ride, and his companion had been scared to death by the realistic, robotic zombies.

As they neared their hotel, the argument broadened to their decision to come to Nostalgia City in the first place. "Why'd you bring me along, anyway?" the woman shouted. "And why did you bring *that* with you? You're nutty, y'know?"

Lyle's authentic 1973 small-town taxi didn't wall in passengers behind Plexiglas. The woman's increasingly jumbled screams vibrated through the car as she waved her arms in the air. He glanced in the mirror and saw the man grab the woman's wrist and shout for her to quiet down. Her response increased the decibels in the car to a level slightly below a Led Zep concert.

A previous set of passengers had unnerved Lyle for different reasons. Three men got in the cab in the middle of Centerville and asked to be dropped off at the parking lot beyond the park's main gate. All three squeezed in the back. A beefy guy in a suit and knit shirt sat on the right. The man's square head rested on his shoulders like a concrete block. Lyle could feel him staring at the back of his head. A bearded man in the center, wearing jeans and a white dress shirt, kept looking from side to side at his companions. Lyle guessed him to be in his early thirties. He couldn't get a good look at the other man who sat behind the driver's seat.

"We're more than fair. You know it," the heavyset man said to his seatmate when Lyle got underway. "It'll work out easy."

"Besides the financial side," said the man behind Lyle, "there are other incentives. The work must be finished." Something in the man's low voice gave Lyle a chill.

The bearded man in the center said something, but Lyle lost the words when his cab's radio squawked out the voices of two drivers arguing over a fare. Lyle slowed at an intersection and when he had a chance to glance in the mirror, the man in the middle had his head down.

Lyle stopped at the last aisle in a dim corner of the parking lot. The large man who'd been on the right walked around to Lyle's window and paid him in cash. Lyle turned to get a look at the man who'd been sitting behind him, but all he could see was his back as the man walked away. The heavyset man joined him, swaying side to side on stubby legs. Both men disappeared into the darkness.

The third man had walked a dozen yards behind the cab. Lyle watched him stop, take a few more steps, then stop again as if he were unsure where to go.

Lyle craned his neck and shouted through the open window. "You okay buddy?"

The man waved an arm over his shoulder and continued walking.

Before Lyle could say anything else, the voice of his radio dispatcher told him to pick up a party at a restaurant. A half hour later, he transported another fare before he picked up the intoxicated redhead. She would be his last passenger. The balance of time left on his shift Lyle would spend helping to clean out his cab.

"I'm, I'm just way sorry," the woman said, slurring her words.

"Just relax. We're almost there." Although the Arizona theme park spread out over many square miles of high desert, nothing was too far away. Lyle drove to the park's cluster of 1970s-style hotels, an eight-minute trip from the center of Centerville.

*Drunk, but she must be pretty well off.* Lyle knew Nostalgia City's most expensive accommodations, the Desert Sunrise Hotel, catered to the well-heeled senior. Red was no senior, but her room doubtless contained a duvet-covered memory-foam bed to help her sleep off the alcohol and a lavish whirlpool soaking tub to blunt the morning's hangover. Room service would be ready with coffee and whatever else she needed to recover.

Lyle pulled up to the hotel and stopped under a bright portico lit with floodlights rivaling the central Arizona sun at noon. He surveyed the backseat landscape and saw it would be better for Red if she got out on the right.

He ran around the rear of the cab to open the door. His passenger put one unsteady foot on the ground, leaned out of the taxi, then almost fell backward. Lyle grabbed her shoulders and pulled. She landed on her feet, clutching Lyle for support. He needed only one arm to steady her. A bellman in an indigo uniform with brass buttons strode over. Before he was six feet away, he halted. His expression said he'd picked up the scent.

"I got it covered," Lyle said, and the porter gave him a grateful smile.

Lyle steered Red, who still clung to him for support, through a revolving door into the lobby. He imagined he caught a trace of perfume or shampoo when the top of her head brushed his face. He marveled he had any olfactory function left.

"I'm on the tenth floor," she said. "Eight, nine, ten, bingo."

Lyle found the elevator bank. As they waited, he noticed a reproving look from another guest. He saluted her by touching the brim of his cabbie hat, then looked down and saw Red was wearing portions of her dinner on one shoe and a pant leg.

"You have your key?" he asked.

She gave him a wobbly nod that she repeated as she stepped into the elevator alone. The other guest decided to catch a different car. Just as the doors were closing, Red put her face close to the opening. "What's your name?"

"Deming. Lyle Deming," he said, and the doors closed.

. . .

Lyle talked to himself as he headed to the park's transport center. The evening's sideshow of passengers crowded out his brain's frequent worry cycle. For that he was thankful. After a few minutes, he pulled into the taxicab wash facility.

Tomás, the friendly young guy who washed the cabs, opened the taxi's back door and looked inside. "One of your fares puke, huh?"

"It's pretty foul. A woman was sick." Lyle got out and set his hat on the front seat. He pushed his wavy brown hair off his forehead and grabbed a plastic dustpan from a nearby rack.

He opened the cab's left rear door. In the enclosed carport, Lyle's taxi smelled like a frat house bathroom after a freshman party. He scooped at some of the vomit with the dustpan but had to back out as his gag reflex threatened to kick in. Sensitivity had been one of his liabilities in his former profession.

"I'll clean it out with this," said the attendant, now wearing a mask and wielding the wand of a wet-dry vac. Standing at the back door, he shoved the nozzle under the front seat and worked toward the rear. The noise of the muck being slurped up sounded little different from when it was deposited.

After a moment, Tomás leaned back out of the car. "I see why this person threw up," he said. "Look what she ate."

Lyle glanced inside the car. On the floor, amid a slurry of bile and partially digested food, he saw a human finger.

# CHAPTER 2

H e said he was going to *kill* him?" Kate asked.

"Yes. But Cory wasn't serious. Besides, that was *before*."

"Before rehab."

"That's right," Stephanie said. "He spent time in a mental health facility. Now he's cleaned up his act, and he's ready to work again. That's what they told me."

Kate Sorensen tried to take it all in. Stephanie Tyler, first assistant director at Appropriate Brand Pictures, had just flown into Flagstaff's Pulliam Airport to help finalize an agreement to shoot a Vietnam-era crime movie at Nostalgia City where Kate was VP of public relations. *Murder for No Reason* was scheduled to start shooting soon.

They stood in baggage claim as Kate's longtime friend explained that the infamous Cory Sievers was going to replace a popular actor in the film's lead role.

"Why didn't someone tell me about this?" Kate said.

"I'm sorry, I thought you knew," Stephanie said. "It just happened at the end of last week. Steve McClintock had to drop out. Something about a contract conflict. These things happen. Wes Moody, our director, had to deal with it. Cory was a last-minute replacement."

Kate didn't follow the lives of celebrities, but it would have been difficult not to hear about the aberrant antics of Cory "Psycho" Sievers. The actor had a record of assault accusations, arrests for drugs, and a hair-trigger temper. Kate could imagine him going off the deep end in front of park guests, or worse. Not exactly the image she had in mind for an upscale theme park.

"So the actor that he threatened to kill is *also* in this picture?"

"Yes, Julian Russo. He's a great guy. The argument with Cory was a long time ago."

*Sounds like it was more than an argument.* "And Julian is a friend of yours?"

"Yes. I haven't had a chance to talk with him. I hope he's forgotten all about it."

Kate frowned and stared at the bags moving on the luggage carousel. "The first publicity has already gone out. Our guests'll be disappointed. And now we have to publicize Psycho Sievers? Really?" She struggled to relax the knot in her stomach. Playing college basketball, she'd trained herself to channel tension into positive energy. Was it working?

Stephanie grabbed her bag and pulled out the handle. "C'mon," she said. "We can talk on the way."

Kate led her through the airy terminal. Recently enlarged to accommodate the masses of travelers heading to Nostalgia City, the Flagstaff airport lay north of the park, closer than Phoenix Sky Harbor International to the south.

From the sound of her voice, Stephanie still maintained her bubbly enthusiasm for the movie project. Initially, Kate liked the idea, too. A movie fan since her early teens, Kate had spent Saturdays at the multiplex with friends. Weekdays after school she watched movies on her family's VCR, *Dances with Wolves*, *Home Alone*, *Beauty and the Beast.* Her favorite had been *Thelma and Louise.* Although her parents worried over Kate's fascination with the film, she knew the story and its suicide ending were just fiction. Mostly she liked the movie because the two women took an aggressive approach to life.

They didn't take crap from anyone, and at thirteen Kate felt as if she had to take crap from *everyone*. In her darker, adolescent days, when girls teased her about her height and boys were intimidated by it, the tall young woman often took refuge in drama on the screen.

Her love of the cinema stretching back 30 years—and not her practical side—had prompted her to persuade Nostalgia City founder and CEO Archibald "Max" Maxwell that hosting a film company shooting would be a great idea for the park. Now it didn't look so great.

Coordinating a film crew with gawking tourists, park employees, and concessionaires who operated stores and restaurants—all with different priorities and expectations—would challenge everyone. And now she had to deal with Psycho Sievers, too? As head of public relations, she'd be the chief troubleshooter. But, she told herself, quieting conflicts in one of the country's most elaborate theme parks was part of her job.

"Don't worry about this," Stephanie said when they reached Kate's SUV in the airport lot. "It will work out fine."

Kate lifted Stephanie's bag into the back of the car and they got in. "You got your hair cut. I like it. Makes you look like Anne Hathaway."

"Thanks," Stephanie said. "You are gorgeous as usual. With your blonde hair and blue eyes, you could be a star in one of our pictures." Kate wore a dark floral print midi dress tied at the waist, her long hair in a loose chignon.

"Thanks, I'd rather be *watching* pictures," she said.

"The location manager and the others will be here on an afternoon flight. They're running late," Stephanie said. Half a head shorter than Kate, she still stood tall for a woman.

"That won't be an issue. They're meeting with Dustin, our Centerville operations manager. He's always late."

Several months before, Stephanie had traveled to Nostalgia City with members of the film company's production crew to work out details of the extended location shooting at the central

Arizona theme park. Supplies, trailers, and equipment were shipped to the park. Only a few last-minute details awaited.

"It will be like, a long stay," Stephanie said. "But it will come together."

Kate pulled out of the lot and headed south.

"Everyone at my company is in love with Nostalgia City," Stephanie continued. "Even at the back lot of Premier Studios in LA where we rent soundstages, we'd never have an entire 1970s town to work with. And you don't have false fronts like movie sets. Centerville is a genuine town with functioning stores, theatres, clubs, everything."

"There'll be inconveniences, but the idea of Hollywood stars roaming around and having the park featured in a movie appealed to Max—because he thought it would attract visitors." *But now I have to break the news to our CEO about Sievers.*

Stephanie glanced at Kate. "We'll be good guests. When we're on location, we try to leave a setting the same way we found it. Not all companies do that."

Kate and Stephanie had become friends years before in Las Vegas. At the time, Kate was public relations director for Max when he ran a Vegas strip hotel-casino and Stephanie directed TV commercials for ad agencies.

Traveling south, they drove through stands of lush green conifers that gradually merged with red rock bluffs as the elevation dropped in San Navarro County. Eastern tourists were often amazed to see pine trees in a state they associated with sand and saguaros.

"How are you getting along with Tori Malcolm?" Stephanie asked. "She should be a big help with the publicity."

"Your PR guru is certainly detail-oriented. We met last month to divide the responsibilities."

"You're organized as usual. Just a word to the wise. Keep Tori up to speed if you can. She tends to be a little—"

"Controlling?"

"You didn't hear it from me."

Kate stared down the road. After a few minutes, Stephanie broke the silence. "I'm looking forward to us spending time together."

"Of course. Me too."

"And we've got a great cast for the picture. Lots of good people. Julian is a fine character actor and a close friend. He helped me learn the ropes when I got to Hollywood. I want you to meet him."

"Sure."

"It's sad, I guess," Stephanie said, "that Julian will have to be in the same movie with Cory, but it'll be alright. Jules doesn't hold a grudge."

"Uh-huh."

"There won't be any problems."

# CHAPTER 3

S o you're the one who gave me the finger." San Navarro County Undersheriff Rey Martinez leaned forward and stared across his desk at Lyle. He held his lips together.

"You've been waiting all morning to say that, haven't you?" Lyle said.

Rey's frown gave way to a smile and he leaned back. "Doesn't happen every day. A deputy called me this morning. Said you found it in the back of your cab."

"Craziest thing," Lyle said. At mid-morning, with his next taxi shift hours away, he wore his customary off-duty uniform: jeans and a Hawaiian shirt. "First time anyone's ever thrown up in my cab, too."

"The deputy said maybe someone swallowed the finger, then spit it up?"

"Sounds too gross. We washed it off before I put it into a bag. Stomach acid would have degraded it."

"Thoughtful. And you even saved some vomit for us."

Lyle shrugged. "Part of the service."

"I gave it to the ME first thing this morning. She was intrigued. She doesn't get too many unattached fingers to examine." Rey often wore a suit at work, but this morning the tall, lean sheriff's second in command dressed in his tan uniform and light blue tie. "Seems like ever since your theme park got built in this county, we've had more bizarre crime than you see on a month's worth of cop shows."

Crossing paths with Rey on some of the crimes had helped form their friendship. "Just giving you something new to work on. To break the monotony."

"Like calling hospitals," Rey said, "to ask if anyone's come in with a finger missing."

"Yeah. Any luck?"

"We got *nada*. Deputy said no hospital in a three-county area has treated anyone for an amputated finger."

"I don't think the redhead who got sick swallowed the finger. She was drunk. Falling down drunk. But no one would eat a finger, would they?"

"*Chicken* fingers."

"This wasn't deep-fried. But it did come with dipping sauce."

"Mmm, *delicioso*," Lyle's friend said. "If the woman didn't puke up the finger, where'd it come from?"

"One of my other passengers?"

"Any of them cut off a finger in your cab?"

"Not that I remember."

"The doc said based on the size of the finger and the amount of hair on it that it likely belonged to a man. And the presence of blood shows the finger was probably cut off while its owner was alive."

Lyle felt a brief, involuntary shudder. "So it *had* to happen in the cab?"

"Not necessarily. It could have been cut off before someone got into the cab. Maybe it was frozen or refrigerated to preserve it after the amputation."

"And if it was kept cold you couldn't tell how long ago it was amputated, right?"

"There ya go. And somehow it wound up in your back seat."

"It was a weird night. The vomit girl was just the last part of it." Lyle explained the man and woman who argued violently and the suspicious men he drove to the parking lot.

"I'd like to have a detective talk to the woman who got sick. Can you identify her and your other passengers?"

Lyle shook his head slowly. "We don't always log names if passengers just flag us down, and unless they pay by credit card or put it on their park account, we don't have a record. Oh, there was someone else, too. Orpheus the Great."

"Who?"

"Orpheus. A magician. I don't know his real name. He's been playing at the Centerville Showroom. The guy didn't stop talking the whole time he was in my cab. He said he could make my taxi disappear, if I wanted him to."

"Could he make someone's finger disappear?"

"Maybe. I heard he's very good," Lyle said. "Makes a bowling ball appear out of thin air. Maybe he does a trick with a finger."

Rey wrote a note. "We'll ask him."

"I don't think you'll be able to, right away at least. His last show was yesterday. I gave him a ride to connect with the airport shuttle. He was carrying bags."

"We'll have to find his agent and see where he's performing next. And what about the woman? A redhead?"

"That won't be tough. I promise you the hotel staff will remember her. Did you get a fingerprint from the finger?"

"Yeah, but we couldn't match it."

"At first I thought it was phony. It was sliced off so cleanly."

"That's what the ME said, but she can't be sure *how* it was cut. She's going to send it to a Phoenix lab. They'll check the DNA too, but she said finding a match is a long shot."

"And the DNA will take weeks," Lyle said.

"Affirmative."

"I have an idea. Why don't I take it to the taxi office and put it in lost and found?"

Rey smirked. "So how would someone prove it was theirs?"

Lyle's cell phone rang. He pulled it out of his pocket. "Yes?

Yeah, that was me. Okay. I'm in Polk at the Sheriff's Office. I can be there in about a half hour."

Lyle put down his phone. "That was my dispatcher. A woman named Sarah Needham called. She wants me to meet her at a restaurant in the park. She wants to apologize for throwing up in my cab."

# CHAPTER 4

L yle detoured past three film company trailers on his way to the restaurant, reminded that they would soon be shooting a movie at the park. He walked around a corner and found The Ranch House between a boutique and a leather goods store. Lights burned inside, but a "closed" sign hung in the window. Was it the right place? He wanted to pull out his phone and confirm the message with his dispatcher, but employees were prohibited from using twenty-first-century technology in the park. How could you maintain the illusion of the 1970s if employees chatted on cell phones? Stores used old-style cash registers or rudimentary computers.

Lyle turned to go, then heard his name.

"Mr. Deming?" The redhead from the night before stood in the open doorway. "Mr. Deming, please come in." She held the door for him.

Lyle walked into the foyer. He noticed she was a little younger —mid-twenties—and more attractive than he'd remembered. Her long hair was curled up and pulled behind her head.

"I'm Sarah Needham." She extended a hand. "I wanted to thank you in person if I could. I didn't just want to call, y'know?"

She wore a name badge on her peach blouse—a shade matching the color scheme in the restaurant. She was a *server*?

"You were sick. I'm glad I could help."

"You were wonderful." She looked at her shoes and clasped and unclasped her hands. "I'm so, so sorry. I don't do things like that. You see—" She paused and looked up. "Can I get you a cup of coffee? We're not open for lunch yet, but I just brewed a pot."

Lyle didn't need more thanks, or more coffee, but he wanted to ask about the finger. "Sure. Thanks. Just black."

He took a seat at a nearby booth. He'd eaten in The Ranch House before but hadn't noticed Needham. The faux rustic charm of the place said 1970s, but it looked not much different from present-day restaurants that affected a country atmosphere. Knotty pine wainscoting, gingham curtains. Wagon-wheel chandeliers hung above.

Needham returned with two mugs, set one in front of Lyle, and sat down opposite him. She took a breath and Lyle could sense another effusive apology.

"Did you enjoy the Desert Sunrise Hotel?" he asked. *If she works as a server, she must have saved up for two years to stay there.* He'd heard rooms *started* at $450 per night.

"The hotel? Yes, sure. It's perfect." She stopped, swallowed, and licked her lips. When she picked up her mug, she hugged it tight and took a long drink.

"Hangover?" Lyle asked.

"Yeah." She breathed in and held it momentarily. "Mr. Deming, it's like, y'know—"

"Please call me Lyle." The *mister* Deming sounded old. But he *was* old, at least twice her age. Where did the time go?

"I'm not a big drinker," she said. "It's just that my BFF from high school came down for a visit to cheer me up. We did some pub crawls during the weekend."

Did Sarah have a low alcohol tolerance? Perhaps a couple of stiff drinks was all it took.

"My girlfriend paid for the hotel. I'd never be able to afford it.

I barely make anything in this job, and I have a three-year-old daughter."

She glanced up for a moment. Lyle remembered the blue-green eyes.

"My friend is so caring. You see," she said with a catch in her voice, "my boyfriend dumped me." She clutched her mug and looked down again.

Lyle debated about reaching out to touch her hand. He sympathized. It was several years since his wife divorced him, but he remembered the emptiness. "So you just drowned your sorrows. I understand."

"He didn't even give me a reason," she said, looking up for a moment. A watery sheen coated her eyes. "He just said it was the best thing."

She looked at her hands. "We met here at the park. We've been going out for a year."

"Sorry."

"We were going to go out that night. Instead, he just came over and told me we were through. I thought…" She stopped and took a breath as if she'd forgotten to breathe. Her right hand abandoned the coffee mug and wiped away a tear.

"Is your girlfriend still here?"

"She had to fly home yesterday. That's why I was by myself last night." Needham looked up. "I'll be okay."

"It gets better," Lyle said. "Eventually."

She touched his hand.

Soaking up Needham's emotions, Lyle felt embarrassed about what he came to ask. "I have a question." He thought of the worms sometimes found in bottles of mescal.

She gave him a weak smile.

When he finally asked her if she swallowed a finger, she laughed.

"I wasn't that drunk, was I?"

He explained finding the finger in his cab. "I had to report it to the Sheriff's Department. Maybe it has a simple explanation."

# CHAPTER 5

MONDAY, ONE WEEK LATER

B uilding B-6," Lyle said. "What's so important?"

"It used to be called Ride Engineering," said Howard Chaffee, the park's security chief, "but they finally painted over it."

Lyle and Howard walked along a sidewalk into a backstage section of Nostalgia City called Park Attraction Development or PAD. Unlike retro Centerville, the collection of grey one-story stucco buildings looked like an industrial park with each building identified only by a letter and number.

"Industrial security 101," Howard said. "Do not identify high-value targets."

"Targets?"

"It's common sense. If you're here to commit a serious crime, a building name could tell you right where you want to be. That's why the numbers and letters."

"Serious crime? Is that why we're here?"

"Just wait."

Lyle paused occasionally to get a closer look at a part of the park he'd rarely seen, but Howard kept up his pace with a determined walk that would have made Jack Webb proud. Chaffee, a former San Francisco police commander, had shed part of his official bearing since coming to the park, so Lyle guessed he might be auditioning for a part in the movie being filmed at Nostalgia City or, more likely, he was pissed off about something. Howard's gray suit seemed to match his mood.

"Hang on, Howard," Lyle said. "Where's the scene of the crime?"

"This way," he said without slowing down.

Lyle hurried to catch up. He wore loafers and Dockers, his version of getting dressed up for a meeting. Soon he saw a chain-link gate with fencing extending in only one direction. The fence ran for hundreds of yards and wrapped around a building, but it didn't connect to the other side of the gate. Howard pulled out a card and held it in front of a panel.

"Wait a minute Howard. The fence stops here. We can just walk around the gate." He suppressed a smile. Using a gate that enclosed nothing reminded him of a Mel Brooks movie.

"When it's completed, it will encircle the entire PAD complex, to give us a perimeter. Prox cards will be required everywhere at PAD. Finally." Howard pushed open the gate. "Just testing," he mumbled.

"Prox cards?"

"It means proximity. You just wave the card. These are the newest high-tech versions. We'll be phasing them in all over the park."

They approached a building labeled B-2, also identified by the large Nostalgia City NC logo on its glass doors. The doors opened into a small reception area. The room featured framed blueprint-like sketches of NC rides and attractions on the walls and furniture in a style deemed futuristic in the 1970s. Even the behind-the-scenes engineering types had an eye for retro. Lyle followed Howard to a reception desk staffed by a young woman with a pageboy haircut and abundant eye makeup.

"Oh, Mr. Chaffee," she said. "Mr. Owings is expecting you. Someone will be out in a minute."

Before they could settle, a door opened and a woman in slacks and an off-white jacket ushered them into a wide hallway. After a short walk along deep carpeting, they reached double doors. One door swung open and Max Maxwell walked out to meet them.

"Thanks for coming, Howard, Lyle." The theme park's septua-genarian founder habitually wore a white shirt, his tie often askew. He wore his thinning hair cut short. He led them into a long, narrow room. Four people sat at one end of a conference table that ran the length of the room. No one smiled.

Maxwell gestured to empty chairs and before Lyle and Howard could sit down, he made introductions. Everyone seemed to know Howard. Lyle immediately forgot the names and titles of three of the people—two men and a woman—but recognized the name of Kerry Owings, a senior vice president who was respon-sible for the PAD department which created all park rides and attractions. He wore jeans that probably cost $400 and a blue chambray shirt with rolled-up sleeves. He stood to shake hands.

"Okay," Maxwell said standing at the head of the table, "we need to get going. Lost too much time already. Our security has been crap. I know, partially my fault. Howard's been writing reports and telling us we need to protect our *ass*-sets better. Any of us listening, *now*?" His voice threatened to pierce the walls.

Howard slowly nodded, his jaw tightened.

"So here's the problem," Maxwell continued. He looked at Lyle. "Our computer system has been compromised and secrets stolen. Not just copied—stolen. Gone. What's missing? Plans and programs for the highest high-tech attractions ever developed. Stuff that's genuine magic. Ideas to drastically change the industry and possibly influence other fields." Max made a fist and started to pound the table, but the motion died and his arm fell to his side. He took a breath. "We've been working on this for years. You can't put a price on it."

# CHAPTER 6

                    DEWEY

I didn't kill nobody. We were playing pool
when it happened. Don't be an asshole. I told
you I was there with Javier until at least
four o'clock.

                    RALPH

The police think you were involved. They came
here looking for you. I'm getting tired of
having to protect your ass. If you're telling
me the truth, okay. You'd better be. Now if
you had stuck with that job—

                    DEWEY

Screw your job. I know what I'm doing. I have
*plans*.

K ate flipped through the pages of the *Murder for No Reason* script, then glanced out her office window. More tourists on the street than usual. A week after her last meeting with Stephanie and other film company crew, she still labored to make the location shooting—scheduled to start that morning—smooth and successful. Maxwell, her boss, had insisted on seeing a final revision of the script, and he simply shrugged when Kate told him about Sievers. Maybe he didn't follow Hollywood news.

Glancing at a clock, Kate gathered up the script and hurried out of her office. Although closed to guests, the Maxwell Building administrative offices occupied a public street in Centerville. Before she'd gone a block, she met Dr. Drenda Adair, the senior vice president of history and culture. Barely above five feet, Dr. Adair, PhD, established and maintained the historical accuracy of the park.

She and Kate paused in the shade of an awning over a beauty parlor's front window. Inside, a row of plastic hair dryer hoods looked like space helmets from a sixties sci-fi movie.

"Kate, what's the prognosis? Are we all ready for Hollywood comes to Nostalgia City?"

"I hope so," Kate said. "I'm heading to the set."

"Cory Sievers," Drenda said. "Doesn't he have a rather tawdry reputation?"

"You need to get out more. Sievers is the *leading* Hollywood bad boy. In his last incident, he started a fight, trashed a hotel room, then jumped off his balcony into the swimming pool."

"That sounds vaguely familiar. It wasn't recent, was it?"

"About a year ago." Kate took a step back under the salon awning to keep the morning sun out of her eyes. "Sievers dodged serious criminal charges, but they placed him in a rehab facility. I've been reading up on him."

"Did the plot of the movie change?"

"Not that I can see. It's still a Vietnam homecoming gone bad."

"It's a trifle dark. Sievers must play the police detective. That's the star role. He's torn by loyalties to the law and to a society wracked by protests and the trauma of war. Does Sievers have the level of profundity for the part?"

"We'll find out."

"How did Sievers ever get the role in this movie?" Drenda asked.

"Good question. My friend Steph—she's the first assistant director—told me when rumors circulated that Steve McClintock was leaving the picture, Sievers's agent begged the company for the role and called in favors from everyone he knew in Hollywood who had sway."

"Is Sievers a Hollywood pariah?"

"I don't know. His early films were big hits, so he still has a name. Steph says he's eager to revive his career." She pulled out her phone to check the time. "Sorry, I need to run."

Soon Kate waded through a crowd as she headed for the movie set. Tourists sweated in the sun as the temperature rose into the eighties. The air smelled of warm bodies, sunscreen, and popcorn. Park visitors decked out in floppy hats, T-shirts, and shorts sloshed drinks in paper cups or took awkward selfies, arms above heads, despite the park's policy that guests limit cell phone use. And everyone strained to see whatever it was that drew the people in front of them.

At the edge of the set, Kate found Stephanie glancing from her tablet computer to the front of a café. They would shoot the first scenes in front of an NC restaurant renamed Bobby's Burgers and Malts. Cables like black snakes crisscrossed the set connecting spotlights, power supplies, and electric gear. Actors in period casual clothes loitered in front of the restaurant.

"Are you ready to get started?" Kate asked.

"Just awaiting the star," Stephanie said.

"Is he late?"

Stephanie looked at her watch. "Not for five minutes."

"Stephanie," said the man who appeared next to them. "Get someone to move that restaurant cart and the table next to it. They're in the wrong place."

"I see what you mean. Just a minor adjustment." Stephanie paused for a moment, then introduced Kate. "This is our director, Wesley Gordon Moody."

Kate had missed the director when he'd visited the park on exploratory trips. The man's thick brown hair, streaked with gray, stuck out in all directions. He looked at Kate with dark eyes and smiled as they shook hands. "Please call me Wes. Everyone does."

"Do you like Nostalgia City?"

"It's flawless. As you can probably see, our set decorator didn't have to change much."

"Our historian used to be a university professor," Kate said. "She makes sure everything here is *period-authentic* as she likes to say."

"You have a nice crowd today, but they're a long ways away."

"We wanted to give you plenty of room, but this is not what we planned. I need to find Dustin, our operations manager, and we'll coordinate with Stephanie."

Kate imagined all movie directors as either brooding or hyper. Only Moody's name matched her mental image, otherwise his smile, relaxed stance, and earnest look said he was comfortably in charge.

Stephanie glanced at her watch again. "I've got to get going. Find Mr. Sievers."

As Moody walked away, Kate heard the murmuring of the crowd increase, then fall silent. The star had arrived.

Sievers jumped out of the electric cart that brought him down Main Street, past the crowd held back by ropes. He wore a dress shirt and tie, his suit coat draped over a shoulder. He walked across the set stopping to greet the crew members. Everyone received a smile, some a handshake. Sievers's light brown hair was long—in the style of the 1970s—but still conservatively cut and combed, and he displayed his well-known sardonic grin.

He seemed to share a joke with two crew members before he walked up to the director, grinned, and saluted. Sievers then took a seat on a tall folding canvas chair and two other actors stood and took places on a narrow patio in front of the cafe. Kate moved forward to get a better view.

Jana Osbourn, the picture's blonde co-star, wearing a multi-colored sundress, took her place in front of the camera. She stood next to a restaurant cart that held glasses, napkins, and utensils.

The director stepped toward Osbourn and asked her to move a little to her left and lean on the cart before they started shooting. She placed a hand on top of the cart—then screamed. Her shriek traveled across the set, cut through the spectators, and echoed down the block.

Osbourn held her hand up in front of her face. Cory Sievers jumped up and rushed forward along with Moody and a security officer. The officer reached the actor first. He looked at her hand then talked into his radio. He held the star's arm as she walked toward the street with Moody on her other side.

Kate hurried in their direction. Moody, Sievers, Stephanie, and others hovered around Osbourn. In a moment, an electric cart arrived.

"Where's the nurse?" Stephanie shouted. A young man in a white jacket appeared. He and the security officer helped the trembling actor into her seat.

"They'll take you to the infirmary right away," the officer said to Osbourn. Her lips tightened and her blue eyes became large. "God it hurts," she murmured.

Moody touched Osbourn's shoulder and whispered some-thing. The emergency driver, also a uniformed security officer, released the brake.

"Wait, I'm going too." Moody jumped into the rear seat and leaned toward Osbourn. The cart sped toward the crowd then turned out of sight.

Stephanie, a cameraman, and others looked down the street, then at each other.

Kate pulled another security officer aside and identified herself.

"Sorry, I've got to run," he said. "They forgot this. They need to see it at the infirmary."

He held up a clear plastic bag, and Kate saw something she'd only seen in photos.

He said, "I think it's a *bark* scorpion."

# CHAPTER 7

Maxwell roamed the conference room. Lyle often thought of him as an energetic, impulsive teenager housed in a short, wiry 75-year-old body. Or was he older? "When did we discover the hack?" Max said looking at Owings.

The PAD senior vice president sounded matter-of-fact: "We went through the logs and access files Friday," he said. "It's routine. But after we found discrepancies, we reviewed all our systems over the weekend and we knew something was wrong."

"Sort of an understatement, isn't it Kerry?" Maxwell said. "We've spent millions on these plans already. Millions. We created programs, engineering studies, simulations, drawings, models. Yup, something is *wrong* all right."

Lyle glanced at the woman seated across from him. Some-where in her early forties, she parted her hair in the middle and it hung ragged on the sides. Jane Fonda in the '70s? Or maybe some-thing new. She sighed and lowered her head as Maxwell spoke. Was she to blame?

"I contacted the FBI," Howard said. "Agents who specialize in economic espionage and computer crimes are coming out."

"That's fine Howard, but we have other problems too, don't we? Our patents."

Max looked at a man in a dark tailored suit and charcoal tie who could either be the park's chief legal counsel or a mortician. "Usually we file for protection as we go along," the man said, "and we have done this for some initial elements of the project we're calling PDE. But there are issues.

"First, artificial intelligence is a complex and evolving element of the law. It's not like seeking a patent for a new type of can opener. And software is challenging, too. If it's tied to particular apparatuses or engineering creations, obtaining a patent is not as problematic. But we're not just seeking a patent for a specific ride, are we?"

"So much for the jargon," Max said. "Are you saying you couldn't do it?"

"Of course not, but work on the project slowed for a while, and then it received a top priority. The innovation continued yet the legal department did not receive enough information, things we need to draft patent applications."

"Max," Owings said, "as you know, PDE was not finished. We were getting close, but there are a few challenges left and now we're—"

"So you're both saying our ass is hanging out. Our secrets are gone, and we don't even have the ideas patented." Max's stare, always penetrating, seemed to bore through Owings and the attorney. Lyle wondered if they might soon be looking for work.

"You two get together. Get as much detail into patent applications as you can. Do it yesterday. And I want a progress report in three days. Understood?"

Owings and the attorney exchanged glances. Perhaps they could carpool to the unemployment office.

"So much for patent protection," Maxwell said. "That brings us to our computer *genius,* Tom Wyrick." Max stood at the side of the room opposite where Lyle sat. "We have indications he is responsible, and now he's *disappeared*? Not a coincidence, is it?" He moved to the front of the room. "Anyone have more information?"

Except for Owings, the people around the table seemed to be examining the far end of the room.

"I know Tom was the big brain behind this. Can we reproduce the project without him? Don't we have any details saved in the patent work?" He looked at Owings, whose mouth turned down in an almost imperceptible frown.

"That's what I thought," Max groaned. "Here's where Lyle comes in. Used to be a Phoenix homicide cop. Solved lots of cases."

Lyle could see where this was going. "But now I drive a—"

"Lyle works in the park," Maxwell said. "Transportation. But he's helped us out before. Some of you probably know this. Saved our bacon. Lyle's going to find Wyrick. *Did* he steal the secrets? Something happen to him? Maybe he'll just walk in the door tomorrow. Ha. We need to find out—now."

"Did we contact the sheriff?" Lyle said.

"Due time," Maxwell said. "Now Howard, when the FBI gets here…"

Lyle tuned him out momentarily. So this was why Howard dragged him down here on his day off. Max is scared. Could one guy create a new type of ride technology, then steal it? Could missing the latest whizbang jeopardize the future of the park? No more cab driving? Yeah, he'd helped the park out of trouble before, but as a result, he'd also been visited with the same anxiety that ultimately pushed him out of police work. So now he was back to detective mode? It would have been nice for Max to *ask* him first. And why didn't he call the sheriff?

"As you know, Kerry," Maxwell concluded, "I have an idea who might be responsible for this. It's not just Tom Wyrick. So we talk to the FBI, right Howard?"

Maxwell looked at his watch and nodded in Lyle's direction before starting for the door. "I want you all to give Lyle your cooperation. Tell him about Tom, the projects he was working on and the plans we think he took. Anything he wants."

"Ah, Mr. Maxwell," said the woman opposite Lyle. "There's a matter of confidentiality. Do you—"

"Mr. Maxwell," Howard cut in. "I think Ms. Pitts is talking about an NDA. We can take care of it."

# CHAPTER 8

The man outside the Nostalgia City burger joint held a gun. He waved it around, the muzzle inscribing a dangerous pattern in the direction of the film crew and guests. The actor smiled. Obviously he was joking. His actions caught the attention of the first assistant director. Stephanie rushed over to him. Kate stood on the edge of the set, too far away to hear what her friend said, but the actor put the gun down, nodded his head, then looked at the ground. Fortunately, any park visitors who might have seen the gun probably took the incident as part of Hollywood dramatics, and no one seemed concerned. Except Kate.

"Was that a real gun that guy was waving around?" she asked when she caught up with Stephanie. "An actor is just stung by a scorpion, now someone's playing with a gun?"

"It looks like a real gun, but it's modified. It doesn't shoot. Only blanks."

"Okay. That was still scary."

"I know. I'm going to talk to Brandon, our weapons master. He needs to keep a closer eye on the guns. Actors are not permitted to have weapons except during a specific scene."

"Is there going to be gunfire here today?"

"No. One actor will be wearing a gun, but that's all."

"But the script does call for gunfights."

"Yeah, it's a crime movie. But we'll warn all onlookers before the scenes and be sure everyone is a safe distance back. No worries. I'm way careful about guns. So is Wes."

"I don't see him around. Have you heard anything about Ms. Osbourn yet?"

"She's going back to her room. She'll be okay, but she's in a lot of pain. Has trouble moving her hand. I guess that bark scorpion is really dangerous. Wes told me to set up for a new scene. He's on his way back."

Kate watched crew members moving light poles and flood-lights when she felt her phone vibrate. She reached in her pocket and glanced at the screen. "I better take this. It's Max."

She scurried around a corner where she could talk—out of sight of guests.

"What th' hell's going on down there?" Max said. "Sounds like chaos."

"One of the stars got stung by a scorpion."

"I heard. Is she okay?"

Kate relayed the details she'd just heard from Stephanie. "It's painful."

"I'll bet," Max said. "Spoiled her day."

"Anything wrong, Max?"

"I'll tell you later. What are you doing?"

"I'm at the movie set. I was planning to go back to my office."

"What's the problem with the crowd? We're getting complaints. Tourists say they're so far from the movie they can't see anything. And concessionaires on Main Street are pissed because customers can't get to them."

Kate muttered under her breath.

"What's security doing?" Max said. "Who's in charge of this? Nobody told me they were going to block off so many damn stores. How can they sell anything?"

"Security is following orders," Kate said. "The operations manager is supposed to be supervising this."

"That's Dustin Isley, isn't it? He's an idiot."

"He's supposed to have obtained agreements with all concessionaires. The park's compensating them for the few days they're inconvenienced."

"Dustin effed up. Can you please fix this? And do the guests have to be chained off so far away? They came here to see stars."

*Max is in rare form today.*

The park negotiated with Appropriate Brand Pictures to find a way that kept crowd size—and noise—to manageable levels but still provided tourists opportunities to watch the filming. Dustin should have kept Max up to date. When she hung up, she called Dustin and told him that Max was on the warpath and that he had three hours left as an NC employee unless he fixed the problems on Main Street.

She walked back to the set to ask Stephanie to keep her posted on Jana Osbourn's condition. Her friend stood talking to a man in his fifties with close-cropped hair. He wore a tailored sports jacket and held a clipboard under his arm.

"I have some suggestions," the man told Stephanie, "but I haven't seen the whole damn place yet. I wanted to discuss an idea with Wes." He paused as Kate walked up, looking at her appraisingly.

"Kate, this is Alan Clappison. He's our associate producer."

He extended his hand as Stephanie said Kate's name and title. Two vertical lines, wrinkles really, appeared between his eyebrows.

"Alan has just finished a VIP tour of the park."

From a distance, Kate had misjudged Clappison's age. Balding slightly, he was forty, tops. He wasn't overweight as she'd guessed. Muscles filled out his jacket.

"The tour didn't include the whole park. I was hoping to find new locations where we could film, possibly save some time."

"Dressing rooms and mechanical areas are for employees only," Kate said. "Is there something specific you'd like to see?"

"Thanks but I'm good for now." He turned to Stephanie. "Let's do some spitballing right after lunch."

"You know where I'll be."

"Associate producer," Kate said after he stepped away. "Is he a big shot?"

"For sure." Stephanie smiled. "Not. Associate producer can mean almost anything. I haven't seen associate producers on the set a lot, but I wouldn't necessarily know who they are. They usually work in finance, not on location. Sometimes the associate producer is just the executive producer's nephew who needs a job."

"He doesn't look like a bean counter."

"I wouldn't go there. Some of the crew think that's exactly why he's here. He just joined us last week. Rumor is that he's here to look over our shoulders, second guess, cut corners, slash budgets."

"Watch out," someone cried from the other side of the set.

Kate turned to see a light standard topple over, hitting other metal poles that cascaded to the ground. A voice cried out in pain.

# CHAPTER 9

I t's a non-disclosure agreement," Joseph Arena said. "It just means you may not share any information about the park and our technology with anyone. There are penalties."

Shortly after the PAD executive meeting broke up, Lyle followed Arena to his office in another building. He sat looking across a desk at the dark-haired man with olive complexion and a bushy mustache.

Lyle signed the paper quickly and handed it to Arena. As vice president and director of PAD information technology, Arena's responsibilities included all computer hardware and software that made park attractions run. Tom Wyrick reported to him, so Arena was the logical first person to talk with.

"So how long has he been missing?" Lyle asked.

"Technically just a few days."

"Technically?"

"Well, he called in sick on Tuesday, and when we hadn't heard from him for a few days, someone called him. There was no answer. We left messages. My assistant and I called several times."

Lyle leaned back in his chair. "Just because he didn't answer his phone doesn't mean he's missing."

"I suppose, but—"

"Is he married?"

"No."

"Have a partner?"

"No."

"Does he have any family?"

"Not in Arizona."

Arena was going to be a wealth of information. "Somewhere else?"

"I believe his parents live in Washington State."

"Has anyone been to his house?"

"Uh-huh. Larry, he's a software engineer and a friend of Tom's. He went to Tom's condo in Polk over the weekend, and Tom wasn't there."

"Did he go inside?"

"I don't know." As Arena talked, his mustache covered the upper part of his mouth. Not walrus whiskers, more like a shoe brush. "Larry's one of the few other people who know about the intrusion."

"So Wyrick is not married and doesn't live with anyone. How old is he?"

Arena hit the keyboard on his desk a few times. He looked at his screen. "Thirty-three."

"Could I see his file?"

"Uh."

"I signed the agreement."

"But that's not related to personnel files."

*Don't you remember Max telling you to give me everything? Never mind. I'll get it from Howard.* "Would it be a violation of confidence for you to give me a photo of the person I'm supposed to find?"

"Of course not." He touched his keyboard again, and a printer came to life. Lyle glanced around the room. Abstract art and drawings of park rides decorated the walls. On a bookcase sat a model of the park's monorail.

"Sorry, I'm...distracted today," Arena said. "We're still trying to figure out how this could have happened. But I'm sure Tom isn't involved in anything."

"How *was* the information stolen?"

"Someone accessed files using the ID of someone who wasn't working that day."

"How does that implicate Wyrick?"

"Paul Vang claims Tom was paying too much attention to his log-in protocol one day. He said he teased Tom about it but forgot about it until the intrusion."

"And it was *Vang's* files that were hacked?"

"Between Tom's file access and Vang's that covers the core of the project."

"And you have nothing left? How's that possible?"

Arena looked away. "Whoever did this took the current files and substituted much earlier versions, and even those versions had gaps. That's why it wasn't immediately obvious that anything had happened. It didn't look like files were missing. Not just anybody could do this."

"And backups?"

Arena shook his head. "The intruder knew how to access those, too."

"But you don't think Tom did it?"

"I know Tom. He's smart. He wouldn't do this."

"Yeah?"

"Max called him a *genius.*" He held up fingers to make air quotes. "And he *is.* He got two degrees in engineering from Cal Poly before he switched to Computer Science at Berkeley. Tom's not just a programmer, he's an engineer and computer scientist. He taught for a while and worked for me as a contractor at Maxwell's hotel in Vegas."

*Sounds like a profile of someone savvy enough to steal all the secrets and leave NC with nothing, not even backups.* "What did he do for you in Vegas?"

"Same thing we do here. The hotel has a subway and other rides. Maxwell wanted everything cutting-edge. We designed and programmed everything. Tom created some special-effect rides from the ground up. When Maxwell left Vegas to open this park, I came along with him. I hired Tom to join us."

Arena's printer had become quiet. He rose and picked up a sheet of heavy paper from a tray and handed it to Lyle. Tom Wyrick had medium brown hair cut short, light eyes, and the kind of expression one usually has when getting a picture taken at the DMV.

"Could I have Wyrick's address and phone number?" Pretty please.

Lyle jotted down the information then said, "So tell me, why would Wyrick—" he held up a hand to head off objections—"or *anyone* want to steal the plans, programs, or whatever you call it?"

"For other parks, of course."

"Steal our ride ideas?"

"Absolutely. It's happened before."

"*NC* secrets stolen?" Lyle asked.

"Not here, but other parks."

"I've never heard of it."

"It's often covered up," Arena said. "Hushed up in court or simply ignored. You don't want to admit your security is full of holes. Especially if you're a publicly-traded company. Sometimes parks copy rides *after* the original rides are up and running and successful. Virtually every park in the country built a flume ride after it had been the most popular ride at Knott's Berry Farm for years. Now there's a growing interest in finding out what the competition is doing *before* they announce new attractions, especially with advanced technology coming online."

Lyle stopped writing in his notepad and looked up at Arena. "Everyone wants to have the next big thing."

Arena nodded.

"Max mentioned other applications for the technology?"

"This is so revolutionary we don't yet know how it might aid other fields. We just can't even *calculate* the value."

*So why did Howard have to browbeat the geeks into being more care-*

*ful?* "If that's the case, shouldn't you have had more safeguards in place?"

"Maxwell was upset. We *are* security conscious—to some extent, anyway. We try to keep projects compartmentalized, but it's not always possible. Programmers, engineers, and specialists in other fields have to work together at times. But generally, no one knows *every* detail."

"Except—"

"Well, it's just that—"

"Ultimately you need good security *and* trust in the people you work with," Lyle said.

"That's the truth."

"Has anyone checked Wyrick's office?"

# CHAPTER 10

H is office? Uh, yes we have."

"May I see it?"

Arena led Lyle out of his office and down a corridor. Rough textured fabric like unbleached burlap covered the walls, and instead of the cushy carpet of the admin building, programming had wooden plank flooring. Lyle's heels tapped on the floor as he walked. After 50 feet, they passed open double doors to a room that looked like a toy store. Dozens of scale models of cars, trains, and other Nostalgia City rides sat on tables, counters, and deep wall shelves. Lyle walked in.

"Tom's work area is this way," Arena said, pointing down the hall. "This is the Conceptularium."

*Sounds like the name of a mental hospital.* Conceptularium? *Is that coder humor?* Lyle saw keypad locks on the doors, but they were propped open.

"Quite a place." Lyle looked around. Part toy shop, part design studio, the vast space contained models and mockups of all sizes. Many of the detailed models, painted in lifelike colors, represented dark rides, the industry term for indoor attractions. More than half of NC's Fun Zone attractions were elaborate dark rides often patterned after 1970s movies, TV shows, or news events. The models surrounded a gathering of chairs and tables where one woman worked on a laptop. Lyle leaned over one model that recreated an old west scene with wagons passing through a town.

"That one didn't quite work out," Arena said as he motioned Lyle back toward the door. "We were going to base the ride on several '70s TV westerns, but the problem was the wagons. We couldn't get enough people through the attraction in an hour."

"Do these move?"

"Some are motorized."

"Where's the switch for this one?"

Arena nodded toward the door. "Mr. Deming."

Lyle tapped saloon doors in the western model and they swung back and forth. "This is fascinating. We could charge guests admission to see this."

"That wouldn't be a wise idea," Arena said. He ushered Lyle toward the hallway.

"So some attractions never get beyond the motorized model stage?"

"It depends. Sometimes they are useful to brainstorm new ideas and they help explain our concepts to management."

Lyle thought Arena *was* management. *He must be talking about Max. Probably needs help visualizing.*

He followed Arena down the hall to an airy room where two dozen people worked, separated by low cubicle walls. Many of the employees stared into computer screens. In a wide-open area to Lyle's right sat a Foosball table and kitchen counter with a shiny espresso machine.

Wyrick's cubicle, larger than the rest, occupied a corner of the room and included one of the building's few tall, narrow windows.

As they approached, a man in jeans and a short-sleeved shirt strolled over from across the room.

"No word, huh?" the man asked Arena.

"Not yet." Arena glanced at Lyle, then back to the other man.

"Larry, this is Lyle Deming. He's working with security to see if we can find Tom."

Probably about the same age as Wyrick, Larry Michaels introduced himself as a "team chief" and friend of Wyrick's.

"When was the last time you saw him?" Lyle asked.

"Last Monday afternoon as we were going home."

"Then he phoned in sick the next morning," Lyle said.

"Yes."

"No one has heard from him since, so you went to his home?"

"Yeah, I went out there yesterday. He lives in a new condo on the east side of Polk. I knocked on the door and called to him, but no one answered. I couldn't see anything through the windows."

"But you didn't try to get in."

Michaels shrugged. "I didn't know what to do."

"Do those condos have garages?"

"Yeah, but no windows in 'em." Michaels turned to go. "Sorry I have a meeting."

"Mr. Michaels, I'd like to talk with you further."

"Okay. Ah, can you call me after lunch?"

Lyle jotted down Michaels's number, then looked toward Wyrick's work space. "If someone had called the sheriff right away, deputies could have already checked hospitals and accident records," he mumbled.

"What?" Arena asked.

"Nothing, just talking to myself."

A colorful Arizona Diamondbacks schedule and the major league standings and scores clipped from a newspaper were stuck to one wall of Wyrick's office. An iMac sat in the middle of a spacious, L-shaped metal, glass, and composite desk, its keyboard resting at a slight angle to the large screen. The office appeared orderly. Lyle picked up one of several binders lined up along a side table and flipped through pages containing drawings of a new attraction, Yesterday-Today. He pulled open a bottom desk drawer not knowing what he was looking for.

He reached in and fished through a row of coiled computer

cables. Then Lyle noticed a woman at a desk across the aisle watching him. When he made eye contact, she looked away, paying attention to papers in her lap.

"We've gone through everything already," Arena said when Lyle pulled open another drawer. "We thought we might find the name of his doctor or something."

Lyle saw nothing of interest in the office, notably no photos of family or friends—or a girlfriend. Wyrick obviously liked to keep a neat space, almost sterile. But in contrast, when Lyle pulled open the shallow center desk drawer it revealed a hodgepodge of small items: paper clips, scissors, nail clippers, a fancy fountain pen, notepad, dry-erase markers, a smartphone charging cord, several pencils. Before he closed the drawer, he picked up the pen. The white star on the cap identified it as a Montblanc. Printed on one side of the cap in gold script was Wyrick's name, on the other side in smaller letters, *Crossroads Casino*.

# CHAPTER 11

A scorpion sting, a light-post accident, concessionaires ready to riot, what next? At least Kate's cat was getting over her tummy problem. Although she lived close to the park in Timeless Village, a housing complex mostly for NC employees, Kate rarely enjoyed the luxury of going home for lunch, but she wanted to check on Trixie. And Lyle had offered to pick up Mexican food.

People at the park who knew Kate and Lyle suspected they were "seeing each other," a euphemism for their ill-defined relationship. Kate identified the relationship by how she felt and their many common values and interests, not by how many times they had sex. She'd lost track. She knew Lyle shared her feelings— some of them anyway—but they'd rarely talked about it.

"Here's lunch," Lyle said, setting two tall brown paper bags on Kate's kitchen counter. He put his arms around her, tilted his head up slightly, and brought his lips to hers. Her slight height advantage didn't appear to matter to him. In fact, he'd once told her that her height was one of the things that attracted him. And at nearly six feet, he was tall enough for her. She gazed from his deep brown eyes to his lips and firm jaw. She could feel the warmth of his trim body.

"Good afternoon, Mr. Deming." She gave him a smack on the

lips and turned to the food. "My dear cat. She had me worried, but I think she's better. I gave her canned pumpkin."

"Pumpkin?"

"It helps her digestion."

"A couple of beers with this Mexican would help my digestion, but I've got to go back to work. How was the first morning of shooting? The filming started today, right?"

"A little short of disaster," Kate said as she unloaded enchiladas and tostadas on her dining table. "A scorpion stung the co-star, Jana Osbourn."

"Ouch. She okay?"

"I think so. It was a bark scorpion. That's the most dangerous?"

"Yes, but it can just be like a wasp sting. Or worse."

"It was on top of a restaurant cart in the set. No one knows how it got there."

"Lots of scorpions here. You have to be careful."

"I'd never seen one since I moved here. Jana was short of breath at first. Her hand was swollen, and she said it continued to hurt all morning. I didn't talk to her. My friend Stephanie did. She's the first assistant director. Jana's got the rest of the day off. Oh, and then a light pole tipped over on the set."

"Anyone hurt?"

"A painful bruise. Not a good start. I hope no one is superstitious."

"Hollywood people superstitious? Don't bad things come in threes? Or is it show business deaths? Was your big star there?"

"Yes."

"And?"

"Charming. Completely charming. I watched him on the set. He said 'hello' to most of the crew members when he arrived. He even gave Steph a peck on the cheek."

"I'll bet."

"No, he was polite. He got a little upset when Jana got stung, but everyone did."

Lyle lifted a bite of enchilada. "You said the movie's about Vietnam?"

"Yes, Sievers is a cop who investigates a series of robberies pulled off by disillusioned ex-GIs just back from the war. One of them, Dewey, has all these problems. Anxiety, changes in mood, intrusive memories."

"PTSD."

"Yes, but they didn't call it that back then. You know that." She glanced up at Lyle for a moment.

"I didn't have PTSD. It was different. I never shot anyone when I was a cop. I only got shot at once, and it wasn't close. One of the Phoenix PD shrinks said I had PTSD. They pigeon-holed me to force me out. I was just stressed. Too many victims, too many wrecked families, too little time."

Kate had heard this before. Lyle left the Phoenix Police after two detectives could not get him to look the other way when they manufactured evidence. They claimed Lyle's anxiety was a sign of mental illness. He refused to dispute it because he just wanted out. She said, "But that's over."

"You know, the stress comes and goes. Today, I'm—"

"Maybe you could help me make concessionaires behave," she said. "Max is on my case. The first issue is the crowds. Tourists are coming here to see the stars, but thousands of them can't squeeze into every square inch of Main Street. Too much noise, too much congestion. Some shops are blocked, but we're compensating the store operators."

"What's the second issue?"

"Dustin Isley."

"Who?"

"He's the Centerville ops manager. I caught up with him at the Control Center," she said, referring to the video surveillance office where security personnel monitored the park's thousands of CCTV cameras. "He just stood there staring at the crowds on the Main Street video feeds. He didn't expect we'd be jammed with guests?"

"If it's Isley's responsibility, why does Max—"

"Spin doctor to the rescue."

"You'll manage. You're tough. So how's Stephanie doing?"

"Amazing." Kate put her fork down. "She's had to roll with the punches. The first assistant director is in charge of virtually everything."

"I thought that was the director."

"He works with the actors and the camera operators. Steph does everything else. On the set she coordinates the wardrobe, makeup, electrical, lighting, all those departments that go into making a movie. She's like a first sergeant, at least that's how she described it to me."

"I saw them setting up," Lyle said.

"This is a bigger project than anyone in the park expected."

"It'll work."

*Maybe, I hope.* "And no matter what you say about *Sievers*, lots of park visitors today acted all gaga overseeing a big movie star like him."

"Lady Gaga?"

"Funny." She paused when her small gray and tan cat peeked around the corner and let out a tentative meow. "Hey sweet girl, how are you?"

Lyle reached down, scratched the cat's head, and made a soothing sound. "At the risk of adding to your PR concerns," he said, "there's an issue you should know about. I don't know if it'll get in the news or not. Maybe this guy just took a mental health week."

Kate swallowed a mouthful of beans, then said, "Who did what?"

"Tom Wyrick, a hot-shot programmer and engineer in Park Attractions Development disappeared. He's been gone a week."

Lyle explained that park secrets were stolen and that Wyrick was suspect number one. "Max and all the brass in R&D are chasing their tails over this. And of course Max wants *me* to find Wyrick. Obviously, the theft of park secrets is all hush-hush. But I thought Wyrick's disappearance could hit the news, then you might need to be ready if you get calls. You didn't hear about it?"

*So that's what was upsetting Max. He could be so infuriating. He kept things to himself, then scolded me for not being proactive. Here we go again.* She got up and followed Trixie to her bed. "He hasn't told me about this because he doesn't want anyone to know. But when the disappearance hits social media or the evening news, he'll want to know what I'm doing about it. Where do you think this guy is?"

"On the run? In Rio? Applying for a job at Disneyland?"

# CHAPTER 12

W e're not talking about one particular ride. Theme park bloggers have been theorizing developments like this for years. *How it's done* is the big question."

After lunch, Lyle met Larry Michaels at an outdoor employee lounge behind one of the PAD buildings. A sculpted metal awning shaded them from the relentless Arizona sun. Michaels settled his heavy frame in a swivel patio chair. Lyle sat opposite. A handful of employees scattered about the patio dodged the sun under umbrellas, drinking coffee, chatting, or working on laptops.

"How do you make a new ride different?" Lyle asked.

"You make it unpredictable." Michaels pushed a baseball cap off his forehead. "Think about Disney's Pirates of the Caribbean."

"I've been on *that* a few times."

Michaels sipped sparkling water from a green glass bottle. "Every time you go on the ride, the pirates do the same thing. One of them chases a woman, one drinks rum, others fire canons."

"Sure, that's how it works," Lyle said.

"Just listen." Michaels adopted an instructive tone. He sounded like a smart-ass millennial, but maybe he only wanted to put technical concepts in layman's terms.

"What if the pirate ride didn't always work that way?"

Michaels continued. "What if a pirate stopped drinking and tried to shoot you as you went by? And the next time you took the ride, that pirate wasn't there at all and a villager stepped out and begged you for money. It becomes unpredictable, see? It's like a different ride each time."

Some theme park rides, no matter how creative, got boring after a while. Lyle could see the advantages of mixing things up. "Our Night of the Living Dead Ride isn't always the same," he said. "I just realized that."

Michaels nodded with a knowing smile. Lyle noticed his nose looked crooked. The tip didn't line up with the center of his lips. *He must know that.*

"On the Living Dead," Michaels continued, "not all the zombies try to grab you each time. Their actions are randomized."

Lyle started to ask a question, but Michaels carried on. "Fun, but basic. Zombies, by their nature, move with herky-jerky motions. That's last-century technology. Imagine a ride with robots that moved with smooth motions, more like humans or animals. And what if they spoke to you about the clothes you were wearing or called your name. What if you could talk to them and have them respond?"

"So this is the type of stuff stolen in the break-in? Programmed rides with almost unlimited variations?"

"Some of it. But even this is pretty basic. Our group is working with interactive technologies. We want to let the guests control their ride, change course, be spontaneous. Two people could leave the same ride having had totally different experiences." He paused. "I know you're cleared for everything but—"

"Artificial intelligence?" Lyle said.

"Uh-huh."

"Augmented reality?"

"We call it XR now. Extended reality."

"Motion simulators?" Lyle wasn't a complete Luddite. He'd heard the names of the technologies but had only vague notions of how some of them worked.

"Of course I only worked on a part of PDE, but we incorporate haptic technology, a technique Tom developed that's like holography, and more. It's our interfacing, our *blending* of methodologies that create a new type of theme park experience. We call it the perception deception effect or PDE. This puts us years ahead of anyone. Tom invented a whole new way of viewing the world."

"And it's worth stealing?"

"Oh yeah. That's why we have security."

*Apparently not enough.* "Who would want our secrets?"

"Other parks. In the US and overseas. Ride manufacturers, crooked consultants. PDE is not a ride that someone would copy, but tools to create the most sophisticated attractions."

"Have you noticed any evidence of spying here before?"

Michaels shook his head and took a thoughtful drink of his water. "Not until this."

"Tell me about Tom Wyrick. You went to his home. He wasn't there. You've tried calling him?"

"Correct. Tom and I are buds. I don't think he's involved. I *tried* to reach out to him. Phone calls, text, IMs."

"IM?"

"Instant message." He said it in a tone you'd use to explain technology to a toddler. "I don't know. I don't know what he's doing. Where he is."

"Do you know of anyone who would want to harm him?"

"Tom? No. Can't imagine it. He's awesome. Why do you ask that? Did someone say something?"

"Has he acted strangely recently, anything out of the ordinary? Something that might be related to his disappearance?"

"No, ah, the only thing is, he broke up with his girlfriend." He lowered his head and pulled down the brim of his hat. "He said she was too clingy. Funny, I didn't see it. Sarah doesn't seem like that kind of a person to me."

"How long ago was this?"

"I dunno. A couple of weeks ago. Maybe a little longer."

"Do you know Sarah's last name?"

"No. She works at the park, in Centerville."

"Does Tom gamble?"

"Yeah. He bets on sports. Always talking about the odds. He goes to the Indian casino."

"Does he win?"

"He says he does, sometimes."

"How did he act the last time you saw him? Nervous? Suspicious?"

"I feel like it was the breakup with Sarah. Maybe he was just sad or disappointed. I didn't expect him to disappear."

# CHAPTER 13

Anyone else I could talk to?" Lyle said. "Other friends here at work?"

Michaels took another swallow from his mineral water and glanced at a young woman sitting thirty feet away. "Allison over there. She's working with Tom on the Yesterday-Today attraction. But I know she hasn't seen him either."

Lyle saw the woman who worked in the cubicle opposite Wyrick's office, the one he'd noticed that morning.

"You can talk to her," Michaels lowered his voice. "But remember, you can't discuss the intrusion."

The two walked over to the other table. Michaels introduced Lyle to Allison Byers. "Mr. Deming works here. He's trying to help find Tom."

"He's maybe just chillin' somewhere," Byers said with an expression that could have been a smile. Her casual dress made Lyle think of someone on vacation, not a programmer at work. She closed her laptop and adopted a serious look. "He's sick. That's why he didn't come into work."

Lyle sat opposite her at the metal mesh table as Michaels walked into the building. "Possibly," he said. "If he was sick, do you know where he might go?"

"Home I guess. Should we be worried?"

"How long have you worked with him?"

"Since I started at Nostalgia City about six months ago."

"And you're working on the Yesterday-Today attraction?"

"Yes. And I'm learning a lot from Tom. He's an outstanding teacher."

Byers had a habit of brushing her light brown hair back. It looked windblown but was probably one of those styles that was supposed to look windblown.

"When was the last time you saw him?"

"Um, before he called in sick."

"Did you notice anything unusual about his behavior? Anything out of the ordinary?"

She thought for a moment. "No. We were both totally busy. They, like, wanted us to make some changes in the routines for one part of the Yesterday ride—on short notice."

"Was Wyrick upset about this? Angry?"

"Maybe a little upset, but not angry. We've changed it a few times before, y'know."

"Did he argue with anyone about it?"

"No. It wasn't like that. He didn't argue. We just got to work. Stuff happens."

Byers' pale blemish-free skin gave her an adolescent look, but her full lips and figure, what Lyle could see of it above the table, made him wonder if she was the reason Wyrick broke up with his girlfriend.

"Did you ever see him at his condo?"

She breathed in and moved her head from side to side. "Um, only a few times to pick up materials or talk about files we were working on."

"You never went out with him socially?"

She wrinkled her brow. "Only with a bunch of us after work."

"Where did you work before you came here?"

"Excuse me, but um, what does this have to do with finding Tom? Do you work in security or what?"

"Sorry to be a bother. Programming has always fascinated me." He waved a hand in the air. "How you do it. Coding is like magic to me. How did you get a programming job at a theme park?"

"I was a programming intern at Benzvo Technologies in the Bay Area. It was okay, but I wanted to grow, y'know. Work on different tech."

And make more money, probably. "Oh, you came from Silicon Valley, of course. Thanks." Lyle got up. "One last question, can you think of anyone who might want to hurt him?"

She pulled her head back. "No way. Why would anyone?"

"I'm just asking questions. Thanks for your time, Allison."

Lyle looked at his watch. The Ranch House restaurant would be open now.

# CHAPTER 14

"K ate, I need your help."

*Now what?* "What is it Steph?" Kate held her cell phone in one hand, the other flat on her desk.

"My friend Julian Russo got in trouble."

"Is it Sievers?"

"No. Nothing like that. Your security stopped him."

"What happened?"

"Julian is the sweetest guy. I owe him a lot. He's sorry. He didn't know. It's just that he's really into drones."

Steph was usually clear-headed. "Drones?"

"Julian's crazy about them. He has like this big collection of them. He builds them, flies them, takes videos—"

"So what's the problem?"

"He was flying a drone around warehouse buildings. It wasn't dangerous. Nobody was around. Then this security guard asked him what he was doing. He told him the area was restricted, then he took his drone away. He tried to escort him out of the park, but Julian told him he was acting in the movie. Can you help us?"

*Here's a problem I didn't expect.* "Where are you now?"

"I'm on the set, inside a variety store. No one can see me on the phone."

"Okay. Stay where you are, and I'll walk over."

Kate took the back way to the store and found Stephanie standing at the doorway to the shop, shading her eyes from the sun with her computer tablet.

"So what's going on?" Kate said.

Stephanie repeated what she'd said on the phone, adding, "I tried talking to that security guy, Chaffee. He just said as soon as he finishes with his scene, Julian had to come to the security office for a background check."

"We don't allow drones in the park," Kate said. "You guys should have been told. And we do have areas behind the scenes marked *employees only*. Where is Julian now?"

"He's over there." She pointed to a small man in his sixties standing across the street. "He's scheduled for a scene in about an hour."

Kate thought she recognized him but wasn't sure. She stepped inside the store to get out of the sun's glare. "He's a close friend?"

"The best. I met him on one of my first feature films. I was third assistant. I was supposed to herd a crowd of extras around. The director told me what he wanted, but I misunderstood. I would have spoiled this big, elaborate war scene if it wasn't for Julian. He told me what I needed to do. He helped me on other stuff that day, too. Probably saved my job. We've been friends since."

"I can talk to Howard Chaffee for you, but I'd like to know exactly what Julian was doing with the drone."

"Just playing, I'm sure. I can go get him."

Stephanie walked across the street, negotiating cables and equipment. She talked with the actor for a few moments, then the two of them walked into the deserted variety store.

When Kate saw Julian up close, she knew she'd seen him in movies. Not a leading man. Character roles, mostly. She struggled to remember some films. He played father figures, bank managers, family friends.

"I didn't mean to get Steph in trouble," he said, standing

against a store counter. His stooped shoulders made him look even smaller than he was. His pale, flat face sagged in places. He looked at Kate with searching eyes.

"She's not in trouble," Kate said. "I can help sort this out if you'll tell me what you were doing."

"I guess Steph told you about my drones. It's a hobby. I got into it a few years ago. It's challenging to get proficient at flying. And it actually helps me relax. You have to focus. Every drone flies a little differently." He gestured with his hands as if he were controlling a craft. "I was over that way." He started to point but put his arm down. "Somewhere. They looked like just plain storage buildings, so I didn't think anyone would mind. I practiced some maneuvers."

When he finished talking, his face settled into an expression of resignation.

"It doesn't sound like a problem," Kate said, "but drones are banned. We tell guests not to bring drones into the park, and employees know better. I'll check this out for you."

A half hour later, Kate found Howard in his office.

"You know we don't allow drones on the property," he said.

"Of course, but—"

"It's certainly not seventies, is it? And besides those buildings are all PAD, ride development. It's off limits to visitors. Everyone knows it's a secure area."

"Obviously not everyone." Kate sat down opposite Howard's desk.

"You know what I mean. Normally, I wouldn't even be involved in something like this. But a supervisor brought it to my attention because we're trying to increase security to protect our, ah, engineering areas."

"I'm sure that's important." Howard was a friend, but a friend responsible for safeguarding a multi-billion-dollar enterprise. The suspected hacking and the disappearance Lyle had told her about were likely prompting a new focus on security. But she was not supposed to know. She maintained a neutral tone of voice. "I know we have employee-only areas, but I didn't quite realize how serious it was."

"How are you involved in this, anyway?" Howard asked, sounding like a cop for a moment.

Kate explained that Steph, the picture's assistant director and a longtime friend, had asked her to intercede. "Julian Russo is an actor in the cast. Drones are just his hobby. He plays with them to kill time. So much time on a movie set is spent just standing around." She raised her palms and turned them up.

"Most drones have cameras and—"

"I met him. He seems genuine. I think he was embarrassed. He's a serious actor. You'd recognize him."

"Did he tell you how he reacted when the guard asked him to land the drone?"

"No. What did he say?"

"My officer said he refused to cooperate. Told him to leave him alone."

"But he gave up the drone."

"Reluctantly. My officer thought at first there might be a scuffle, but eventually Mr. Russo calmed down. All in all, not a pleasant experience."

"Too bad it happened that way. I'm sure Julian's sorry."

"Okay, but I still want to talk to him."

Kate leaned forward and made eye contact. "Could I have his drone back?"

"I suppose so. But he needs to come see me."

"He will. Thanks, Howard." Kate stood.

"It's of little evidentiary value, anyway." He pointed to the drone on a table across his office. "We looked at the video and it's just bumpy shots of sky, buildings, and pavement."

# CHAPTER 15

L yle thought Sarah Needham looked better this week. Even coiled up behind her head, her red hair shone. She gave him a smile of recognition when he walked into the restaurant. He wondered why Wyrick dumped her. Too clingy? He knew other reasons for breakups.

"Can I talk to you for a few minutes? It's about Tom."

"What about him?"

"I'm trying to find him."

"Is there something—" she paused when a customer seated nearby waved to her. "I can take a break in about 15 minutes. Can you wait?"

Lyle nodded, took a seat at the counter, and ordered coffee. He pulled out his phone, cradling it below the counter, and scanned his email. Max Maxwell. What now?

FBI is coming early tomorrow morning. They want to talk with you. Call me.

He felt a tap on his shoulder. "No, no. You're not supposed to use that here."

He looked around. The elderly woman with silver-blonde hair looked at him through outsized sunglasses. "Don't use your phone in public. Naughty. It spoils the atmosphere, the masquerade." The woman was enjoying herself. She gave him a mischievous smile.

"You're right." He raised a finger to his lips. "Shh. Sorry. Don't turn me in." Luckily, he was wearing street clothes and didn't have his name badge. He winked and tucked the phone in his pocket.

After a few minutes, Sarah arrived and led him to an empty private dining room. She set her purse on one of the five tables and sat down with a sigh.

"I only have a few minutes, Mr.—Lyle. What's going on with Tom?" She foraged through her purse with unsteady hands. "Isn't he at work? Is there something wrong?"

Lyle sat next to her. "We're talking about Tom Wyrick, right?"

"Yes. I told you about him."

"You didn't tell me his name."

"Then how—" Her eyes were more green than blue today, and he'd forgotten about the freckles.

"I'll explain. First, let's be positive." Lyle reached in his jacket pocket and placed the picture of Wyrick on the table.

"Yes. That's Tom."

Lyle noticed her questioning look. She pulled her hands out of her purse and held a box of nicotine gum. "I'm trying to quit smoking. I'm doing okay, but I need to keep chewing this stuff, and I can't when I'm on duty." She looked at the photo again. "This must have been taken before I met him. He has a beard."

"Mr. Wyrick works in PAD."

Sarah nodded.

"And he hasn't been to work for a week. He called in sick, but his co-workers are a little concerned. They haven't been able to contact him."

She looked away for a moment and opened the box in her hand. She popped a piece of gum in her mouth. "But if Tom's just sick, why are you—do you know him?"

"No."

"Then…"

"Before I drove a cab, I did some investigation work, so the park asked me to help find him. When was the last time you saw him?"

"It was about two weeks ago now." She tapped her finger on the gum box. "We met for a date, and that's when he told me."

"It was later then that your friend came to visit and you stayed at the Desert Sunrise."

"Uh-huh. And you picked me up and got me into the hotel." She stopped toying with the box and put it back in her purse. "Is he sick or what? Is he *missing*?"

"Probably a mix-up. I'm just asking around. Maybe he'll be checking back with work soon." He picked up the photo. "No one told me he had a beard."

"Yeah, his beard is—wait a minute." She went back into her purse. "I don't know why I kept this." She pulled out her cell phone and showed Lyle a photo on the screen.

He stared at the picture. In it, Sarah's smiling face was next to a young man who looked something like the man in Wyrick's company photo, except he had a full beard. Did he look vaguely familiar now?

"I don't know why I kept this," Sarah said. "I erased all the others."

"The beard changes his appearance." He tried to read Sarah's expression. "Someone told me Tom likes to go to the Indian casino."

"Yeah, we went there a few times. I was kind of bored."

"Thanks for the help, Sarah. Could you send me the photo?" He gave her his cell number and watched her click on the photo. Her hand trembled momentarily, then she stabbed the phone rapidly and set it down with a thud.

"You've got it now. I'm done with it, with him." She looked as if she were trying to smile, but she just pressed her lips tightly together. Her eyes became moist. "Here, you might as well have this, too." She tossed a door key on the table. "It goes to his condo. Just give it back to him."

She glanced at her phone again. "Oh, I've got to get back to work. My boss is on my case. Says I'm not fast enough."

She pulled the gum out of her mouth and looked for a place to put it. She found a tissue in her purse. "You know, it was Tom who persuaded me to stop smoking."

# CHAPTER 16

Kate felt self-conscious walking through the Lantana Inn lobby. She held the drone and its controller in front of her and walked to the elevators. The device reminded her of a giant black insect.

The hotel served as headquarters for Appropriate Brand Pictures. Several meeting rooms were turned into film company offices, and a portion of the cast and crew stayed in the hotel. Kate reached Stephanie's room on the sixth floor. She had to knock with one elbow.

"Oh, you got it," Stephanie said when she opened the door. "Thanks so much. Was it a problem?"

"No. Howard wasn't going to keep it."

"Just put it on the table in the corner." The first assistant director rated a mini-suite with a small seating area and kitchenette to the left and a bedroom to the right. "Julian can pick it up when he gets here. He's parked his drones in my room before, last time we were together on location."

"What, does he fly them in your room?"

"No, he just likes to show me new models he's bought or video he's shot in the air. When he's not acting, he's tinkering with drones or reading about them."

Kate sat on the couch. Stephanie, still dressed in the slacks and a *Murder for No Reason* T-shirt she wore on the set, stood by a window.

"So you guys hang out?"

"We do."

Kate raised her eyebrows and nodded as a sign for her to continue. Clearly the wrong signal.

"Don't look like that. Julian is super. It's not sexual. Anyway, he's old, isn't he? We're just friends—good friends."

Kate glanced at the big-screen TV on the wall. "I've seen him in movies."

"It's sad. His career's been up and down," Stephanie said. "He's been in dozens of pictures. Some bigger roles, some not. Then he lost his wife two years ago. Cancer. He misses her badly and he's lonely. I know he was drinking heavily for a while, but he said he stopped."

"Does he have other family?"

"A son. He doesn't talk about him much. I get the feeling they're estranged. I could be wrong." She gazed across the room. "Now he gets a good part again and who is a last-minute replacement but Cory Sievers."

"What exactly happened with Sievers?"

"This was when Julian's wife was dying. He had a bit part in a picture with Cory. I wasn't there, but I heard stories. Cory kept forgetting his lines in a scene with Julian, and he blamed Julian for it. He said Jules was giving him the stink eye, then he blew up and threatened him."

"*That* sounds more like Psycho Sievers."

"But I hope he's changed. Julian told me once that—"

A knock on the door interrupted Stephanie. She walked around the corner. "Jules, how did it go?"

Julian grunted and walked into the room. "Hi, Ms. Sorensen. I see you got my drone."

"Safe and sound."

"Thanks. I appreciate your running interference for me."

Stephanie sat in one occasional chair, Julian slumped in the other. "Sorry again, Steph, for causing a problem for you."

Stephanie shook her head.

"I don't know why it happened," he said. "I tried to fly someplace where there were no people around."

"Did they interrogate you?" Stephanie asked.

Howard wouldn't *interrogate* him, Kate wanted to say.

"Oh, it was friendly enough," Julian said, "but he asked me lots of questions. I told him I was just practicing some low-level maneuvers."

As he spoke, Kate imagined him as a down-on-his-luck suspect in a crime movie. Maybe a role he'd played.

"I told him the security guard surprised me. He was just a kid, but he started ordering me to stop and put down my controller. I didn't know what the fuss was about."

"Not only is it a safety issue," Kate said. "But drones don't fit with our seventies atmosphere."

"Okay, I can see that. But why was the guard so jumpy?"

Kate didn't think she needed to apologize, but Julian plainly was not a threat to anyone. She said, "I'm sorry."

"I thought they were just ordinary warehouse buildings. No one would mind. Except I see you're building a fence and locked gate around them. Top secret?"

# CHAPTER 17

Lyle found Tom Wyrick's condominium complex on the outskirts of Polk. An adobe wall adorned with "Acacia Creek Vistas" in distressed wrought iron letters marked the development's entrance. Lyle knew of no creek or other waterway in the area, and Polk's eastern flatland provided the condos with vistas only of neighboring condos. Nevertheless, the project's landscaping looked inviting with cacti, mesquite, and ground cover dotted with wine-red flowers.

Lyle drove through the development listening to an old Bay City Rollers's hit while looking for Wyrick's address. He'd called Rey wanting to know: A, if Rey had been told about the disappearance and B, if he was interested in checking out the missing programmer's home. The person at the other end of the sheriff's business line told Lyle the undersheriff was "in the field" and Rey's cell number went directly to voice mail. Without constabulary cooperation or consent, Lyle would have to be careful.

Fortunately, Wyrick's two-story condo sat on the edge of the property facing undeveloped scrubland. Lyle parked his Mustang next to several other vehicles in visitor parking. Walking to Wyrick's unit, he passed other condos but saw no one. To get to Wyrick's front door without walking in front of neighboring units,

Lyle continued along a gravel path then stepped over an artificial dry stream bed. Perhaps this was Acacia Creek. When he reached Wyrick's door he knocked several times and waited, glancing over his shoulder as casually as possible, but no neighboring windows were close by. Bad for the unit's security, good for Lyle.

When no one answered, Lyle put on his driving gloves and opened the door with Sarah's key.

"Mr. Wyrick? Tom Wyrick?"

Silence.

He took cautious steps across an entry area, past a polished wood staircase, and stood in Wyrick's living room. Everything seemed well-ordered. Flat-screen TV on the wall, an overstuffed couch and chairs, a low bookcase in the corner. On the walls hung two desert landscapes and a framed baseball poster. He walked into the kitchen. A cup, two glasses, and a used coffee pod on the counter next to the sink were the only items reflecting any recent comings and goings—but how recent? The sink and glasses were dry, and a shaft of late afternoon sun illuminated a thin layer of dust on the counter. The cabinets and drawers he opened revealed no secrets.

He poked around inside the refrigerator, usually the best indicator of recent activity. The sliced meat wrapped in butcher paper had the color of tarnished metal. It might have been ham. No amount of culinary magic could resuscitate the Chinese food in the cardboard container. The fridge had been untouched for probably a week. He didn't need to smell the carton of milk. The lapsed sell-by date was sufficient.

As he turned to go, he saw light reflected off a small object on the floor. Tucked up next to the baseboard, he saw a piece of broken glass. The three-inch shard curved as if it might have been part of a jar or drinking glass. Something left over from a fight, or a remnant of a forgotten accident?

He walked back through the living room and took the staircase. An open area at the top of the stairs contained a table, desk, and chair. Framed photos sat on a shelf. Still wearing his gloves, he picked up one showing Wyrick—without his beard—and two other young men smiling from the deck of a sailboat afloat on blue water somewhere. The portrait of an older couple—Lyle's age—could have been Wyrick's parents.

The door to the master bedroom stood open. He looked through the closet and pulled open a dresser drawer looking for signs that Wyrick had cleared out. Then someone knocked at the front door.

Shit, were deputies already here? He'd have to have a good excuse. He walked to the top of the stairs and listened.

"Tom?" said a female voice. "Tom, are you home?"

She knocked again.

He started down the stairs to look through the peephole but heard his hard heels tapping on the wood stairs. When the woman called to Tom again, he froze.

After a minute, the knocking stopped. He went to the door. Through the peephole, he saw only desert landscaping and no sign of anyone out the front window. Whose voice had it been? He'd been too far away to recognize it. Maybe if he heard it again.

Returning to Wyrick's desk upstairs, he saw a charging cord for a laptop, but no computer. Unopened junk mail, an adhesive tape dispenser, and two highlighters told him nothing. Going through the drawers, he held out no hope that he'd come across bank statements or cancelled checks. Computers and the internet had robbed cops and nosy PIs of those handy resources, but he did find a stack of Crossroads Casino betting sheets showing the odds for sporting events. The most recent games were weeks old. Next to the papers, Lyle found a clear plastic sports bottle. Why put a water bottle in a desk drawer? For a quick shot of Gatorade while working? Or maybe something stronger?

He unscrewed the cap and sniffed. No identifiable scent. The only printing on the bottle was an abstract logo and the ubiquitous "Made in China." As he started to fit the lid back on, he noticed its weight, heavier than it should be. He examined inside the thick cap. Was it two pieces of plastic? Along the edge, just below the drinking spout, he spotted a small hole. He turned on the desk lamp. Was the hole a camera lens? With his pocketknife, he pried off the cap's inside liner and found a battery, memory card, and what was probably a tiny camera. Apparently Wyrick was set up to take secret pictures, but of what—computer screens, plans, passwords?

His first thought was to put the bottle in a bag, to protect any fingerprints, and take it to Rey. Immediately he knew his finding the bottle could taint it as evidence—if it was needed—so he put the cap back together. He then placed the bottle and cap on top of the desk. Why not make it just a little easier for Rey's deputies to find it?

Driving out of the condo complex, he called a friend who worked in the accounting department at Crossroads Casino.

After a few pleasantries, Lyle asked, "How big of a gambler does someone have to be to get one of your personalized Montblanc pens?"

"Depends. You need to have a fairly sizeable credit limit and use it."

"Five figures?"

"That would do it. The pen's just one of our gifts at that level." She lowered her voice. "Why are you asking?"

"Max has me working as his own personal private dick again. You worked at the park. You know how paranoid he can be."

"I heard stories."

"Yeah, they're true. So could you tell me how much a guy has been spending there?"

She still talked in a whisper. "That's confidential, you know that."

"I know, that's why I called you."

"*Lyle.*"

"This is very important to the park. And I *have* to keep it super-secret."

"But Lyle…"

"No one will know where I found out. I promise."

# CHAPTER 18

Imperturbable, that's what Lyle liked about Rey Martinez. When Lyle's thoughts roamed all over the desert in search of a solution to his errant concern of the day, Rey exuded calm. He provided a grounding. Kate was like that too, sometimes.

Lyle didn't know if Rey would be on duty after five o'clock, but the Sheriff's Office was on the way, so he stopped by. He found Rey at his desk, his tie loosened, his suit coat on a hook in a corner of the room.

Lyle picked the more comfortable of Rey's two guest chairs. "You're drinking coffee at quarter after five?"

"I don't work a fixed shift like you," Rey said. "What are you looking for, cab driver?"

"Just thought I'd give you a little update on a case, but if you're busy—as I can see…"

In his mid-thirties, Rey had proven himself a savvy cop and administrator as well as a friend. Lyle wanted to tell him everything he'd learned about Wyrick and then persuade Max that the sheriff should take over the disappearance and let him get back to his taxi.

"I suppose," Rey said, "this has to do with the disappearance of Tom Wyrick and the suspected hacking."

"Hacking?"

"Uh-huh."

"I got the impression we—they—weren't eager to report this. Max is, shall I say, overly cautious with bad news about the park."

"Howard called this afternoon."

"Well then, you know Wyrick is a computer genius. He's apparently disappeared and someone hijacked confidential files about new ride technology we're developing."

"Howard also told me that Max assigned you to find Wyrick."

"Yes, and I told *him* he should call the Sheriff's Office. But you know Max."

"Uh-huh."

"So I did a little work today." Lyle told him about talking with Arena, Larry Michaels, and Allison Byers. "And I found an expensive, gold engraved pen in Wyrick's desk. It's a thank-you souvenir from the Crossroads Casino. Wyrick's a gambler. Bets on sports."

"The park thinks Wyrick is the hacker. And if he's a high roller, gambling debts could be a motive."

"I don't know exactly how much he bets, but you could find out." So could I.

"Hell, Lyle. Too bad I assigned detectives to this. You've already done the work."

"As much work on the case as I'd like to. But you know the expression, when Maxwell speaks—"

"You jump?"

"Not quite. He is a good arm twister, but he pays extra for legwork. And I've got something else for you, a picture of Wyrick."

"I've seen it. His office already sent it over."

Lyle pulled out his phone, tapped it, and set it on Rey's desk. "Who's this?"

"Look closely. Behind that beard is Tom Wyrick."

Rey picked up the phone. "Where'd you get the picture?"

"It turns out that Sarah Needham, the redhead who threw up

in my cab, was Wyrick's girlfriend. Until two weeks ago. She told me she got drunk and puked because her boyfriend dumped her —without a reason. She didn't tell me his name, but when Michaels told me Wyrick broke up with a girlfriend named Sarah," Lyle waved his hand in the air with a flourish, "I figured it out."

"There ya go. Deductive reasoning at its best," Rey grinned. He looked at the photo again. "So he grew a beard since the office picture was taken."

"Yeah. Needham gave me the picture. She was next to him in it, but I cropped her out. I had to tell her his office was looking for him, but I didn't get too specific."

"How'd she react?"

"She says she's over him, but I don't think so. Says she has no idea where he might be. That I believe."

"Here," Rey said, handing Lyle's phone back to him. "Text me a copy of that picture. FBI agents are coming out tomorrow. I'll give them an update."

"Max wants me to talk to the FBI. I can tell them everything I just told you about Wyrick and his coworkers. Then, I hope, I can bow out."

"The sheriff is out talking to Maxwell."

"Your boss and Max? I bet that's a fun conversation." Lyle got up.

"One other thing," Rey said. "We didn't learn anything from the leads you gave me on the finger. At least the people we talked to said they knew nothing about it. And nothing helpful yet from the Phoenix lab."

Lyle paused at Rey's door.

Rey said, "Anything else?"

# CHAPTER 19

Q uiet on the set," Stephanie said.

Kate stood amid a small crowd of tourists flanking the rear of the street-scene set. She moved forward to get a better look.

"Roll sound," Stephanie continued.

"Speed," said another voice, "action."

Cory Sievers in a suit faced another actor dressed in jeans and a T-shirt. They stood on the sidewalk near the cafe. Kate stopped walking and listened.

"Look Dewey," Sievers said, "I know you had it rough over there, but—"

"Over there?" said the other actor. "Yeah, but that was in 'Nam. Now I'm talking about the good old US of A."

"What do you mean?"

"I got drafted. I should have gone to Canada instead. But I did my God-damned duty. I spent my time over there in the jungle and almost got my ass shot off. Then I find out the government lied to us, I can't find a job, and protesters are calling me and my buddies 'baby killers.'"

"Okay," Sievers said, "I know this has been tough on you and why—I mean—something... oh shit." He shook his head and slapped his arm against his side. "Sorry. I'll do it again."

"Take five," the director said.

Kate had returned to the set early that morning to see Dustin Isley's solution to the crowd problem. It seemed to be working. A large section of Main Street was still roped off, but security officers and tour guides escorted batches of guests to a closer vantage point.

She didn't want to wait to see if Sievers flubbed his lines again, so she started back to her office. A few steps away from the set, she saw an ambush coming. A man with a shaved head and a script in his hand headed her way. She kept moving.

"Hey, are you Kate Sorensen, the PR lady?" The man jogged after her.

At six-two and a half, Kate was easily recognized around the park, even when she didn't want to be. Her abundance of natural light blonde hair and unblemished skin also worked against anonymity.

"Yes, may I help you?"

"I'm Wyatt Lewis, Cory's agent. I've got a great idea for you. I know you're busy. I'll make this quick. I can set up some short video interviews with Cory—"

"Mr. Lewis, Tori Malcolm handles all the publicity for the actors and the movie. We do stories strictly related to the park. You should—"

"That's what I'm talking about, Nostalgia City." Lewis's smooth head emphasized his protruding ears. If he had dark glasses perched on top of his head and a half-unbuttoned dress shirt, he might better fit Kate's stereotype of a brash theatrical agent. Instead, he wore slacks and a knit shirt tucked in to contain his belly. He looked at least ten years older than his star.

"We'll highlight landmarks with one-minute interviews with Cory standing in front of your city hall, malt shop, stuff like that. Real retro. It'd go viral, guaranteed. We're calling this

'Cory's Comeback.' You know, it's an alliteration and everything."

"I'll think about it, but really—"

"I didn't mean to spring this on you at once. They told me what you looked like so I just thought…" He paused for breath and looked almost embarrassed. Almost. "Maybe I could come by your office later?"

"Quiet on the set." Stephanie's voice spared Kate further cajolery. Lewis's idea actually had merit, but did she want Cory Sievers as a de facto spokesperson for the park? She held up a hand, feigned interest in the filming, and took steps back toward the set. Lewis released her as he too walked forward, presumably to watch his client perform.

"Action," Moody said, and the actors repeated their lines. When Sievers got to his troublesome line, he stopped mid-sentence then said, "Dammit. Would somebody stop Julian. His fucking drone is driving me crazy." He shook both hands in the air. "Stop it."

Kate saw Julian at the edge of the set. He held a tiny motionless drone in one hand and a controller in the other.

Sievers left his spot in front of the camera and charged Julian. "He's been doing this all morning," Sievers said. He slapped at Julian's arms, the strength of the blow spinning the older actor around. Sievers stood only slightly taller than Julian, but he was 30 years younger and fit. Julian's drone and controller shattered on the pavement. Julian retreated, pulling his arms into his body. He said something to Sievers Kate couldn't hear.

In the next moment, people jumped to action. Lewis pushed through the film crew toward Sievers. Stephanie rushed toward Julian. The director stalked toward the two actors. An NC security officer took two steps forward, then stopped, unsure what to do. The crowd stirred.

*Julian and his drones again—Moody's problem this time, not mine.* Kate strained, but couldn't hear what the director said. After a moment he pointed, and Sievers walked back toward the camera.

He shot dark looks over his shoulder as he went. His mouth moved, but Kate couldn't hear him. Moody talked to Julian. The actor gestured with his hands, palms open. Moody shook his head. Julian's shoulders fell. Finally, Moody patted Julian on the back and walked back to the set. The director said something to Stephanie and several crew members.

Julian picked up the pieces of his drone. He shuffled across the set and disappeared behind a trailer.

# CHAPTER 20

The Asian woman, Lyle assumed Chinese, wore her straight dark hair parted on the side and swept across her forehead. The ends hung just above her shoulders. She had a delicate nose, small mouth, and inquisitive look. Why did he always notice women first?

"Lyle, these are special agents Lisa Peng and Craig Futrell," Howard said when Lyle walked into Maxwell's executive conference room. Max sat at the end of the table glowering over his hawk nose at everyone and no one in particular.

A tablet computer, cell phone, and two stacks of papers spread out in front of the FBI agents seated next to Max. Was this going to be a long meeting? Lyle was thankful he stopped at Bohemian Coffee in Centerville on the way over. He shook hands with the thirty-something agents in suits and acknowledged Howard and Max. He sat down on the opposite side of the table with his coffee in front of him.

"The agents are with the FBI's Counterespionage Division," Howard continued. "They'd like to ask you about Wyrick."

"You're an experienced investigator," Futrell said.

"And you drive a cab," Peng said. "But we know about your record. The sheriff here speaks highly of you."

"We understand Mr. Maxwell asked you to do some initial investigation of Wyrick," Futrell said.

Lyle looked from one agent to the other. "To see if I could find him, yes."

"Would you tell us what you've found?" Peng asked. The petite agent's voice was soft, but Lyle had a hunch she was not.

He explained how he'd discovered that Wyrick had recently dumped his girlfriend, Sarah Needham, that she didn't know where he might be, and that he found a personalized casino pen in Wyrick's desk.

As he spoke, one thought hit him like a stomach punch. He'd made a serious mistake not telling Rey about going into Wyrick's condo and finding the sports-bottle camera. Now he would be guilty of withholding evidence from the FBI. As soon as he got out of the meeting, he'd talk to Rey, see if he could help him head off problems. Like a jail sentence.

"According to Larry Michaels, a software engineer, Wyrick likes to gamble." Lyle tried to collect himself after an unintended pause. "Needham confirmed this. Wyrick bets on sporting events. He frequents the Crossroads Casino, not far from the park."

Peng looked at Howard, then Lyle. "Wyrick's probably not acting alone. We're checking airlines over the past week. By now he could be in China."

Lyle lifted his coffee cup, but his arm stopped halfway to his mouth. "China?"

"At this point, we don't know for sure," Peng said. "But given the scale of Chinese economic espionage, this can't be overlooked. Mr. Owings tells us you're planning to use artificial intelligence to control your new rides. That could be valuable in China. Sounds just like the type of technology they've tried to steal before.

"The Chinese don't always *steal* designs and technology. No, they would rather we just *give it to them*. And we do. Do you know their strategy?" Without waiting for a response, she started tapping her tablet.

Max looked as flummoxed as Lyle felt.

"The PRC identifies US researchers and university professors and gives them honorariums. They invite them to China to be celebrated at symposia. Here's a list of some of the dozens of conferences and meetings set up to attract western experts." She held up her tablet showing a list in small print Lyle couldn't read. "They use terms like *career development* and *fostering cooperation between nations*, but it's a sham. It's all about stealing our ideas."

"Excuse me," Lyle said, "what's PRC?"

Peng wrinkled her brow and stared at Lyle. "People's Republic of China. They invite these experts to give talks and they flatter them with awards. And the scientists are so proud of their research, the secrets come right out of their mouths."

Frowning, Max started to protest.

"Please, this is important," Peng said. "The PRC is eager to lend money to Chinese corporations that want to buy stolen technology. In addition, Chinese business organizations in the US, made up of Chinese nationals, are also involved in stealing industrial secrets. And did you know more than 300,000 Chinese students are studying in the US right now? Most of them in technology fields. They learn from US experts and take the information back home."

"Agent Peng," Lyle said. "You're Chinese—"

"I was born in Chicago."

"I didn't mean to offend, but—"

"We need to know if any native Chinese work here."

Futrell glanced quickly at Max. "This is one theory, of course."

Peng looked at Futrell with a lethal stare, then turned to Max. "In addition, do you have any researchers or engineers who may have traveled to the PRC recently?"

"We'll be looking at *several* ways your secrets could have been compromised," Futrell said, placing a hand on the table next to Peng, "Won't we?"

"The PRC is very good at recruiting." Peng looked from Lyle to Howard. "Contrary to what some in the bureau think, the

Chinese like very much to recruit Anglo operatives in target corporations. In several cases, the Chinese were able to—"

"Agent Peng's worked on a number of important cases of Chinese espionage," Futrell said. "She speaks Mandarin and Wu dialects, so she sometimes tends to—"

Peng gave Futrell a stare that stopped him. It would have stopped a bullet.

The agents' exchange reminded Lyle of a scene from *The X-Files* but with reversed roles. The female, Scully character propounded theories, and the male agent, the Mulder character, offered a restraining influence.

"At this point Agent Peng," Futrell said trying to match his partner's stare, "we need to start by evaluating *all* circumstances."

"The Chinese may have recruited your Tom Wyrick," Peng said turning to Max. "It's especially likely if he has a history of gambling."

Futrell sighed. "Yes, that's a possibility."

Lyle and Max exchanged glances. Lyle had read about Chinese industrial spying in the news but couldn't remember many details. And he wondered how this young-looking pair of agents would help them plug leaks and discover who was trying to steal NC secrets—especially if it had nothing to do with China. *Agent Peng probably thinks the Chinese whacked Jimmy Hoffa.*

When Futrell asked Howard about access to the PAD systems, Max leaned over to Lyle and whispered, "This sounds like hogwash. *You* can find Wyrick. I'll tell you where to look. Come back and see me later this morning."

"China has hundreds of theme parks," Peng said. "They would like to steal some of your cool new rides."

Lyle said, "Did anyone tell you about the finger I found?"

# CHAPTER 21

As soon as he could, Lyle left the meeting and drove directly to the Sheriff's Department in Polk to come clean with Rey.

The San Navarro County undersheriff looked up from a desk full of papers to his computer screen to Lyle. "I'm really busy this morning. What's up?"

"I just left a meeting with the FBI. They wanted to know what I found out about Wyrick."

"And you told them what you told me."

"Yeah. I did. And there's one other thing." He considered telling Rey that he'd only gone into Wyrick's condo that morning and thus hadn't omitted mentioning it the day before. But he didn't know but what sheriff's detectives were already there this morning. He sat down in front of Rey's desk. "I didn't tell you this before, but yesterday I went into Wyrick's condo. Sarah Needham had a key. She told me to give it back to Wyrick." Lyle placed the key on Rey's desk.

He expected Rey to be angry. He just looked hurt. That was worse.

"Why didn't you tell me this yesterday?"

How could he explain that avoidance of conflict was one of the coping mechanisms—the shrinks call it *symptoms*—of anxiety. He'd worried about how Rey would react—even though he was a friend who had already been through serious scrapes with him. Maybe it was getting drafted to search for Wyrick. Maybe it was worry about tainting the evidence. Maybe he was embarrassed.

"I didn't tell you because what I did was a little like unlawful entry."

"Yeah."

"But not really. I had a key."

"You could have told me ahead of time."

"Would you have gone in with me?"

"Maybe."

"That's what I had in mind. I called you, but the office said you were out and your cell went to voicemail."

"The sheriff and I were at a county meeting." Rey leaned back in his chair and stared at Lyle. "Did you find out anything at the place? I assume you left it the way you found it."

Lyle explained finding the water-bottle camera.

"Did you touch it?"

"I wore gloves the whole time. I left it sitting on the desk upstairs at Wyrick's."

"A spy camera. That looks bad for Wyrick." Rey sighed and rested his arms on his desk. "What did the FBI say when you told them?"

Lyle wanted to be anywhere else. What could he say?

"You didn't tell them, did you? You withheld evidence from the FBI. That's why you're here, isn't it? You want help."

"Sorry Rey. I'm a shit."

"And hard to understand sometimes." He glanced at his watch. "Detectives are planning to go into Wyrick's place this morning along with a crew from the FBI. Wyrick's father's flying in. *Hijo de perra.* Lyle, you could have just kept your mouth shut. No one would know and we wouldn't have to worry about tainted evidence." He brought his hands together and stared into space. "The key, that's it, isn't it? Without the key, there's no way of knowing that you were there or that you withheld the evidence. But we *have* the key, don't we? Sarah Needham gave it to you."

"Rey, I…"

"Hmm. Okay. Let's see…. I'll try to forget you went into Wyrick's place. I'll just pass the key along to my detectives and say it came from Wyrick's girlfriend. If the FBI asks, I'll tell the truth and say you got it from the girlfriend and gave it to me. You'd have to tell them you forgot to mention it. Likely it wouldn't be a big deal."

Lyle couldn't tell if Rey's grimace reflected personal or professional disappointment. Really both. "Thanks Rey. I don't know what more to say. I screwed up. I'm sorry."

Rey's face turned expressionless.

"I think Max is going to put me on the road investigating again."

"Are you okay Lyle?"

■ ■ ■

When Lyle got back to the park, Max was still ensconced at the head of his conference room table. He was talking into his cell phone and motioned for Lyle to sit next to him in the otherwise empty room. Into his phone Max barked out questions about internet and computer security, peppering his remarks with the occasional "bullshit." Feeling not at all sorry for whoever was on the other end of the line, Lyle tried to relax as he glanced around the room. Movie posters, probably originals, advertising top films from the 1970s decorated the walls. Lyle glanced at posters for *Rocky, Jaws, Jonathan Livingston Seagull,* and his gaze stopped at a poster for *The Shining* showing Jack Nicholson's maniacal expression.

Max ended his call and put down his cell phone. Lyle looked away from the movie posters and waited.

"You need to go to Atlantic Adventures," Max said.

"The Florida theme park?"

"Yup. That bastard Jack Danneman is president. I'm sure he's behind all this."

Lyle's mouth sagged. He started to speak.

"Dammit, we have to solve this," Max said. "Need to find out for sure what was stolen. I told you this is leading-edge tech. If we don't recover this, our millions will be down the drain and that damn Danneman will have the best rides in the world—at our expense. Find out exactly what they've got and what they plan to do with it." He made a fist. "We've got to stop them."

"Why would Danneman want to steal our secrets?"

"Because he's a crook. When we were building this place, Jack said he wanted to buy into my Vegas casino. Could have been a good deal. I needed cash for this park and he wanted to spread his name around. Except the bastard backed out at the last minute. He violated the contract, tried to copy my ideas, and accused *me* of trying to steal *his* theme park ideas. He's a lowlife, and he likes to get revenge."

"So you want me to go to Florida and talk to this guy."

Max frowned. "C'mon Lyle. Of course not. He'll deny every-thing. Then everyone would be on their guard."

"Then what—"

"You're a damn detective. You'll figure it out. If you want to find Wyrick, this is the place. Danneman probably bought him off."

"What about the FBI and the sheriff?"

"Hell, do you think the San Navarro County Sheriff is going to send people across the country on my say-so? And you heard the FBI agents." He held up his hands and waved his fingers in the air as if he were playing a piano. "They think it's *international intrigue.*"

Max's assignment *did* give his brain something different to focus on. Nevertheless, Lyle reached into his jacket pocket to be sure he had his container of Valium.

"Talk to my assistant. She'll make flight reservations. When you get something concrete on Danneman, we can call in the FBI."

Lyle looked up and saw Jack Nicholson leering behind Max's back.

# CHAPTER 22

Kate stared at a photo on her computer, trying to figure out what was wrong. Less than two days into the filming and she was trying hard not to regret the decision to invite Appropriate Brand Pictures to Nostalgia City.

"You look cheery," Lyle said as he poked his head into her office.

She looked up, startled at first, then thankful to see his face. "Just thinking about something that happened on the set this morning."

"Problem?" He settled himself into a guest chair.

"Two of the actors got in a fight. One of them got kicked off the set."

"Don't tell me. Cory Sievers."

"He started it, but the other guy, an older actor named Julian Russo, got disciplined. The director told him to take a break and not come back to the set until Thursday."

"What happened?"

"I just heard part of it. Sievers flubbed a line, and he said Julian distracted him. He ran over and smacked Julian. Almost knocked him down. Julian didn't fight back, even when Sievers broke a drone he was holding. The director blamed Julian and I think he was embarrassed."

"Uh-huh."

"And Julian is the guy Sievers threatened to kill two years ago."

Lyle stared out the window.

"Hello, Lyle."

"Sorry. Pay no attention to me. I'm not in my Fun Zone today." He nodded at the window toward the park's amusement ride area off in the distance.

She stretched a hand out across her desk. Lyle leaned over, took her hand, and squeezed it. "That helps," he said. "Always."

She felt the warmth of his hand for several moments before she leaned back in her chair and glanced at her computer monitor. "Here's something that may *not* help your mood, but you probably need to know. The Flagstaff paper had a story today about an intrusion and possible theft of a new ride at NC.

"They called me late yesterday for a comment," she said. "I tried to shrug it off and say it was under investigation. I really don't know any details. The *Phoenix Standard* is onto the story, too. *And* I saw an article on a theme park industry website about the theft. It cited a rumor that Nostalgia City had data about rides or technology stolen and that a missing employee might be involved. Only people in the theme park business will see this story. But I'm afraid it's spreading. For now, I'm going to stick with the 'it's under investigation' strategy. At least the fight on the movie set hasn't leaked out yet. It will."

Lyle acknowledged with a vague nod of his head.

"You still fretting?"

"Sorry. Just distracted. And Max is sending me to Florida."

"What for?"

He explained his meeting with Max and the FBI. "The FBI agents, at least one of them, think the Chinese government is probably responsible for stealing the plans, the technology. Howard said we ought to consider the FBI's ideas." He tapped his temples with his index fingers. "Max thinks they're nutty. I might agree with him, except *his* idea is to send me to Florida to investigate this rival of his." He made a face.

This sounded to Kate like a typical Max mess where you didn't know who represented the voice of reason, nor exactly what Max expected of you. "China?"

"Yeah, the agents say China has been stealing American intellectual property for years. And the country has lots of theme parks. So, does that make sense?"

"Obviously not to Max."

"Right. So his assistant booked me on a plane to Miami. And Samantha was going to come up for a visit."

More than once Lyle told Kate that Samantha, his stepdaughter, was the big positive consequence of his marriage and divorce. Lyle had supplanted Samantha's biological father, who rarely saw her, and became her backstop emotionally and, ultimately, financially. He loved her dearly. Now a senior at Arizona State, she visited Lyle frequently.

"You'll see her again soon."

"Yeah," he grumbled. "You worked for Max in Vegas. Do you remember someone named Jack Danneman?"

"Hmm. Danneman, yes. Max tried to get him to be a partner in his struggling World Underground Hotel. But the guy backed out."

"That's not exactly how Max explained it. But yeah, he was a potential investor and Max thinks he wanted to steal his ride ideas back then—only he accused Max of wanting to steal *his* ideas. Danneman is head of Atlantic Adventures in Florida."

"He might have more history with Danneman, but I can't remember. Max wasn't the best-liked casino owner in town."

Kate looked at him and hoped they could spend the night together. It had been several days, and the unexpected tension from several directions, including her cat's condition, refused to submit to her usual remedies. And judging by Lyle's dour expression, some lovemaking would do him good, too. Kate felt their relationship was solid, if restrained at times. They lived blocks apart in Timeless Village and alternated sleeping at Kate's apartment or Lyle's condo, when they slept together, which was intermittent.

"When are you leaving?"

"Tomorrow morning. Early. I'm leaving from Phoenix."

"That's enough time."

"I was thinking the same thing."

Lyle's warm goodbye hug promised more togetherness. Kate went back to puzzling at the photo on her computer, a *Murder for No Reason* cast picture at the entrance to Nostalgia City.

# CHAPTER 23

L ook, I need to see her right now, okay?"
Just back from lunch, Kate recognized the raspy voice of
Tori Malcolm. She didn't sound as if she'd dropped by for a
friendly chat. Kate had an idea what she wanted. Is this what it's
like working in Hollywood? One mini-crisis after another? Maybe
this one wasn't so *mini*. Rather than have the film publicist
ushered into her office, Kate walked out to the reception area.

"Tori," Kate said, "we're getting calls about the incident. How
do you want to handle it? The actors are your territory, but—"

"Just a little trouble on the set. No biggie. Actors are tempera-
mental. It comes with the territory, okay? Right now I need to
know about the news crew that jus' got here from KTEM in
Phoenix. I wish someone had tol' me about it. Bad timing."
Malcolm spoke at California business speed as if she were impa-
tient for a reply even before she'd asked a question.

"Do you want to come into my office?"

Malcolm held a phone in her hand and kept tapping it against
her hip. "I need to get back to the set."

Kate struggled to distinguish genuine emergencies from

Malcolm's normal, everyday rush, rush. "What's the matter?"

"Did you authorize the TV crew?"

"I think so." With everything going through her head of late, she wasn't positive.

"Well, I have someone from a network affiliate coming out. Should be here any minute. I tol' *them* they could do a feature on the historical side of the film and talk to the screenwriter—as an exclusive." She stopped only briefly to take a breath. "I don't want some local indie station getting in the way. I *thought* this historical approach would help Nostalgia City, too." She stole a glance at her phone.

"Sorry if there was a mix-up. My media coordinator, Amanda Updike, schedules all the press. She should have been keeping you up to date."

"I like to talk to the boss."

"I appreciate that. But we need to keep Amanda in the loop. She'll take care of it."

"Okay. Be sure." Malcolm turned to go.

"Wait a minute," Kate said. "What about Sievers and Julian?"

"Yeah?"

"We've been getting media calls, and I need to get back to them."

"Refer them to me. It was just an argument between actors. It happens."

"But Sievers—"

"I know. Cory Sievers. He's a pain, but nothing we can do. Maybe somebody could talk to that agent of his. I don't know why *he's* here. He's not supposed to be on the set."

"What about Julian?"

"Julian gets on people's nerves. He's that way. Send me the calls, okay?"

Malcolm walked out of the office, and Kate turned and saw her secretary standing in the doorway.

"Stephanie Tyler is on the phone for you," Joann said. "Julian Russo is dead."

# CHAPTER 24

"What happened, Steph?" Kate said, picking up the phone in her office.

"Something bad. A detective is out here talking to people." Stephanie paused, and a sob escaped. "He just told me Julian's... his body was found in a canyon near here. That's all he'd *tell* me."

"Are you still filming?"

"So far. We've got a scene to finish right now. Maybe...maybe we'll break early. I don't know what to do. Something was bothering Jules yesterday, and now he's gone."

"Can I help? Do you want to talk? I could come down there."

"We're in the middle of a scene. I gotta go."

When she left her office, Kate tried to visualize Julian the last time she saw him in a movie. Some sort of family drama. *Didn't he die early in the film?* She couldn't remember. What happened to him? And what a shock for Stephanie.

On Main Street Kate walked past a bookstore, art gallery, and hat shop—all closed because of the filming. Hefty lights shined, actors spoke their lines on the sidewalk near the café, the crew stood silent. The director yelled "cut" and crew members started talking and moving equipment. Kate saw Stephanie talking with the director and another crew member, so she wandered around the perimeter of the set. A man in a coat and tie held a notebook and pen as he talked with Jana Osbourn. He could have been a movie cop, but Kate recognized him as a San Navarro County Sheriff's detective. When he finished talking to the film star, Kate walked up.

"Detective Gage, right? I'm Kate Sorensen, public relations VP for the park."

The detective nodded.

"Are you investigating the death of Julian Russo?"

"Do you have some information about it?"

"No, I was wondering what happened. The park may get news media calls."

Gage glanced at his notebook for a moment, then put it in a pocket. "Mr. Russo's body was found this morning at the bottom of Little Buckhorn Canyon."

"The bottom of the canyon? What happened? How did he die? Was anyone with him? Did he *fall*?"

"We're still investigating, Ms. Sorensen. I'm trying to get a picture of who he was and what he was doing out at the canyon. That's all I can tell you. Can you excuse me? I need to talk to that guy over there."

She'd had a feeling she wouldn't get anywhere, but it was worth a try. She made eye contact with Stephanie, and her friend broke away from a group and walked over. Kate put both arms around her.

"Oh God, I don't know what to do," Stephanie said. "They won't tell us anything."

Kate kept an arm on Stephanie's shoulder. "When did you find out?"

"A little while ago." She dabbed her eyes with a tissue and took a deep breath. "We're going to break for the day." She glanced back at the director who nodded his head. "Wes wants me to shut things down. Sorry. I need to go."

Kate could feel her friend's sorrow. As she walked back to her office, she wondered how she could help. While she waited for the elevator, Amanda, her media coordinator, walked in.

"I talked to Tori," Amanda said. "She's kind of wired twenty-four-seven, isn't she?" She stepped into the elevator with Kate. "I told her the TV reporter I invited wouldn't bother her. She goes, 'Okay. I've got the exclusive.' And that was it."

When they reached their floor and got out, Kate stopped. "I have a job for you."

"Sure. What can I do?"

"Julian Russo, an actor in the movie, died today—suspicious circumstances. Something about his body being found in a canyon out past Polk."

Amanda frowned. "Was he...the old guy with the drones?"

"Yes, I guess everyone heard about his trouble."

"Yeah, and there was a fight on the set."

"Something like that. His death is going to be a story, but there's nothing from the sheriff yet. Could you see what hits social media and the local news about this? Julian was well known enough that it will be in the major papers and on TV. We need to be prepared in case we get calls, and I'd like to know what you find." *Maybe the media will tell us what the investigator wouldn't.*

Back in her office, Kate called Rey.

"Sorry Kate, I can't tell you very much."

"Well, they found him at the bottom of Little Buckhorn Canyon. I know the area. Was he hiking or did he fall? Was there a fight? Was it murder?"

"We're in the middle of the investigation."

"I know. I saw Detective Gage out at the movie set."

"So you know deputies are still working it. I won't know anything until I see their reports, talk to them, and then hear from the medical examiner."

"It might affect the park. I was just trying to be—"

"When we release information to the public, I can probably answer your questions."

"In other words, you'll tell me what you release to the press."

"We *really* don't know much yet. We're talking to witnesses—"

"There were *witnesses*?"

Rey groaned. "I can't always mix my official duties with people I know."

"People you know? It's me. We worked on that murder case? You know what you tell me won't go anywhere. Could you give me an idea?"

"Why don't you ask Lyle."

# CHAPTER 25

A sixteenth-century Spanish galleon sailed past Lyle's vantage point, cannons blazing. The crew, a half dozen teenagers, laughed and wiped the water from their faces as the ship splashed through a wave then vanished around a rocky point. Soon another small-scale ship carried its six passengers across the artificial lagoon.

Lyle sipped the dregs of his lukewarm coffee. He turned his attention away from the Atlantic Adventures Spanish Main ride and back to the nonstop flow of theme park tourists walking by. He'd been sitting in the coffee shop patio for nearly an hour trying to fight off jet lag with caffeine, staring at the multitude, and wondering how he'd get the goods on Jack Danneman. He absently reached for the rubber band on his wrist, forgetting it had broken the day before. A sharp snap of the band was an antidote to anxiety, making him clear his head and focus on the present moment. He didn't really need the help now, anyway. His problem was more stupor than stress.

Checking out the theme park itself sounded like a good starting point. Did Atlantic Adventures have high-tech rides similar to the ones stolen from Nostalgia City? Did they need new ones, or would the NC innovations be out of place in the Florida park? Loosely patterned after events in Southeast history, park attractions ranged from traditional thrill rides to elaborate dark rides in cars and other conveyances.

He had arrived in Miami late the previous afternoon, tired but unable to sleep. He called Kate at midnight eastern time. She told him that character actor Julian Russo had died under what she thought were suspicious circumstances. So far there were only rumors about how it happened.

Lyle also talked to his friend who had finally called him back from the Crossroads Casino.

"Tom Wyrick paid off his debts with us about ten days ago," the accountant said.

"Could you tell me how much he's lost there?"

"Over the last eighteen months, the house has won more than one hundred and eighty thousand."

"Casino talk, huh? Winnings. Bottom line, Wyrick has dropped more than a cab driver makes in two or three years." *How could he afford losses like that? Where'd he get it? Did a programmer make that much? Gambling debts could be why Wyrick quit academia for a corporate paycheck.*

"We haven't seen him here since he brought his account current," she said.

"He paid off and left? Period?"

"That's what it looks like. No recent activity in his account."

Wyrick's big debt could easily be his reason for selling out, yet it did nothing to tell Lyle how to find him.

As he sat looking at the assortment of faces passing in front of him, they didn't look much different from the tourists who packed the streets of Nostalgia City every day. In fact, he'd seen one face before. A man in his thirties walked by with a child in tow. Where had he seen this guy? How did he know him? It wasn't someone from his cop days, not likely a criminal. With dark hair trimmed close and black plastic-framed glasses, he looked more like a professional of some sort. He walked slowly with a rangy gate. Maybe he was from NC or had ridden in his cab. Lyle dropped his coffee cup in a trash container and followed the pair.

The man and boy—he assumed a father and his six- or seven-year-old son—strolled through the muggy air, taking in the panorama of rides, food carts, and souvenir shops shaded by palm trees. Lyle followed the stream of tourists moving around the bow of a life-sized looking freighter as it lurched slowly up and down in an inlet, beckoning guests into a ride called the Bermuda Triangle Voyage.

A crowd made it easier to tail someone without being seen. Lyle tagged along at a safe distance and watched the pair approach a historical, narrow-gauge train ride. The queue for the ride snaked back and forth through rows—theme park style—but the man led his son away from the entrance to an open space where they could observe the trains and locomotives pass by. As a train passed, picking up speed rapidly, the man knelt down, pulled out his cell phone, and appeared to take pictures, either of the locomotive or its running gear. The man waited and looked to be taking pictures of more than one train. When he finished, he and the boy got in line.

Lyle followed, keeping about a dozen tourists between them. The young boy could not be still, and he climbed on the railings and looked all around, once making eye contact with Lyle. After a half hour, they reached the boarding area. The man and boy chose an open-air car on the Jacksonville, St. Augustine & Halifax Railroad. Lyle took a seat a few rows behind them. As the train pulled out, the man pointed his phone at the control panel staffed by young people dressed in period costumes.

The ride took them across faux mangrove swamps that Lyle thought might not be so faux. At times the tracks became submerged in murky water, and the lurking alligators, real or artificial, looked at Lyle as if he were a Big Mac. Suddenly the cars shook, the regular click-clack of the wheels replaced by grinding, groaning metal. The cars tilted until Lyle felt they were going to topple into the water.

After the ride, he had still not remembered where he'd seen the man before, but he was getting close.

"Who is this guy?" he said as he walked.

The pair then led him to a dark ride where tourists drove horseless carriages through turn-of-the-century Charleston. This time, Lyle decided not to follow. He knew where they would exit. As before, the man pointed his cell phone at control panels and ride mechanisms. Just before the pair's car entered the ride, the man turned his cell phone camera on his son—almost as an afterthought—and told him to smile. Not your average tourists.

After the pair left the ride, the boy led his father to an outdoor restaurant. They bought hot dogs and drinks and sat at a metal table under a market umbrella. By now Lyle was pretty sure he'd seen the man at Nostalgia City—recently. He bought a drink and sat down with one table between him and the father and son.

He couldn't hear their voices clearly, but it didn't matter. Lyle looked at his watch. It was early in the day in Arizona—three hours to the west. He pulled out his cell phone and aimed it at the man with the boy. To anyone watching, Lyle was checking email or posting on social media. In truth, he took a close-up picture of the guy. Then he texted the photo to Howard, hoping Chaffee was somewhere he could respond. Lyle's accompanying note read:

I'm in Florida for Max. Do you know this guy? He's at a theme park here. I've seen him at NC.

Lyle sipped his drink and looked at his phone. After a few minutes, the father and son were finishing their meal. The boy got up and tossed his plate into the trash. He tugged on his father's arm.

Where was Howard? Maybe he didn't get the text.

The boy picked up his drink. His father rose to leave.

# CHAPTER 26

Kate opened her eyes before the alarm went off. She'd spent part of the evening consoling Stephanie and listening to her tell anecdotes about Julian and his movies. Above all, Stephanie had worried over the cause of his death. Would filming continue today? *Get out of bed Sorensen and find out.*

Kate abbreviated her makeup—she needed little—and was out of her apartment on time, after checking her cat's food, water, and litter box. Trixie was on the mend.

The evening before, she'd also talked to Lyle. He'd called her from his Florida hotel.

"I miss you," she began.

"Me too."

He sounded tired, anxious. She told him about Julian's mysterious death and asked him how long he'd be gone. He didn't know. She forgot to ask him about Rey's strange comment. Actually, she didn't want to risk stressing him long distance. It could wait. She said she'd call him tomorrow evening.

Before going into her office, she wandered down Main Street again toward the movie location. A street sweeper had been by recently. Pools of water glistened with the morning sun and reflected a cloudless sky. She knew Stephanie was often the first person on the set, and she found her friend seated at a portable table tapping on a laptop.

"Did you get any sleep?" Kate said. "You looked beat last night."

"Thanks for holding my hand. I kept thinking about Jules and couldn't sleep. Then I remembered I made a mistake on the shooting schedule and I got up to fix it, but I couldn't concentrate. I'm just scared." She looked up from her computer and seemed to have trouble focusing on Kate. "I'm afraid of what might have happened."

Kate put a hand on her shoulder.

"I let him down, Kate. I realized that last night." She took her hands from the computer and rested them on the table. "I let him down, and then he was murdered."

"We don't know that." Kate sat next to her on a folding chair. "Maybe it was an accident."

"No, no. He was too careful. He wasn't afraid of heights that I know of, but he didn't take chances. He said as he got older he got more cautious. Jules wouldn't have stood too close to the edge. No, Kate. He got killed because I let him down."

"What do you mean?"

"We had dinner together. He was distracted. He said something about being followed. When he heard a noise, he would turn and look around the restaurant. One time he knocked over his water."

"What was he worried about?"

"I don't know. He started to tell me, then someone from the crew came over to our table to ask me a question." She paused and seemed to collect her thoughts. "Lots of cast and crew in the restaurant that night. Jana was across the room with someone, and later Alan Clappison came in and sat near us. I worried that he'd bother us, too. Our check came and Jules never finished telling me."

"Did you tell this to the detective who was here yesterday?"

"Yes." She tightened her lips and looked at her friend. "But I let Jules down." She took a breath. "He wanted to hang out after dinner and talk, but I was exhausted—worrying about him and his problem with Cory—and I had more work I *had* to get done before I could get to bed. This is the biggest picture I've worked on, and Wes is picky. I said good night early."

And the next morning he went off the cliff. "I tried to get details yesterday from a friend at the Sheriff's Department," Kate said, "but he was being a hard-ass."

"It was Cory. Cory, Cory, Cory." She repeated the actor's name over and over until her voice trailed off. "It's a nightmare to think about." She banged her hand on the table. "It was Cory. He did it."

After a fight on the set with an unstable actor, Julian plummeted to his death. Kate repressed a shudder. "We'll find out today." She gripped Stephanie's hand.

Slowly crew members walked onto the set, tested lights, arranged scenery.

"Are you going ahead with the filming?" Kate asked. *The show must go on?*

"We're going to replace—*they're* going to replace—Julian in a few days. Julian had only filmed one brief scene. No delays. Time is money with a big crew working," she said with an edge in her voice.

"Stay busy. That always helps me. "

"I don't have a choice. I have to keep things running."

. . .

Later that morning, Amanda appeared at Kate's office door. "I've been monitoring the suicide in the media like you asked, and a Flagstaff station has—"

"Suicide? Is that what the sheriff said?"

Amanda scrunched up her mouth. "No, I didn't see anything from the sheriff, but it looks like suicide. Channel Fourteen in Flagstaff had an interview with a witness. I emailed you a copy of the clip."

Kate swiveled her chair around and reached for her mouse. She found Amanda's email and clicked to start a video clip. A woman, probably in her late sixties, wearing wire-rimmed glasses, gestured with her hands as she talked into the camera.

"I was hiking, hiking with my friend Joyce." She nodded to the woman next to her. The speaker wore a long-sleeve T-shirt and a vest with flapped pockets. "We were on the Little Buckhorn Trail near the bottom of the canyon. There's this little up-hill part where the trail does a U, so we had to go slow. I was just lookin' around, y'know, and I sees this guy way up there just standing on the edge."

Wild strands of hair fanned out below the brim of her tan canvas hat. She pushed the hat back as her voice rose. "There he was. He just stood there for a minute without moving, then he jumped off. It was horrible. He sorta goes like this." She swung her arms around as she took a step forward.

"I couldn't look, y'know. I screamed at Joyce. She saw him go down somewhere off into the canyon."

"So you were at the bottom of the canyon, looking up," said the TV reporter holding a mic. The hiker bobbed her head up and down.

The reporter turned to the camera. "Deputies said Russo fell at least three hundred feet into the canyon. His body was recovered and delivered to the morgue."

"I hope I never see anything like that again," said the wide-eyed witness. "I think I'm still shaking."

Kate stopped the video. "It does sound like suicide. Did you find anything else?"

"One Phoenix TV station had a brief mention," Amanda said. "They just said the sheriff was still investigating. *The Phoenix Standard* today has an obit mentioning that his wife died two years ago, and it lists some of his movies. A news radio station website said Julian Russo had a troubled past. They said after his wife died he was treated for depression. Gossip on social media was mostly about suicide."

# CHAPTER 27

Drained from his cross-country flight and baked by heat and humidity intense enough to strip wallpaper, Lyle didn't know what to do. The father and son he'd been trailing were leaving. Then his phone hummed.

Howard's message read: The guy is Rob Napier, a PAD engineer.

*Who needs facial recognition software when I have Howard?* Lyle could think of a couple of reasons why Napier was visiting another theme park, but he decided just to ask him.

He stood. "Rob Napier?"

Napier looked at Lyle with a noncommittal expression. "Yes?"

Lyle introduced himself, said he worked for Nostalgia City, and said he recognized Napier having seen him recently, probably earlier in the week at the PAD offices.

"I was there Monday morning," Napier said. "We were scheduled to fly here sooner, but I had to come into the office early Monday to um, analyze some issues."

"That's when I must have seen you in one of the offices. They called me out there after the hacking."

Napier presented a perfect poker face. "Oh?"

"I know about it," Lyle said. "I'm looking for Tom Wyrick. Arena briefed me. Could we talk for a minute?"

Napier invited Lyle to sit with them. He introduced Lyle to his son. "Do you work for security?"

"Sometimes. Right now I'm working directly for Maxwell." He paused. "I'm an ex-cop."

Napier's son sipped his drink, but his attention was obviously drawn to an otter enclosure nearby. "You can go look at them," his father said. "Just stay where I can see you."

He watched his son for a moment, then turned to Lyle. "So you know what happened at the park."

"I know there was a security breach," Lyle said. "I know Wyrick has been gone from work for more than a week. You may know more than I do. So, why are you here?"

Napier glanced back at his son. "We're on vacation."

"Sure." Napier wasn't a bad liar. "I really do work for the park. We can call there if you like. Talk to security or maybe get Max on the line."

Napier raised a hand. "It's okay. I think I've heard of you." He paused and smiled. "No big deal here. I'm just here keeping an eye on the competition. Someone from PAD visits the other parks regularly. We take turns. The engineers mostly. We know what to look for."

"Is Howard in on this?"

"Mr. Chaffee? Yes, he's coached us." He lowered his voice, "on spying without being too obvious."

Napier sounded like he might relish the role as a Nostalgia City secret agent.

"This time I brought my son with me."

"Father and son," Lyle said. "Fits right in. Have you seen anything interesting?"

"Not really. The park hasn't innovated much recently."

"So they could use an infusion of new high tech?"

"Possibly." Napier looked over at his son again. "They bring new rides on line when they need to. It's an irregular pace, something like ours. Why do you ask? Do you suspect something?"

"Do you know Tom Wyrick?"

"Yes. I've worked with him. He's an amazing conceptual thinker. He can leave you behind in a technical conversation because his brain has leaped ahead."

"Genius?"

"Uh-huh."

"How about Vang?"

"Paul Vang? Yes, I know him. He's a developer. Sharp guy."

"Honest?"

"Uh-huh. Straight arrow. Paul's not—"

"No." Lyle said, "unrelated."

So Vang's story about Wyrick stealing his log-ins was probably right.

Napier glanced at the tables to their right and left. He lowered his voice. "*Do* you think Atlantic Adventures might have put Wyrick up to this?"

Napier *did* like the espionage stuff. "I have no idea. The PAD people I talked to say theme parks do steal from each other—news to me—so here I am."

"Our operational tests have been very promising. Any park would love to have our new formulations."

Napier had a habit of using his thumb and forefinger to adjust his glasses by the top corner of the frame. Lyle saw it as a mannerism showing wisdom or experience, something a '70s TV doctor might have done while dispensing medical advice. Maybe Napier didn't know he was doing it.

"PDE is a technological game-changer," Napier continued. "Very unique. From what I've heard, it could be cost-prohibitive to replicate from the beginning. I've only worked on a few elements of it, but I understand our technology could shave years off somebody else's project development and then only if they knew where to start."

PDE, that was the perception deception thing that Larry

Michaels talked about. "So this is like a blueprint for the next generation of rides?"

"That's a simplification, but yes. Unless someone invents a transporter room or time machine, once it's finished, PDE could be the vanguard for more than a decade."

*If Max's hunch—more like wild-ass idea—was right, Danneman would have to know about PDE before he bought off Wyrick. How did he find out?* "If you wanted to peek into the ride engineering and programming offices here, where would you go?"

Napier's eyes widened for a moment. "Want me to show you? We can walk over there."

Maybe engineering wasn't exciting enough for Napier. "You've got your son here. I'm sure I can find it." Lyle pulled out a park map from his pocket. "Maybe you can show me here."

Napier started drawing on the theme park map, pointing out ways to get into employee areas. "The administrative offices, research, and fabrication are all in buildings right here. Most of them don't show on this map." He drew an arrow. "You can go in right here."

Lyle now had the *where* of his search for Wyrick, next he had to figure out the *how*.

# CHAPTER 28

N o, but I need to explain. He didn't. It wasn't. Not suicide. Murder."

Everyone in the conference room heard the disjointed words from a loud voice Kate recognized as Stephanie's. All ten people looked up when an anxious clerk opened the door and searched the faces around the table. Kate saved her time. She got up and went outside.

"Kate," Stephanie cried when she walked into the anteroom. "I've been thinking about this all day." She stopped and wiped tears away. "He did not commit suicide like they say. He was murdered."

The clerk hovered, looking concerned and obviously curious.

Kate led her friend to an alcove in the Maxwell Annex's broad hallway. They chose a corner couch and sat together. She looked at Stephanie's red eyes, her uncombed hair. She was losing it.

"Your office said you were here. I *had* to talk. The paper, did you see the paper? It's bullshit. The story in the paper today?" She pulled her tablet out of her large purse and frantically tapped on it until a story from a Phoenix newspaper appeared under the headline:

**Suicide Suspected in Actor's Death**

Kate had already read the wire story. It quoted Rey's boss, the San Navarro County Sheriff, saying the death was being treated as a suicide. According to the investigation, Julian had jumped off a cliff at a canyon overlook. An autopsy was performed in Polk. The story quoted the witnesses Kate had seen on TV. A statement from Julian's long-time agent lamented his death and praised his work.

"It's not true." Stephanie pulled a tissue out of her purse, took a deep breath, and wiped her eyes. "Jules would never. He couldn't."

Kate touched Stephanie's shoulder and whispered. "The story says that he tried to commit suicide before."

"That was years ago after his wife died. He blamed himself for her death. He suffered, Kate. But he never tried suicide again." Stephanie paused for a breath. "After he swallowed the pills, he knew he'd made a mistake. That's what he told me. So he called for help right away. He didn't really mean to do it."

"You said the other day that he was worried or depressed."

"He wasn't depressed." She raised her voice. "I've thought about this a lot. He was nervous, maybe frightened."

Footsteps sounded in the hallway. Kate held up her hand until she heard a door opening and closing.

"I deserted him," Stephanie continued. "I was just too damned busy with work to bother with him."

Kate moved closer. "Something like this is *not* your fault. You had to do your job. Julian knew that."

"It wasn't suicide." Stephanie shook her head and stared at Kate. "He wouldn't. He had plans. He was going to be in another picture this year. They were going to shoot in Europe. He looked forward to it." She looked up quickly, her eyes wide. "And also, I forgot. He said his agent was close to getting him a role in a TV series. He didn't jump off that cliff. He got pushed."

"So you think—"

"Cory Sievers *killed* him."

She shouted the last sentence and Kate heard her voice echo down the tiled hallway. "Steph. Not so loud. You can't say that here."

"You should have heard him on the set this morning," she said, curling her lip. "Greeting everybody and smiling. He was flat-out happy. Bastard. And then he even tried to tell me he was sorry to hear about Julian. He said they *had their differences,* but Julian was a fine actor. Oh, the son of—"

"Did you accuse him?"

"No. I wanted to, but no one would believe me. Cory hated Jules. I tried not to worry when I saw he was going to replace McClintock in the movie. I hoped he'd forget. I wanted it to work out." She made a noise between a laugh and a cry. She touched Kate's arm. "But now he's dead."

"How much of this did you tell the detective the other day?"

"Not much. I just… I don't know."

"You should talk to Detective Gage again. I know people in the Sheriff's Department. I could take you down there."

"I want him arrested."

"Can you get away this afternoon?"

"Oh shit. Look what time it is. I'm supposed to be arranging a shot for tomorrow. Maybe they'll fire me. I don't care. Hell, I gotta go."

"Call me."

Stephanie wiped her eyes again, stuffed her tablet back in her purse, and rushed down the hall. Kate walked back toward the meeting room wondering how many questions she'd have to answer after the managers meeting broke up. She walked to the door, hesitated, then kept walking.

It was nearing five o'clock. She went back to her office. Wyatt Lewis had called, wanting to talk about Cory's casual videos. Depending on developments, she might have additional reasons to talk to Sievers's agent but not now. She picked up a stack of news stories about Julian that Amanda had collected. The printouts included samples of social media posts, and Amanda had even added a few articles from two years before about the death of Julian's wife. She'd been in show business, too. Kate read one obituary.

### Hollywood designer dies after long battle with cancer

*Award-winning Hollywood costume designer Eloise Russo passed away Wednesday after a long battle with cancer.*

*She came to Hollywood from Cincinnati in the late 1970s and worked in the wardrobe departments of several studios before her designs gained recognition.*

*"Mom came out to Hollywood as a kid," said her son Gary Russo. "She always designed her own clothes and wanted to see some of her designs worn by film stars. But it took a long time."*

*In 2008 she won the top Filmwear award for the science fiction costumes in Wesley Gordon Moody's Crusade of the Planets. A year later she received the Costume Designers Guild Award for Excellence in a period film for "The Mushroom Scandal."*

*She is survived by her husband, Julian Russo; a son, Gary Russo; a brother, Will Malcolm; a sister, Iris Edison; an aunt, Phyllis Hallowell, two nieces, and three cousins. Services will be held at Wee Kirk O' the Heather at Forest Lawn in Glendale, Calif.*

Tributes to Julian and biographical stories would come out over the next few days. Kate put the printouts into a folder and set them on her credenza.

No word from Stephanie. Kate tried calling. It went to voice mail. Kate could easily imagine Psycho Sievers losing his temper and killing Julian, but at a scenic canyon overlook miles from Nostalgia City? It seemed to be more a place where someone would go to leap. Regardless, Stephanie should talk to the detective again. It might help her.

After six and she didn't want to go home and fix dinner. The idea of fast food made her scowl, so she walked to the executive dining room to treat herself to a real meal. She saw Howard seated by himself at one of the red Naugahyde booths.

"May I join you? You working late too?"

"The movie shoot has brought us more guests and a few more troublemakers," he said after Kate sat down.

"Anything serious?"

"Just lots of routine stuff. And I need to walk the park after dark. I haven't done it for a while."

A server whose name badge said he was originally from Albuquerque took their orders and suggested a wine. Kate ordered a glass of chardonnay. Howard, iced tea.

Howard wore a camel blazer. Lyle was right about the ex-San Francisco cop adopting a more casual look, perhaps in keeping with the slower-paced southwest. He must have read her mind because he complimented her on her pinstripe pantsuit then said, "Is Russo's suicide causing you any grief? Sounds like it's not going to stop them from filming."

"Not so far. A murder might be another story." She meant to surprise Howard, and she did.

"Murder? Who's saying that? The evidence looks pretty conclusive."

"From what I've read so far, you're right. But just between you and me, the first assistant director—Stephanie is a friend of mine —doesn't think Julian killed himself. I'm taking her to talk to the detective on the case first thing tomorrow. I tried to find out more details from Rey the other day, but he stonewalled me."

"The sheriff's been really pushing him to find out what happened. That could be it. I don't know if Max had any influence in this, especially as it hasn't affected the park that I can see. But all in all, Rey's been feeling pressure to resolve the Russo case. There were witnesses to the fall and a sheriff's detective even found out that Russo was drinking and singing the blues in the Copacetic Bar in Centerville the night before."

*That last item wasn't in the news stories. Howard obviously has a better pipeline than I do.*

Their food arrived, and Howard stopped talking until the server had gone. "I see that expression on your face. Yes, I talked to Rey. He called about something at the park, so I asked him about Russo. Now that he's almost finished with the case, Rey may have more time to talk."

# CHAPTER 29

The receptionist had pleasant features: a round face, wide-set hazel eyes, Florida tan, glistening light brown hair. Her nameplate said she was Amber Neff, and she was an Adventure Experience Associate. Odd title for a receptionist, but the term *adventure experience* had promise. Maybe this building housed the people who developed the Atlantic Adventures experiences. Amber smiled at Lyle and asked how she could help him. He took a breath and became calm. He'd rehearsed his response.

Earlier that morning, coffee and scrambled eggs had helped him shake off a disoriented feeling. He sat in his South Florida hotel's coffee shop and thought about how to search for Wyrick when going to the beach was a much better idea. The ocean wasn't too far and Florida had miles of soft, sandy shore. A beach chair, the sound of waves, and a good novel on his lap. Oh yeah, and a beer or two. Max should give him a vacation rather than send him on a search for the runaway Tom Wyrick.

At least he now knew a little more about his quarry, thanks to his friend from the Crossroads Casino. Wyrick's record with the casino was interesting, but it could mean several things. In addition to his casino line of credit, he could have been in debt to others, loan sharks if he was desperate. Was the theft *his* idea? Did he steal the secrets to pay off *all* his debts? And how did he find a buyer for the technology? He probably didn't post it on eBay.

Conversely, an inveterate gambler with debts could be a target for blackmail. But the blackmailers would have to know about Nostalgia City's tech breakthrough and know about Wyrick's habits. Either way, finding Wyrick remained daunting. He could be in South America. Or lounging on one of those soft, sandy Florida beaches working for Jack Danneman.

"Funny," Lyle murmured, starting another of his habitual out-loud conversations with himself. "Why didn't I go through this thought process before?" He knew the answer. He'd thought a missing persons case belonged to the Sheriff's Department, so his NC interviews had been pro forma. Ditto for his hasty foray into Wyrick's condo. He'd figured that Wyrick might never show up or, however unlikely, might walk in to work the next day.

He pondered how he might approach Atlantic Adventures as he sipped his third cup of coffee. As Max had said, walking in and asking if they happened to have secret technology developed at Nostalgia City was definitely out. Asking after Wyrick might be the better choice. Lyle didn't have a yellow pad, his usual tool for solving problems, so he sat in the restaurant and made notes on his phone. What excuse could he use? Why was he looking for Wyrick? As usual, he wanted to make a list. His smartphone's reminders app was the closest thing he had to a lined pad. After a few minutes of note-taking, he was using the cell phone to make phone calls.

He called local law firms. He picked attorney names at random from law firm websites and asked for them. It took him several tries before he found an attorney who was out of the office for several days. That done, he signed his breakfast tab and went back to his room. He pulled out the only suit he'd brought with him. A little out of date. Weren't lapels narrower now? It was clean and unwrinkled, so it would have to do if he wanted to look like a lawyer.

Fortunately, only a short drive brought him to the last law firm he'd called. He went into the office and asked for the attorney he knew was out of town. He confirmed that Brent Gallagher would not return until the middle of next week. Perfect. Before he left, he helped himself to a bunch of the absent attorney's business cards.

Next, he drove to the theme park. In the parking lot, he left his engine running to keep the A/C going and called Rey. It took him straight to voice mail.

"Rey, it's me. I heard from a friend of mine at Crossroads Casino. Wyrick ran up huge losses betting on sports. It might be worth a warrant for his records, so you'll have financial evidence you can use, if necessary. Please don't tell anyone I told you.

"One other thing I thought of: Someone should find out who at the PAD office talked to Wyrick when he called in sick. See if it was really him. I missed that one. My heart wasn't really in this, which is maybe why I didn't wait for you to check the condo. I wanted to be done with it. But big surprise. Here I am now in South Florida playing gumshoe at a theme park Max thinks paid Wyrick for all our secrets. Look, I respect the hell out of what you do and value our friendship, and I regret compromising you with the shortcut. It was not what I intended at all. Now, maybe you'll know why.

"At the time we first talked, I knew you'd be upset about my going into Wyrick's condo. I couldn't handle the conflict right then, so I didn't mention it. I know it's hard to understand. I'm sorry."

He hung up and looked down at the Atlantic Adventures map on his lap. Time to get going.

Pulling a little trickery—*fraud* made it sound as if he was doing something illegal—should have made him terminally anxious, but it had the opposite effect. Naturally, he felt a little surface tension, but pretending to be someone else or pulling a similar scheme required intense focus. It demanded the relaxed concentration that forced out the past and future. There was only now. That's what people said about meditation. Running sometimes made him feel the same way.

The map helped him navigate his way on foot to a complex of office buildings on the outer edge of the park. Damn. Howard was right. Hiding the identity of offices and buildings behind letters and numbers or, in this case, Florida place names, made it difficult to know what was what. He chose a building named Kissimmee with a reception area visible beyond double glass doors. The building looked like a cube, as tall as it was wide.

Marble or granite floors reflected indirect lighting flowing from gold abstract shapes in the ceiling two stories up. Tall, three-sided kiosks displaying back-lit photos of park scenes stood to the right of a bank of elevators. Beyond the photo display several people sat behind a long, polished wood reception counter. At the far end sat Amber.

"My name is Brent Gallagher," Lyle told her. "I'm a lawyer, and I'm looking for one of your employees on a very urgent matter."

# CHAPTER 30

Stephanie got out of the SUV first. Kate lingered. "C'mon," Steph said. "Let's do this."

Kate stepped out finally and they approached the entrance to the San Navarro County Sheriff's Department. Unimposing except for the sign with a large, star-shaped sheriff's badge, the recently enlarged single-story tan stucco building spread out for a half block. Palo verde and mesquite trees cast shadows along the walls.

"I'm going to tell him everything I told you," Stephanie said. "Cory Sievers killed Julian."

Stephanie had appeared businesslike—nervous but determined—when Kate picked her up early at her NC hotel. During the twenty-minute drive, Stephanie apologized again for breaking into Kate's meeting the afternoon before, and they decided it would be best if Stephanie talked to the detective by herself.

When Detective Gage led Stephanie back to the detective bureau, Kate remained at the front desk. She had not made up her mind if she would talk with Rey, or what approach she'd take. But a minute after Stephanie left, Rey walked into the front office. He wore a shirt and tie with his pistol clipped to his belt. He seemed surprised to see her.

"How are you, Kate? Is there something we can do for you?"

He sounded normal, Kate thought, as if he hadn't dismissed her on the phone the other day. "Have you got a few minutes to talk?"

He opened a swinging gate and followed Kate back to his office.

"You're a good detective," she said, sitting down in front of his desk. "I'm sure you can guess what I'd like to talk about."

"The Russo case."

She explained that she came to the department with a friend of hers who wanted to talk with Gage. "Julian was a good friend of hers, and she's convinced that he did not kill himself."

"I had more than one person working on this, and the evidence is substantial."

"Stephanie says that Julian had plans to appear in an upcoming movie and TV series. She said the day before he was killed, he was worried, nervous. Always looking over his shoulder. There was a fight on the set—"

"With Cory Sievers. We know about that. And Sievers has a reputation as a hothead. But there's no evidence he pushed Russo off the cliff. We talked to him. He says he was at his hotel and in his trailer Wednesday morning. And why would he do it, because Russo made him *nervous*?"

Rey sounded amiable this morning. She set her purse down on the floor, crossed her legs, and relaxed a little. "I understand. I've had the same thoughts, too. But he *has* been accused of assault in the past *and* Stephanie is so sure that Julian wouldn't kill himself."

Rey glanced at his computer and looked back at Kate. "Alright, let me tell you why we think this is a suicide, okay?" He turned the monitor slightly so Kate could see it. He tapped on his keyboard and the screen changed. Scrolling down, he stared at the page.

"First, Russo had been treated for depression. His wife died two years ago, and later he went to a therapist. Second, he tried to kill himself once before."

"But Steph says he regretted it immediately and called for help."

"That was the first time—that we know of. Many people who *attempt* suicide, eventually succeed. That's number two. Third," he looked at the computer screen, "Russo was drinking at a Nostalgia City bar the night before and complaining about how life wasn't fair."

*Howard was right.*

"And I believe your friend Stephanie told Gage that Russo had been a heavy drinker, but she thought he stopped. I guess he didn't. Now combine these factors with Russo's being insulted and embarrassed by the director after the brief fight. Some of the crew told us that Sievers was the aggressor, but it was Julian who was kicked off the set."

A deputy stepped into the office. "Rey, excuse me, I need to ask you about the patrol schedule."

Kate began to see the case for suicide, but she still had questions. When the deputy left, Rey looked back at his computer screen. "Where was I? Let's see number four—no, five. We have witnesses."

"I know. I saw them on TV. Weren't they a long way away when Russo fell?"

"They were, but detectives asked them more than once if they saw anyone else on the cliff. Anyone who could have pushed him. The answer was 'no.'"

Kate let it sink in. "Where exactly was he standing when he went over?"

"We think he was just to the right of a wooden guardrail at the canyon's Number Two Overlook."

"Did he leave a suicide note?"

He shook his head. "But a majority of suicide victims don't leave notes."

"You did an autopsy?"

"You want the whole thing, don't you?" He paused.

Was he thinking the autopsy would become public record,

anyway?

"The ME found no bullet wounds or any other evidence that he'd been hit or injured before he fell." He leaned back in his chair. "There ya go."

Kate picked up her purse, then remembered a last question. "He was sixty-eight, I think. Could it have been possible that he had a stroke or heart attack that caused him to fall?"

"Whoa, you're a pretty decent detective yourself."

*You should know that after our last murder at the park.*

"Not many people would think of a heart attack in a situation like this. But the ME does. And as far as she could tell, there were no medical issues that could have caused him to fall."

"We found his car parked in the lot by the Number Two Over-look. His keys were in his pocket."

She hadn't quite expected this wealth of evidence. She slid to the edge of her seat, about to stand up. Rey started to swivel his computer screen back around, and something caught Kate's attention. "What's that note there at the bottom? Telephone calls?"

Rey hesitated. He glanced at the screen. "Russo received two calls on his cell phone the evening before. One from his agent and one unknown. Probably a burner phone."

"Thanks, Rey. I appreciate it. Oh, tell me, what was it about Lyle that you mentioned on the phone the other day? You said to ask him something?"

Rey looked past her for a moment. "He was acting a little strange—out of character. I think stress is getting to him a little more than usual. I got a voice mail from him today. He sounded better. Have you noticed anything recently?"

She had.

. . .

"I don't think he believed me," Stephanie said as they drove back to the park. "He asked me, 'what was the nature of your rela-tionship?' Hell, can't two people just be friends? This was a nightmare." She hit her fist on the dashboard. "He told me to call if I thought of anything else. But his mind was made up."

"I talked with Rey Martinez. He's the second in command at the department." *And apparently still a friend.* "He was understanding, but the evidence of suicide is, well, pretty strong. She explained Rey's list, unable to avoid the heartbreak of trying to persuade Steph that Julian killed himself.

At every point, except the apparent absence of another person on the canyon rim, Stephanie shook her head and challenged Rey's arguments.

"Corey Sievers killed him. Will you help me prove it, please?"

# CHAPTER 31

Amber, the receptionist, glanced at the business card Lyle handed her. "Who are you looking for?"

"His name is Tom Wyrick. He's only worked here a short time."

"Is he a guide?"

"No. He does programming."

"We have lots of programs for guests. What type of programs does he do?"

"No, he doesn't *do* programs."

"Does he do tours?"

"No, he's a *computer* programmer."

"Then he wouldn't be working in Adventure Experience Guides."

"Right. He probably works where you design new rides."

"Um, our rides are made by several different departments. But they're not on the tour."

Amber's cheerful demeanor and adorableness didn't quite compensate for her lack of perception. "So," Lyle said, "is there an office or building here where he might be working? Or where I could find him? Or someone I could ask?"

"Why don't you try the Human Resources Department."

*That's your first good suggestion, Amber.* "Can you tell me how to find human resources?"

She pointed to the elevators. "Third floor."

He wanted to snatch back the lawyer business card, but he had others. As he started to step away, Amber raised a hand. "You'll need a visitor badge."

She stopped him from asking what it takes to *get* a badge by pulling out a plastic clip-on ID holder. She looked at his business card and wrote his alias on the badge.

■ ■ ■

Human resources occupied the entire third floor. Dozens of chairs, many filled with teens and twenty-somethings, covered a large open area on the right. Everyone wore a badge like Lyle's. Clerks stood behind a counter that ran along the far wall. Wire racks held stacks of literature. *Obviously, this is where you apply for a job. Take a number. Let's see if there's someone else I can talk with.*

He walked down a hallway, following signs for Employee Development. Behind wooden double doors he found another counter, this one considerably smaller and with only two people waiting for the attention of the smartly dressed assistants. When it was his turn, Lyle smiled at a young man in a shirt, tie, two earrings, and a name badge. He explained who he was, flashed a business card, and said he was looking for Tom Wyrick. "He will only have been working here for maybe a week or so. Would you be able to find out which department he works for?"

"What is this in regards to?"

Lyle hated that expression. Bureaucratic, trite, ungrammatical. His grievance, a legacy of majoring in English and, he thought, of his common sense. "It's an urgent legal matter I need to discuss with him."

The young man obviously didn't know what to do. He told Lyle he needed to go speak to his supervisor and he stepped away. After a five-minute absence, he returned to the counter with the news that his supervisor authorized him to say that no one named Tom Wyrick worked for Atlantic Adventures.

*Swell. I could have found this out on the phone. But it had been a longshot, anyway. If Wyrick was a runaway hacker, would the folks in ride engineering—or whatever the hell they called it here—set him up through HR with a job interview and an employee handbook? Probably not.*

He'd try a fresh approach. He still had cards left from the accommodating attorney.

Back outside, he walked around the collection of buildings. With determination in his step and his dark suit—which made him long for a shower and a tall G and T—he hoped he wouldn't look out of place as he examined buildings obviously not designed to welcome casual visitors. After walking for a half-mile at least, he passed an industrial building with a broad loading dock at the rear. Entrance at the other end of the sprawling single-story structure was a door controlled with some sort of security protocol.

He ambled toward the door, wondering how he would get inside. A speaker hung next to an access panel, maybe a card reader. He wished he'd found time to talk to Howard about the latest security systems. While he pondered how he might talk his way into the building, a man bustled toward him from across the street, heading for the door. Lyle slowed to let him pass and watched as he used a key card and pulled open the door. Right behind him, Lyle reached for the door, offered a "thanks," and walked in.

The man wore expensive-looking casual clothes. He paused and glanced at Lyle's badge. "Are you applying for a job? You need to see Human Resources."

"Oh, the badge," Lyle said, glancing up at a sign. "Bob said I should check in with systems integration."

"Oh, okay." The man paused only a few seconds. "Do you know where it is?"

"Probably this way," he said, pointing in the direction of the *Systems Integration* sign. "Thanks."

The man continued down one hallway leading from the foyer, and Lyle was glad someone named Bob worked nearby. Often a safe bet. He then noticed a framed diagram of the building. According to the layout, the middle of the building looked to be a place where rides were designed and prototypes constructed.

He found the central room to be a combination of small offices and an open computing center. Bingo. Belatedly, he pulled off his badge, stuffed it in his pocket, and approached a counter with desks arranged behind it.

"Can I help you?" asked a middle-aged woman seated at a worktable equipped with several computer monitors.

"I hope so. I'm an attorney, and I'm trying to locate someone on a personal matter."

That seemed to get the woman's attention, so she walked up to the counter. "What is this in regards to?"

Uh oh. Nevertheless, Lyle proffered one of his stolen business cards and gave the woman a moment to digest its authority. He said he was trying to locate a programmer, but instead of saying Wyrick's name, he pulled out his phone.

"This is the man I'm looking for," he said, displaying the Wyrick photo Needham had given him. The woman bent over and looked. Lyle watched her reaction closely. "His name is Tom Wyrick."

The woman looked up shaking her head. Lyle flipped to Wyrick's NC ID picture without the beard. Still no reaction.

"Do you suppose there's anyone else here who might—"

"I've worked here longer than the boss, and I know everyone in the building. Anyone involved in rides. I've never seen your guy. Is there a problem with him? Someone sick?"

"No, it's more of a business matter."

He thanked her and looked for the exit.

Driving to his hotel, listening to *Evil Ways* by Santana, Lyle realized he'd missed lunch. He imagined an immediate future that included a drink—or two—an early dinner, and a flight reservation for Arizona. He'd spotted a good-looking fish restaurant near Atlantic Adventures. It had to be here somewhere. Turning on a vaguely familiar-looking street, he noticed the car behind him making the same turn. Hadn't that car been behind him when he left the Atlantic Adventures parking lot?

Lyle saw his restaurant ahead, but instead of continuing, he made a sharp right turn into a block-long strip mall's parking lot. The Nissan SUV behind him continued straight ahead. Lyle glanced quickly at the driver. Was he Chinese? Lyle watched the car go by. It turned right at the next street, then right into the strip mall lot.

Rows of cars blocked Lyle's view. He couldn't see where the Nissan stopped. Maybe the guy pulled into the line at the fast-food joint at the end. Lyle waited a couple of minutes then pulled back onto the street heading for the restaurant. He didn't see the Nissan. Must be the heat and anxiety. He'd get a drink.

# CHAPTER 32

Scallops and shrimp preceded by a gin and tonic put Lyle in the mood for a nap. His hotel wasn't far. He checked out flights on his phone and zeroed in on one the next morning. Back in his room, he'd call Max, tell him Wyrick was not to be found at Atlantic Adventures, then book the flight.

Before paying his tab, he called Howard to get the latest on the investigation from his end.

"You find Wyrick yet?" the NC chief of security asked.

"Nope."

"We got almost zilch here, too. Deputies found a water bottle with a spy camera at Wyrick's condo. But the memory chip was unused. His car is missing. It wasn't in his garage. And none of his credit cards have been used since he disappeared. All in all, not much to go on. Without his credit cards it means he either found another way to pay for things or maybe..."

"He's dead," Lyle said softly so as not to alert diners nearby. "I'm planning to come home. Max's idea didn't pan out."

He walked out to his car parked on the side of the restaurant looking casually around, what cops call situational awareness. Primarily, he was aware of the humidity and the absence of any Nissan SUVs.

Later, he walked down his hotel's fourth-floor hallway, heading to his room. Lyle pulled out his keycard and tapped it against the panel above the doorknob. He pushed the door open —and someone hurled him into the room. He tried to stay on his feet, but his assailant hooked a foot around his ankle. Lyle crashed face-first onto the carpet. He broke his fall with his hands and spun around to face whoever attacked him.

His young, dark-haired assailant didn't look intimidating. Lyle scrambled to his feet. He stood at least half a head taller than the other guy. *Okay, shorty.* Lyle opened his mouth and raised a hand as if he were gesturing with a question. Instead of speaking, he grabbed the man by his coat collar. In about three seconds, Lyle felt himself flying through the air. Fortunately, he landed flat on his back on his bed. He braced for what was coming next.

Lyle didn't have a gun. He figured he wouldn't need it unless he ran into the FBI's dreaded Chinese Mafia—and here it was. He rolled over and looked up at the young man standing over him. "You're Chinese."

"No, I'm not Chinese, you asshole. I'm Korean."

"*North* Korean?"

"I'm Korean American. Where were *you* born? Obviously somewhere they didn't teach geography—or self-defense."

"So you're a purple belt in Hapkido, huh kiddo?"

"That's a black belt, and just be glad I didn't use Taekwondo."

Lyle propped himself up on his elbows. "That's the kicking one, right?"

"Boot to the head."

Lyle was beginning to like this guy. "So what's the deal? Are you selling martial arts lessons? Or working your way through college beating up old men."

"I wouldn't want to harm a hard-working local attorney, Mr. Gallagher." He pulled a business card out of his shirt pocket and tossed it toward Lyle.

Lyle knew what was on the card. "I *thought* this might be connected to the park."

"You were all over Atlantic Adventures offices today, Mr. Deming."

"You followed me after all."

"Yes, from a distance. If you had kept going, I wouldn't have been able to keep up after you spotted me. But you stopped at the restaurant after a few blocks. Made it easy."

His interrogator lost his threatening mien and showed no sign of a weapon—not that he needed one. Lyle sat up on the bed and relaxed. "So you work for park security?"

The man nodded.

"How do you know my name and that I'm not Brent Gallagher, esquire?"

"Local attorneys rarely drive rental cars. The paperwork had your name on it."

"You broke into my car."

"I didn't break anything. You notice anything broken?"

"So what's your point? You going to have me locked up for impersonating a barrister, Mr...."

"My name is Yoo. And we'll talk about calling the cops after you tell me what you were doing in the park yesterday and today."

"Yesterday? How did you—oh. Never mind."

*Once he knew my name, he could check recent credit card admission purchases and see that I bought a ticket yesterday. But how in hell did he do it this fast? Could we do that at Nostalgia City? Smart kid.* He did like him, but his back was hurting.

"Okay Yoo. First, show me some ID that says you work for Atlantic Adventures."

After he complied, Lyle asked him to sit down and make himself comfortable. "You see Yoo, I'm a headhunter and I was trying to locate someone who came to me looking for a job. I think I found him a job, but now I can't find my client."

"You do recruiting for Nostalgia City?"

"I have a variety of clients and—" Lyle stopped when Yoo smiled and started shaking his head.

"You work for Nostalgia City, but I don't think you're in employee recruitment."

"Well hell, if you know everything about me, why ask questions?"

"If you want to be incognito, it pays to keep your name out of the papers."

Lyle tried to control his public exposure as he had when he was a cop, but some of his previous exploits for Max had generated local publicity. "You know as well as I do that we monitor the competition. Just like you do. You've never had anyone check out *our* park?"

"This is possible. But it is not what you were doing. I want for you to talk with one of my superiors."

"Why don't you just send a nasty complaint to Nostalgia City and get out of here."

"Atlantic Adventures would like to see you prosecuted for trespass, fraud, attempted theft of intellectual property, and then of course you just tried to assault me. I have a detective friend in the police department. Should we talk down there?" Yoo pulled out his cell phone.

Lyle knew better than to try to bodily eject this guy from his room, and likely he could talk his way out of this. He might even find out something useful about Atlantic Adventures. "Buy me a drink afterward?"

• • •

Back at Atlantic Adventures, Yoo surprised him by leading him past signs for park security and into an office next to the ride development building he'd last visited. The reception area's Victorian brocade couches and chairs with ornately carved arms and legs reflected the park's historical theme. The nineteenth-century extravagance, complete with plush carpeting and gold-framed mirrors, also told Lyle this was not maintenance or janitorial offices. Maybe he'd get a chance to meet Jack Danneman himself.

He looked down at his suit and realized he was a little worse for wear. He straightened his tie and ran his hand over wrinkles in his coat.

Yoo told him to take a seat and wait. Where would he go? He'd accepted a ride to the park in Yoo's Nissan. Yoo returned ten minutes later and ushered Lyle into an adjoining office. An attractive woman in her late forties stood up behind her desk when Lyle and Yoo entered. Next to her desk sat a man Lyle pegged as a cop or a recently retired military officer—no one wore crew cuts anymore, except at Nostalgia City.

"Have a seat, Mr. Deming," the woman said. "My name is Tracy Galvan. I'm EVP for park attractions. We have a pretty good idea what you've been doing here, poking around our facilities and misrepresenting yourself. But we'd like to hear your story."

# CHAPTER 33

Kate drove her hybrid SUV down the two-lane desert road while she talked with her friend Drenda, the park's PhD historian.

"I know Steph is sure Sievers murdered Julian," Kate said. "I'm *not* sure. She's too emotional about this, but her arguments also make sense. And if I'm going to help, I have to be sure it's *murder*. Right now the evidence for suicide sounds persuasive, but there are holes in it."

"So for the experiment, I'm going to assume the role of Julian Russo," Drenda said, "and stand on the edge of a precipice?"

"Don't worry. It won't be dangerous. I brought a rope along to tie around your waist just to be safe. I'll go over everything when we get there." Kate's adrenaline was up this afternoon. She hoped Drenda's wasn't. With help from Drenda and Steph, she planned a little demonstration that might prove what happened at Little Buckhorn Canyon.

"Steph is driving separately because she may have to get back to the set quickly."

They arrived at the canyon's Number Two Overlook and parked in the small paved lot where Julian's car had been found. The lot accommodated only six cars, and today theirs was the only one. Modest by Arizona standards, rocky Little Buckhorn Canyon, painted in reds and rusty browns, stretched out before them and extended hundreds of feet down. Kate and Drenda walked along the wooden guard rail until they got to the end where, according to Rey, Julian was standing before he plunged off the cliff. The space between the end of the railing and a thicket of bushes and low trees spanned only a few feet. Kate could easily figure where Russo must have stood. Rocky soil spotted with wild grass sloped slightly upward from the parking lot to the edge of the cliff, and a remnant of police tape hung from the railing.

Drenda approached the edge with caution. "What do you think Mr. Russo was doing out here to begin with?"

"That's what I've been wondering. The director had just reprimanded him for a scuffle he didn't start. Was he looking for a peaceful place to think, or…?"

Kate turned when a car pulled in. Dressed in her casual work clothes, Stephanie had obviously just come from the set.

"I'm so sorry about your friend," Drenda said after Kate introduced her.

"Julian was a wonderful guy. Thanks. He was one of those unselfish friends who just help you out when you need it. Like Kate."

"A rare quality," Drenda said.

Kate thought Stephanie might tear up, so she asked the two of them to step to the side of the guardrail.

"I appreciate your help, Kate," Stephanie said, "but how is this going to prove that Cory murdered Julian?"

"In order to get the sheriff to reconsider the case, we need to show that Julian didn't commit suicide." *And I need to be sure, too.* Kate knew it was a risk to ask Stephanie to come out to the scene of Julian's death. Her friend might be overcome, so she got things started right away.

"Okay, can you see the trail way down there? I've jogged in the canyon before, and I'm thinking the hikers could not really see clearly what happened up here. The overhang sticks out and the trail is a long way away. So, Steph, Drenda is going to stand near the edge of the cliff over here and I want you to stand behind her. You'll be someone who wants to push her off the edge."

Drenda and Stephanie looked at each other.

"Don't worry. We'll put a rope around Drenda's waist and both of you will just stand still the whole time. I'm going to drive down to the closest trailhead, then hike in to find the spot where the hikers stood. It will take me a while to get there. I'll call you. *Then* you can stand near the edge."

"What are you going to do down there?" Stephanie asked.

"I'll take pictures and videos from different spots to be sure to cover the witnesses' vantage point."

It took Kate about ten minutes to drive the narrow, twisting road to the trailhead. When she got there, she called Drenda. She and Stephanie had arranged the rope and fashioned a harness that fit firmly around Drenda's tiny waist. No other cars had stopped at the overlook, so they were still alone. Kate told her she'd call when she was in position. She'd come prepared wearing hiking shorts and trail shoes. After fifteen minutes of walking and jogging along the trail, she reached the short, up-hill U-turn the witnesses had described.

She looked up toward the canyon edge and could not see the top of the overlook's railing. She'd brought compact binoculars with her too, and she scanned the ridge. No sign of the women. Before she'd lowered the binoculars, she heard a voice. Two voices. Men.

"You think we'll find anything?"

"Hell no. His drone could have crashed anywhere. Needle in a haystack if you ask me. I thought it was all decided. This is just grunt work."

"What's so bad about this? We're outside and on a trail. Better than sitting in—"

A third, scratchy voice broke in. "You got company." It was the sound of a radio. "She's twenty, thirty yards along the trail."

"Roger that," one of the men said, and the two fell silent.

Kate's first instinct was to duck out of sight, but the rocky terrain afforded little cover. Then she heard a humming noise. She looked up and saw a drone hovering fifty feet above her. The drone's operator had obviously given her away to the two men approaching. Poised to run, Kate waited to see if she could spot the men before they saw her. Through the scrub brush, above on a gradual slope, she saw two sheriff's deputies.

"Afternoon ma'am," said one deputy when they were a few feet away. The deputy was less than ten years younger than Kate. *Ma'am?*

"Beautiful day deputies." The men, dressed in standard uniforms, wore hiking boots. One carried a radio, the other binoculars, and both had water canteens. "You guys looking for something? I see your drone escort."

"Something someone lost," said the younger deputy. "Have you seen anything that doesn't belong here?"

The older deputy scowled. "Just routine. Trying to help someone out."

"Sorry, no."

"Okay. Have a good hike."

The older deputy motioned for the other one to get going. When they were out of earshot and Kate couldn't see or hear their drone, she scanned the rim of the canyon again. Her vantage point was closer to the cliff than she expected. She had to look northwest and not quite ninety degrees up to the edge. The last few feet of the canyon's wall jutted out, blocking Kate's view of anything on the rim. She called Drenda and asked her to put the call on speaker. "I'm in position, Drenda. You can walk toward the edge."

Kate took a quick glance through the binoculars to locate the spot, then put her phone on camera mode. "I still can't see you. How close are you to the edge?"

"Two or three feet. Perhaps a little more."

"Steph, where are you?"

"I'm about three feet behind her. We've got the other end of the rope tied to the park bench to be safe."

Kate took several photos, then moved a few feet down the trail. She asked Steph to stand at the end of the guardrail and raise her hand. It was just enough. Kate saw her hand wave, so she was able to point her camera at the end of the guardrail. "Drenda, be careful, but could you just move a little farther?"

"She's very close to the edge," Stephanie said. "The rope is tight."

"Okay, I see you. Your head and shoulders. You're a long way away."

Drenda waved a hand. "My toes are almost at the edge."

"Yes, I can see you now from the waist up, actually a little more." Kate took more photos and videos. "Now, Steph, would you stand directly behind Drenda?" Their proximity to a death fall made sweat appear on Kate's forehead. *Oh no, just a couple of seconds more.* "Are you right behind her?"

"We're touching."

"Now raise your arm Steph, straight up. Got it. Thanks. Please back away. Be safe."

Kate put her phone away and headed back up the trail. She now knew what Julian was doing out on the cliff and what the senior citizen hikers probably saw—or didn't. If Rey would not investigate further, she would.

# CHAPTER 34

Lyle felt like he was back in an interrogation room at the Phoenix PD only he was on the wrong side of the table. He sat in front of Galvan's desk and eyed the beefy guy with a crew cut who was not introduced. Yoo sat next to Lyle.

"So as you now know, I work at—or maybe I *used* to work—at Nostalgia City. In any event, I'm a cab driver."

Galvan chuckled.

"I can show you my ID and commercial license."

"This is not the time for your name, rank, and serial number," Yoo said. "Tell us what you were doing here."

Yoo still prodded, Galvan had large dark eyes, and the crew cut looked at him like he was a suspect in a one-man lineup. "Okay, I'm just looking for a Nostalgia City employee. What's the harm?"

"And you thought he might be working *here*?" Galvan said.

"Possibly."

"And what does he do at Nostalgia City?"

"I'm not sure."

"I believe Tom Wyrick is a programmer for you," Galvan said, her voice light and conversational as if she were asking if he enjoyed his flight to Florida.

*Hell, how do they know he was a programmer? Amber, the reception-ist. My mistake. She was the only one I told who Wyrick was. But how did they know I talked to her? I never mentioned her name to anyone. Surveillance cameras. They went back and looked at video of the time before I showed up in HR. Damn these guys are good. Least I know what they know about me, which is pretty much everything.*

"Wyrick is a programmer and he disappeared. The park is worried about him so they asked me to look around."

"And you were chosen, not because you drive a cab, but because of your previous occupation."

"Yeah," he said. "I was a Phoenix homicide detective." Did the crew cut's gargoyle expression soften slightly?

"Actually, Mr. Deming," Galvan said, "the only thing we don't know for sure is what Wyrick was working on when he disap-peared. But I can guess. There've been stories. And you were asking around in our attractions development building next door."

*This lady has a complete picture of my actions and motives. As complete as I would have liked for any perp I detained as a cop.* He gave a shrug of surrender and leaned back in his chair.

Galvan turned to the thickset guy next to her. "Thanks for coming over Bill. It's like we thought. I just have a few more ques-tions for our cab driver. I'll give you a call later."

Bill got up slowly, pushed his chair out of the way, and came around the desk. He looked at Yoo and made a slight motion to the door. When they left, Galvan got up and took Yoo's seat oppo-site Lyle.

"Are you working for Maxwell? Hiring an ex-police detective sounds like something he'd do."

Lyle couldn't read Galvan's body language. She sat back in the chair, put a hand on the arm, and crossed her legs. Relaxed maybe, but her brown-eyed stare held his attention.

"Yes and no. I am working for Max, but he didn't hire me. I went to work at the park because it was a break from police work. It takes it out of you. I like driving my taxi."

"You're not driving it now."

"I sometimes do special assignments for Max."

"So one of your programmers has gone rogue and you want to find him before he sells your secrets."

Lyle could play the game, too. His noncommittal expression was as good as anyone's.

"Does it have to do with your perception deception effect?"

*Why don't I just call Joseph Arena and have him explain the technical details to you?*

"You don't have to worry. That term was in one of the trade mags recently. No one knows what it means." She shifted in her chair and leaned forward. "I sympathize with you. We all want the latest and the best, and we all try to protect our own proprietary ideas."

"Which is why Yoo followed me."

"That's right," she said. "I'm sorry if he got too rough. He's young. It didn't sound like you were looking to steal anything. I despise anyone who would steal secrets for profit. Your secrets, our secrets, anyone's. Our engineering team is inspired, and like Edison said, it's ninety-nine percent perspiration. Is this Wyrick going to sell your secrets to the highest bidder or what?"

"Could be."

"Well, I would not buy stolen technology. I can't say for certain that Mr. Danneman wouldn't be interested, but if anyone wanted to sell us new tech, it would have to come through me. And it hasn't."

Lyle was beginning to like Tracy Galvan. Intelligent, attractive. These Atlantic Adventures folks were sharp, straightforward people. Except Amber.

"I know that Maxwell and Mr. Danneman have butted heads —maybe that's putting it mildly," she said. "'No love lost' is the expression. Is that why you're here instead of Sea World or the Magic Kingdom?"

Lyle nodded. She knew it all. "I don't think there's anything else I could tell you that you don't already know, except how perception deception works. And I don't have a clue. I really do drive a cab."

She smiled.

"I appreciate your frankness," Lyle said. She was telling the truth. "I could have saved a lot of time by just talking to you first."

"So where are you going to look next?"

"Does this mean…"

"No, we're not going to press charges. This is just our little secret. I enjoyed seeing what you did, even at our expense. Very inventive. Should keep security on their toes."

"Glad I could provide some entertainment."

"Are you going to IAAPA?"

"I whata?"

"It's the International Association of Amusement Parks and Attractions, the industry's biggest trade show. It's in Orlando every year and it just started. All the big ride manufacturers are there to display their latest bright ideas for theme parks and carnivals. If this Wyrick is trying to sell your ride secrets, he'd probably go to IAAPA."

"I've been told that another theme park would most likely want to recruit Wyrick to steal our secrets, or at least buy from him after the fact."

"Yes, another park could have stolen your secrets, but there's a limited number of parks in the country that could take advantage of leading-edge tech. Your average roller-coaster park probably not. However, there are dozens of ride manufacturers and consulting firms from all over the world that might be happy to sell the ideas to whoever has the most money."

"Orlando is close."

"Yes, about a two-and-a-half-hour drive, depending on traffic. Nostalgia City will probably be there. *We* go every year. I'm going there tomorrow in fact."

*I wonder if Tom Wyrick is registered there.*

# CHAPTER 35

I t's murder," Kate said. She'd kicked off her shoes and poured a glass of wine before she called Lyle in Florida. "Steph was right. It wasn't suicide." Her words reflected the apprehension and excitement over what lay ahead of her. She wanted to share it with him and to hear his voice.

"So the bad luck did arrive in threes."

"The scorpion sting and the light pole crash really *were* accidents. But Julian was murdered."

"Is Rey investigating?"

"Well, he *said* he was finished. He's got a persuasive-sounding list of reasons why it's suicide, but he's wrong. Nothing *proves* it. The eyewitnesses couldn't see what happened. Julian wasn't despondent, and he had concrete plans for the future."

"There were witnesses?"

"That's what *I* said. Two older ladies were hiking in the canyon and they claim they saw him step off. But this afternoon I proved they couldn't have seen anyone pushing him. I took video that verifies the women were too close to the side of the cliff for them to see Julian until he was right on the edge. They couldn't have seen someone standing behind him."

Kate took a breath and set her wine glass on the coffee table.

Here she was, talking matter-of-factly about someone being shoved to his death, something she wouldn't have done a short time before. Things had changed since she went to work at Nostalgia City. And met Lyle.

"I saw the witnesses on TV. When one of them described what she saw, she moved her arms in a circle. That's what you do when somebody pushes you and you lose your balance, not when you take a leap."

"Sounds like you're relishing another investigation."

*I am. And I want to help Steph.*

"You said Rey had a list."

"Everyone assumes a person who commits suicide is depressed. And so you look for evidence of that. I think the sheriff's detectives investigated a suicide, not a suspicious death."

"Expectations influence how you look and what you find."

"That's what I thought. So I called Julian's agent. Steph had told me that Julian had plans for another movie and a TV series coming up. The agent talked to Julian several times before he died. He said the actor was enthusiastic about his upcoming movie, but even more so about being on a TV series. That could set him up well for retirement."

"Set up who, Julian or his agent?"

"You know what I mean. Does that sound like someone contemplating suicide?" Kate didn't wait for an answer. "And he also told me about Cory Sievers. He said when Sievers was in rehab he told friends he would settle some scores when he got out."

"And then what happens?" Lyle said. "Julian winds up in Sievers's first picture after rehab."

"Right. Late today I emailed my canyon videos to Rey, but he just said they *might* talk to the witnesses again."

"So you're going to…"

"Try to catch Sievers."

"He's not going to admit it. And he's an actor."

"I'll think of a way."

"You're not going to vamp him, are you?"

"I don't think it would take much. I've read he'll go after anyone in a dress."

"Wear pants."

"Oh, you do care." She was kidding, but she liked being reminded.

"I know you, Kate Sorensen. Be careful about taking chances."

"I will. So how is your search going for the elusive Mr. Wyrick?"

"Well, I had this great idea when I visited Atlantic Adventures. I pretended to be an attorney looking for him on a *serious personal matter*."

"Any luck?"

"A little. After the park's Korean security agent decked me and hauled me in for questioning."

"*Lyle*."

"Relax. It wasn't as bad as that. I wound up talking to the head of Atlantic Adventures ride development. She told me they had nothing to do with Wyrick's disappearance. I believe her. And I'd already tried to find him two different ways at the park, and I came up empty. Tomorrow morning I'm driving up to Orlando for this big theme park trade show."

"IAAPA?"

"How d'you know?"

"I'm a vice president of the world's most elaborate theme park," she said, smiling to herself. "I know we send people there every year. It's a good place to find out what kind of rides our competition might be buying. Sounds like it would be a good place to look for Wyrick if he's trying to sell our secrets."

"You got it. I already talked to Max. I had to tell him the disappointing news that Joe Danneman didn't hijack his data. But he told me to dig in and find quote, 'the bastard ride consultants who probably stole our ideas because we do all our ride development in-house and don't farm anything out.'"

"That's not exactly true. We do more than most parks ourselves, but we've used outside ride companies before."

"Whatever. Max is generally pissed. Wants this solved tomorrow."

After a silence, Kate said, "I miss you."

"Me too."

Before they hung up, Lyle again told her to be careful and reminded her about Sievers's temper. "If Julian didn't commit suicide, then Sievers or someone else in or near the park is a murderer."

She took her wine glass into the kitchen and absently foraged in the refrigerator while imagining how soon she could talk about murder with Psycho Sievers.

# CHAPTER 36

SATURDAY

The Orange County Convention Center in Orlando looked more like a theme park than a trade show. Life-size dinosaurs with chomping jaws competed for Lyle's attention with roller coasters, robots, rocket ships, boats, and bobsleds. One ride spun visitors around in circles, another threw them along twisting tracks up in the air toward the shiny beams of the convention center's sky-high ceiling. Everything either flashed lights, gyrated, or emitted sharp electronic sounds. Or all three. Enough to give you a seizure.

The day before, after he'd talked to Max, Lyle called Joseph Arena to arrange for IAAPA passes. It was no problem. The park sent people every year as Kate had told him. Lyle's admission would be waiting for him at the gate. Atlantic Adventures helped him get a reservation at a small hotel several miles from the convention center.

"Holy crap," Lyle whispered to himself as he walked into the cavernous, noisy exhibit hall. A badge with his name and *Nostalgia City* on it hung from the lanyard around his neck and he clutched a map of exhibitors. "Where to begin?" Some parts of the floor had aisles that separated the sprawling company displays. In other areas, exhibits overlapped. Bobsled-shaped cars dashed along tracks suspended in the air over virtual reality truck rides that shook and bucked.

Unfamiliar with the names of the ride builders, Lyle arbitrarily started at one corner of the exhibit hall. He looked for company representatives among the crowd of gawkers. Occasionally he saw people in costumes ranging from circus performers to aliens to superheroes. Visitors or vendors, he knew not.

He stopped at an exhibit featuring high-tech bumper cars. The different models sat in groupings like new cars in an automobile showroom. "Excuse me," Lyle said to a casually dressed man with a name badge that matched the bumper car logo. "I'm trying to locate this man." He pulled out his cell phone and showed Wyrick's picture to the bumper car salesman. The man glanced at the photo, then shook his head. Lyle mentioned Wyrick's name, but the man kept shaking his head.

The next exhibit showcased gondolas—the kind that hang from cables strung up the side of mountains or stretched in the air above theme parks. Gondolas in the exhibit hung from cables attached to an elaborate steel beam superstructure.

Lyle peered inside one gondola and saw a man using a straw to sip a light green frozen drink that looked suspiciously like a cocktail. For breakfast? The man's badge identified him as an aerial gondolier, so Lyle showed him Wyrick's photo. The man put his drink aside and leaned out of the car to stare at the picture. Then he looked up at Lyle.

"Dude, you're from Nostalgia City. I've been there. It's way cool. Is this person you're looking for from your park?"

"Ah, yeah," he said, suddenly wishing he didn't have Nostalgia City on his badge.

"Haven't seen him. If I do, should I tell him to call you?"

"Nah," Lyle said. "Tell me, where did you get the margarita?"

Reminded of his drink, the man reached behind him and returned the straw to his mouth for a liberal gulp. "Snow cone place down the way. They have *unique* flavors not on the menu. Ask Bobbo for the special of the day." He winked.

Advertising that he represented Nostalgia City was not what Lyle had in mind. Letting the word out that NC was looking for its absent programmer would get in the way, at minimum alerting Wyrick that he was on his trail. He thanked the guzzling gondolier and headed for the exit.

Less than an hour later, he was back at the convention center having found a FedEx copy shop where he created a visitor ID badge identifying him as Brent Gallagher.

He picked up where he left off and wandered past an exhibit advertising theme parks in Indonesia, Brazil, Spain, and other countries where Jovan Amusements apparently created everything from haunted houses to water rides. A twelve- or fifteen-foot-long working model of a river ride showed flat-bottomed boats cruising on crystal blue water through canyons and wetlands. Two children stood at the edge of the ride and poked fingers in the water.

"You interested in water rides?" said a female voice behind him. The voice belonged to a stout middle-aged woman in a white blouse, red vest, and blue skirt. Scandinavian attire, or perhaps Swiss?

"This river ride is beautiful," he said. "But I'm looking for someone who has been working in the amusements industry." He held up his phone. "Have you seen him by chance?"

"I don't think so. Why are you looking for him?" She looked Lyle in the eyes.

"Inheritance," he improvised.

"Really?" The woman leaned toward Lyle. "He doesn't know about it? Is it a lot of money?"

He let a tiny smile form on his lips and he held up a finger in front of his mouth. "Lips are sealed."

"Hmm." Her eyes widened. "Sorry, I haven't seen him."

Lyle moved on. As he trudged from exhibit to exhibit, it surprised him to see a number of Chinese companies that sold rides and even one that offered to build an entire theme park. After more than an hour, he'd talked to people selling everything from singing penguins to Ferris wheels. No one recognized Wyrick. He was almost ready to ask Bobbo for the special of the day when he saw a familiar face. Across the aisle, sitting in the driver's seat of a glossy red Jeep, sat Rob Napier.

"Rob, still checking out the competition?"

Napier looked startled. Then he remembered. "Lyle Deming."

Lyle frowned and held up his Gallagher name badge. He sat next to Rob in the theme park vehicle. It had no instrument panel and was obviously designed to carry guests through some sort of ride.

"Are you undercover?"

"I'm asking after Wyrick."

Rob lowered his voice. "Did you find anything at Atlantic Adventures?"

Lyle gave him a severely abbreviated version of his inquiries, omitting his get-together with Yoo, but explained that one executive had been helpful.

"You used to be a cop, didn't you?"

Lyle had already told him.

"Good idea to come here," Rob said. "Lots of possibilities."

At that moment, Lyle realized he was making a mistake. One he'd made before. "It's likely that Wyrick is not working alone. It's possible that someone else here is trying to sell our perception deception plans. You probably talk to technical people, the ride engineers and specialists. You might hear something."

He suggested they exchange cell numbers in case Rob came across anything promising.

"I'll keep an ear out for anything that sounds like people transferring or selling new technology," Rob said. "I can ask around."

Lyle imagined Rob was visualizing scenes from a James Bond movie. "Please, don't ask about it. Leave that to me. And don't mention Wyrick's name."

"Okay."

"Just hang out and listen." Lyle made a show of looking around them before he continued in a lower tone. "Yes, just listening is an excellent stratagem."

"Got it."

He gave Rob a subtle thumbs-up as he walked away. He knew now that despite his phony credentials and his attorney story, his mistake was that he still acted too much like a cop. Flash a photo, ask if anyone has seen the missing person. "Stupid," he said aloud as he continued walking. "And I *sound* like a cop, too."

He needed a new approach.

# CHAPTER 37

How do you ask a famous movie star if he's a murderer?

Even though it was Saturday, Appropriate Brand Pictures scheduled a half-day shoot, so Kate set off early to talk with Cory Sievers. She found him between scenes chatting with crew members next to an equipment-laden panel truck.

He must have seen her coming because he stopped talking. She'd chosen a navy midi skirt and simple long-sleeved blouse. Feminine, but businesslike.

"Mr. Sievers, I'm Kate Sorensen. I'm in charge of public relations for the park and I wonder if I could talk with you for a few minutes? Do you have time?"

He smiled, and Kate could see Johnny Caspary, the brash young race car driver he'd played in one of his recent pictures. "Public relations. Kate Sorensen. Yes, Wyatt—my agent—told me about you."

She waited with a polite smile.

"Sure. I did my two scenes for today. You want to walk over to my trailer?"

As they turned to go, Sievers said, "later guys," to the men he'd been talking to. Did one of them give Sievers a knowing grin? No matter. She had Sievers's attention, although he obviously thought they were going to talk about something else.

"These little video vignettes were Wyatt's idea," he said as they walked around the corner from the set toward a parking lot that held several stars' trailers. "He said there's not going to be any script. So I just get to talk. Think I can handle that?" He gave Kate a waggish smile.

Kate hesitated about going inside Sievers's trailer. If a makeup person or someone else was in there, she'd feel safer, but Sievers might not be as candid with the questions she had in mind.

His trailer appeared to be the biggest on the lot. Next to the door, a modest plaque held his name. She made a split-second decision and stepped inside. The main room's furnishings looked like a standard, upscale travel trailer with leather overstuffed chairs, a small couch, lots of polished, dark wood, and a makeup counter and mirror at the rear. She didn't see anyone else inside.

"Have a seat," he said.

Kate sat in a soft upholstered chair next to the door. Sievers took off his sport coat, and she saw he was wearing a gun. He must have seen her reaction. "I hate lugging this around." He pulled off the holster and semi-automatic from his belt and set it on a table at the back of the room.

*Is he supposed to have that off the set? Isn't there someone in charge of guns?*

"Would you like coffee or a drink?"

"No thanks." He might not be very hospitable once she got down to cases. On second thought, she accepted a cup of coffee. *Why not have a little more relaxed intro?*

While he stood at a counter and filled two cups from a carafe, she glanced at the wall opposite and saw photos of Sievers with other stars she recognized. In some, Sievers mugged for the camera, others appeared more serious. Wyatt Lewis was included in one picture. In another, Sievers stood next to a topless red hot rod.

Kate sat back and crossed her legs. She wouldn't tell Lyle she hadn't worn slacks. He was kidding anyway. Sievers took a seat facing her, a coffee table between them. He seemed at ease and she started the conversation with small talk. The weather, Nostalgia City, his trailer.

"You collect cars," she said after a few minutes.

"Yeah, mostly custom jobs, hot rods." He pointed to the car photo on the wall.

"You have a thirty-six Ford roadster that just won some award. Is that right?"

"That's my favorite car." He looked as if he was visualizing the Ford in his mind. "It took first at a car show in San Diego. Do you know about cars?"

"The park is filled with old cars so I at least have to know a seventy-two Plymouth from an eighty Oldsmobile."

"Yeah. Since you do PR, you have to know *all* about the seventies and the park."

Kate nodded and sipped her coffee.

"Is our filming getting in your way? Disrupting your routine?" he asked.

"*Murder for No Reason* is *part* of my routine now. And I'm having to deal with publicity around Julian's death, too."

"That was sad," he said in a flat tone.

"Had you ever worked with Julian before?"

"Yeah, we did a picture a few years ago."

"Do you know of anyone who would have wanted to harm Julian?"

"What do you mean?"

"Who would have pushed him off the cliff?"

"Julian committed suicide."

She set her coffee on the table. "I don't think so. According to his agent, he had another movie coming up and a TV series. I don't think he would jump. He had plans."

"How do you know?"

"I asked around. To be prepared to handle our public image in case the news changes. From what I've gathered, it's more likely he was pushed."

"You're investigating?"

"Just trying to find out what happened."

"Well, a detective talked to me." Sievers shifted in his seat. "He'd obviously heard about our little argument."

"Did Julian get on your nerves?"

"No question. He got on other people's nerves, too. Always fussing with things, like his drones. And he was always complaining." Sievers unbuttoned his shirt and loosened his tie.

"Do you think Wes Moody did the right thing by suspending him?"

"It sounded harsh, but it's not unusual. It gave everyone a little breathing space." He leaned back in his chair.

Kate uncrossed her legs and leaned slightly back, mirroring his posture. "You're not the first person to tell me about Julian's personality."

"Nervous, irritating. Hard to figure out."

Kate watched him set his jaw and stare out the window. She waited.

"You know, I wanted to talk to him. This picture is important to me. We need to finish it."

"Did you talk to him Wednesday?" *Just before you pushed him over?*

"No." Sievers focused on Kate and lowered his brow.

"You told the sheriff you were here all morning the day Julian was killed."

"I was here, yes. All morning." He almost sounded like he was speaking from a script. "But it was suicide. What are you getting at?"

"Well, Julian *was* irritating. I think someone might have argued with him. Maybe pushed him too hard, just by accident."

He opened his mouth then closed it momentarily. "You mean *me*."

"It was probably an accident. Understandable. One slight push."

Lines appeared at the corners of his mouth and creased his forehead. The familiar silver-screen face didn't look boyish. "What th' hell? You didn't want to talk about *videos*."

"Just tell me what happened," she soothed, trying to smooth out any hint of animosity in her voice. "I'll understand."

He moved to the edge of his seat. Kate saw a look she didn't like.

"Some magazine stories have said you had a long-standing grudge against him. But maybe he was the one with the grudge. Was that it?"

"This is bullshit."

"Okay," she said in a lower tone.

"Okay what? I don't know what you're trying to do." He stood up. I had nothing to do with Julian's death. That's what I told the sheriff. You can take your fucking accusations and get the hell out of here."

He strode past her and flung the door open. He started to say something but stopped and glared. He pointed at the doorway. "Out."

Kate stood. "Sorry, Cory. I could help you." But it was too late.

Sievers rapped on the edge of the door. "Dammit. Get out. Now."

He took a half step forward and looked as if he might grab her.

She stepped out of the trailer. She could feel his eyes on her as she walked away. He said something under his breath, but she was not too far away to hear.

"Bitch."

# CHAPTER 38

M usic, electronic beeps, and intermittent laser blasts continued to fill the convention hall. At the next exhibit, Lyle stood face to face with a robot. It looked like an alien from a low-budget 1950s or '60s science fiction movie. Its long arms hung like an ape's nearly down to its knees. It wore an ill-fitting flexible space suit, and Lyle could see dark hair or fur sticking out at the cuffs. On its head, the robot wore what looked suspiciously like a diving helmet.

"I'm guessing you're not exactly the twenty-first-century technology I'm looking for," Lyle said.

"You would be surprised," came a voice echoing from inside the helmet. "We employ the latest in AI communication. What can we do for you, Mr. Gallagher?"

"So you can read badges."

"And I can tell jokes. Want to hear one?"

Lyle turned to the salesman who walked up.

"Hi, I'm Carl Lamont. We *do* have the latest twenty-first-century technology. Interactive robots are the wave of the future."

"This one looks more like the past."

"Don't be offended Alvin," the man said to the robot. Carl dressed in slacks and a pink golf shirt. "He's supposed to be retro," he told Lyle. "And jokes are part of his AI. We like to give our characters a sense of humor. Our clients find it really helps make them more approachable."

*Who, the clients or the robots?* Carl's blond hair was askew, and he wore an expression that hinted he might be spending too much time talking to androids.

"Very impressive, but I'm not in the market for robots. I'm actually representing a buyer interested in the latest in AI-controlled extended reality dark rides." He hoped he got the terminology right.

"For that, you want one of the major amusement companies like Poppy or Meng Industries."

Lyle glanced at other robots standing or sitting in tableaus: a cartoon cat, a fuzzy bear, and a space-suited woman. He left Carl with his friends and walked on.

His new persona was an attorney representing a large—anonymous—theme park corporation. The company hired him to locate and buy the absolute latest technology in dark rides. Something that's never been done before. His corporate client was willing to pay whatever it cost—no limit. And although it sounded melodramatic, he thought about using the phrase, *no questions will be asked*.

After a few steps, he was overwhelmed by the smell of hot oil and scorched popcorn. The exhibit in front of him sold popcorn wagons. He remembered the convention also catered to county fairs and festivals.

Lyle soon found the broad Poppy Attractions Inc. display. Imitation stone walkways led from the aisle into the exhibit. Lyle strolled a path past models of rides, some automated. One model showed four-person cars winding up and down a mountainous road narrowly missing falling trees and tumbling boulders. Escaping the perils of the wilderness, the cars entered a tunnel. Gawking at the models, he must have looked like a serious customer because someone soon approached him.

"Are you interested in dark rides?" The short-haired woman wore a slightly less-than-chic outfit. More engineer than sales rep.

"In a way, I am. I represent a corporate client that's interested in new ride technology. Not the fastest coaster or the usual mine train, but something powered by AI, something that's only been imagined before." He paused and pulled out one of Brent Gallagher's business cards. He thought the gravitas of an attorney doing the shopping might make up for his spotty use of jargon. "My client wants something so revolutionary it's only been hinted at before. It may not even be displayed at the show."

"I think I understand what you're looking for, Mr. Gallagher but..." She frowned momentarily, then smiled. "What brought you here?"

"I was trying to get away from the popcorn smell."

"I mean, how did you hear about our new technology? I think you're asking about our quantum progression, and we haven't even advertised it yet."

*Is this it? Did these guys get our PDE and give it another name?* "My client's executives keep abreast of what's going on in the industry. They hear things. Can you tell me more about this?"

She thought for a moment. "Let me see. Why don't you come in here."

She led him to the rear of the exhibit and through a tunnel entrance that looked like the one in the ride model. A desk, table, and several chairs plus hanging swag lamps made the tunnel a small office, albeit a dimly lit one. She told Lyle to take a seat and said she'd be right back.

A few minutes later she walked in with a thirty-something Chinese man she introduced as Albert, Poppy's director of interactive engineering and a corporate partner. Shorter than Lyle, he had straight black hair and intelligent eyes behind glasses. Lyle read his expression as enthusiastic but apprehensive. He set a large laptop down on the desk.

"I have a simulation I can show you. It's very preliminary. But this will give you an idea. This is a totally proprietary system and the result of, well, a lot of work. It's nothing like what you see on display in our exhibit."

"Well, I can tell you that if your ride technology works out, my client would likely want to take it on exclusively. And would be willing to pay…"

The man opened the laptop and invited Lyle to sit opposite it. "This should give you a little idea of our AI interactivity capabilities."

In the dark room, the colorful computer animation drew Lyle in. It began with a person sitting in something like a bobsled from Disney's Matterhorn Ride. But as soon as it got underway, the ride rushed the passenger through a city that looked like downtown LA. People on street corners—who looked like live humans—waved to the passenger and talked to him.

Before it had been running for half a minute, Lyle realized he had no way of telling whether this was their stolen technology or a five-year-old video game.

"Very impressive," he said, "but I'm afraid I'm not technical enough. Before we proceed, I would like to have one of my client's engineers see this."

The two Poppy employees looked at each other.

"He's actually here in the convention hall. If he could just see your video and ask questions, I think we could progress to the next step of negotiations."

"We would be happy to talk with him, yes," Albert said.

Lyle stood up. "Let me step outside and call him."

When he was out of earshot, he dialed Rob. He explained the situation and said he really needed technical help.

Rob agreed and said he would need to ask them questions.

"That's fine. But don't get too specific. Let *them* explain how it works so you can tell if it's ours."

"Okay. I can do that. Do they look like crooks?"

"No Rob, they look like engineers. You'll hit it off. Do you know how to find the Poppy exhibit?"

He walked back toward the tunnel office. The Poppy engineers *didn't* look suspicious. But anybody could be lured by stolen technology. Scientists sometimes cheated when they couldn't solve a problem, didn't they? Maybe these engineers were front people for more seedy avaricious types who really ran things.

Lyle stepped back into the office, then realized he forgot to tell Rob to hide his Nostalgia City name badge.

# CHAPTER 39

Getting Sievers to confess now seemed impossible. And with no evidence from the scene—based on her conversation with Rey—Kate felt her chances of proving the murder growing dim. In addition, the deputies' search for a drone left her with a question.

Flustered, irritated, mad from her confrontation with Sievers, she couldn't let it go. She needed to brainstorm. With Lyle out of town, she took a chance and showed up at Drenda's front door. The former academic approached problems differently than Kate did, so together they might find a way to tie the murder to Sievers, if she'd agree.

"Positively," Drenda said as soon as Kate asked for help. "I was just going to have lunch, but there's enough for two. Come on in."

Dr. Adair's Timeless Village townhouse, like her office, looked like a combination library and exhibition of sixties and seventies memorabilia: a Pet Rock, eight-track tape player, framed photo of David Cassidy. Kate settled down in a chrome and leather dining chair at her kitchen table while Drenda stirred a pot of pea soup.

"So you didn't have any luck with Cory Sievers."

She explained her interrogation techniques, some she learned from being a reporter early in her career. "I asked him questions I knew the answers to, to see how he responded when he told the truth. I even researched his hobbies so I could break the ice. He sounded for a moment like he was going to talk about arguing with Julian, but he finally got angry and threw me out."

"I streamed a Cory Sievers movie last night. A family comedy. He was humorous and likable. But if you do an internet search you find out his personal life has been well, unsavory."

"I'm disappointed I didn't come up with the right approach with him."

Drenda set two bowls of soup on the table along with muffins and sliced cheese. She turned on her coffee maker. "So what's the next step?"

"That's what I wanted to brainstorm about. There are three ways Sievers could have been on that overlook in time to kill Julian. The first way could have been a coincidence. He happened to be driving by the canyon and spotted him."

"The canyon's a fifteen- or twenty-minute drive from Polk on a county road," Drenda said. "That type of coincidence is not reasonable."

"Agreed. The second way would be if they had arranged to meet there. Rey said Julian received an untraceable call the night before."

"But from here to Polk, then out to the canyon, is at least a forty-minute drive. Why meet way out there?" Drenda paused. "Or why meet at all?"

Kate swallowed a spoonful of soup, then pointed the spoon at Drenda. "No reason. Unless Sievers lured him out there."

"Your conclusion then is that Sievers followed Mr. Russo to the canyon."

"Had to be."

Drenda helped herself to two squares of cheddar and pushed the plate to Kate. "That might be difficult to prove. We'd have to find someone who saw him leave or saw him following Mr. Russo."

"Let's talk about another problem. Why was Julian out at the canyon in the first place?"

"You saw the deputies in the canyon looking for a drone, so can we assume Mr. Russo was flying a drone when he died?"

"Yes, I think so. The first deputies on the scene must have found a controller, otherwise how would they know about it?"

"But if Sievers had pushed Mr. Russo over the cliff when he was flying the drone, the controller would have gone over with him," Drenda said. "Did the witnesses mention it?"

"No. They saw *him*. And if it went over the cliff, the deputies might not have seen the controller and would have no reason to look for the drone. I'll have to try to confirm they found a controller. Police, sheriffs sometimes hold back information they don't want the public to know about. If Rey won't tell me, I'll see if Howard can find out."

"It's a logical assumption that he would fly his drone over the canyon. He could get spectacular photos or videos."

"I met him once, and he told me flying the drone was relaxing. I guess you forget everything else."

"So he goes out to Little Buckhorn Canyon to forget about his argument on the set and…"

"Sievers follows him and kills him. Maybe they had an argument first and Sievers knocked the controller out of his hands."

"That could explain it, but we're still looking for proof."

Kate picked up a corner of a muffin and started to butter it, then stopped. "CCTV."

"What?"

"I think CCTV might be the answer. And most of the stars are staying at the park. We might find a shot of Sievers following Julian driving out Wednesday morning."

"Do we know what kind of vehicles they drive?"

"No. But I think we could find out."

"There's more than one way someone could leave the hotel complex for the highway toward Polk."

"Yes," Kate said. "The main exits have cameras. There may be four or five ways to go. And there's a way to get out on the other side of the park that doesn't pass by cameras. But it's longer. Most people don't use it. Regardless, it will take time to look through the videos."

Drenda finished the last of her soup. "I'm game. Want some help? I don't have a date tonight."

"I'll have to talk to a few people first. Let me call you."

"Do you miss Lyle? If he were in town, perhaps he would be helping."

"Yes. I miss him." *I wonder what he's doing. If it's dangerous.* "But you and I have work to do. Maybe we can catch the murderer."

# CHAPTER 40

Ninety minutes later, Drenda met Kate just outside the park's Control Center surveillance room.

"I called Howard and he set us up," Kate said. "Krystol Robinson is the supervisor this afternoon. She's going to have the videos we need. We can view all the tapes from Wednesday morning."

"It's not actually tape, is it?"

"No. It's all digital. But that's what everyone calls it if you're old enough to remember videotape."

Inside the main Control Center more than a dozen women and men, some in security uniforms, sat at multi-screen consoles watching live feeds from CCTV cameras throughout the park. Broad LED screens, many with multiple camera images, lined the walls. The room was larger, but not unlike the surveillance offices at the Vegas hotels where Kate had worked. The NC facility, however, made Kate think of command centers in spy movies.

"Kate?" said a woman in a security uniform. "I'm Krystol. Mr. Chaffee said you wanted to view recordings from hotel parking exit cameras. You'll have views of four different intersections leading out of the hotel complex. I can show you how to access the times you want."

She led them to a small viewing room where bright screens on two computer desks showed frozen video of park streets. Kate and Drenda sat at adjoining desks, and Krystol explained how to control the video speed and how to switch from one camera view to another.

"Thanks," Kate said. "We may be here a while."

"We have video search software that could save you time, depending on what you're looking for."

"Thanks," Kate said. "We'll try the old-fashioned way first."

"Call me if you need help."

"Looks like we may have to look at hours of recordings," Drenda said, "because we don't know when Mr. Russo left for the canyon." She swiveled in her chair and glanced at Kate's screen.

"We know when the witnesses saw him fall, so we can work backwards from there."

"What types of cars are we looking for?"

"Stephanie told me Julian drove a beige Toyota," Kate said. "So first we have to find him leaving, then see if we see Sievers following him."

"What's the movie star driving?"

Kate leaned back from her desk. "A blue Corvette."

"That should be easier to spot. How did you find out?"

"I didn't want Steph to ask around. I don't want her involved. So I went over to Sievers's hotel and talked to a star-struck desk clerk. She was nice enough to show me Sievers's registration and vehicle ID."

"I have a suggestion. Toyotas are commonplace. Why don't we look for the Corvette and if we find it, we can work back to see if he was following Mr. Russo."

"I knew you'd be perfect for this."

They both focused on their keyboard controls and stared at the screens. But after more than an hour, the Corvette had not appeared.

Drenda leaned toward Kate's desk. "I didn't realize there was so much traffic this time of the morning."

"We're seeing people who just checked out, people leaving to drive to the Grand Canyon, or people driving to Polk or Flagstaff. A lot of early risers."

Even though they divided the work, with Drenda looking at two camera positions and Kate the other two, time crept on. After a coffee break and another thirty minutes, Kate heard, "there he is."

She rolled her chair over to Drenda's monitor and saw the Corvette, Sievers visible at the wheel.

Knowing approximately when to look, it took them just minutes to find Julian's car—with the Corvette a few car lengths behind. They were seconds apart.

"We got him, Drenda."

# CHAPTER 41

When Rob didn't show up, Lyle looked at his watch, then glanced at the cave opening. He excused himself and walked outside. He saw Rob hurrying down the aisle, and he sensed one of the engineers had followed him out of the cave. Lyle held his breath until Rob got closer and he saw he wasn't wearing a badge.

"Rob, this is Albert," Lyle said. "He's a Poppy company partner. Come on in and take a look at their presentation. It looks impressive to me. But you'll be better able to tell if it's something your boss is interested in."

When they entered the office, Albert offered Rob a seat and spoke softly, giving him a summary of the new ride's rationale. Then he played the video. Rob watched attentively, twice asking to stop the video so he could ask questions.

When the program was over, Rob sat back and adjusted his glasses by the edge. "I have a question about the architecture."

Lyle was sure he wasn't talking about the design of the cave. He listened to the technical Q and A. Rob seemed to dig into the foundation of the new ride system. When Albert sounded as if he were reluctant to provide many specifics, Rob would rephrase his question.

Lyle couldn't tell from Rob's comments whether or not this was what they were looking for. What if it was? He hoped Rob wouldn't accuse them of stealing. The easiest thing to do would be to stall the Poppy people, then call the FBI. He wondered again what happened to Wyrick.

"Thanks, Albert," Rob said, breaking into Lyle's thoughts. "This has a lot of promise, but I'm not certain it's what my boss is looking for."

"It's in the preliminary stages of development." Albert angled his head and looked at Rob. "It can be modified to include your input and meet your budget."

"Let me have a card. I'll be meeting with my boss. If we need more information, I'll call you."

Albert pressed him to tell him where he worked, but Rob just thanked him again, complimented the project, and signaled Lyle to get moving.

"So, was it our stuff?" Lyle asked after they'd walked a few feet past the Poppy exhibit.

"No, not ours. It has some things in common, that's to be expected. They have two approaches they're working on. One doesn't fully use AI the way we've been discussing it. Remember, I've only worked on the edges of our project. And their second approach relies on virtual reality goggles. Wyrick's system doesn't require them."

"I'm disappointed. They were so curious how I found out about their new ride concept. Thanks for trying."

"This gave me a glimpse of what they're going to try to sell to our competitors, so it's helpful. And he didn't know I'm from Nostalgia City." Rob finished with a satisfied smile.

"I'm glad you thought to hide your badge."

"Yeah, I took it off just before I walked up. By the way, I haven't told Joe what I'm doing."

"Joe Arena?"

"Yeah. He probably wouldn't mind because we're all freaked

out about the theft, but he always likes a low-key approach to things."

"Now that you mention it, I think it would be a good idea if you didn't tell *anyone* what we're doing."

Rob thought for a moment. "I understand. Just between us. Do you think someone else—"

"No way of knowing. It's just better this way."

At the next exhibit, screaming passengers careered along the tracks of a scaled-down roller coaster.

"Want to take a ride?" Rob asked.

"No thanks." Lyle looked up to see cars spinning slowly at the same time as they dashed forward. He hated roller coasters. Thought they'd give him a heart attack. He'd never even been on NC's relatively slow 1960s-style wooden coaster. It clattered and shook as it raced over the tracks. Roller coasters were designed to separate riders from their lunches. "I've got more exhibitors to visit."

"Are you going to any hospitality suites this evening?"

"They have hospitality suites here?"

"Many, big and small. It might be a good place to corner some vendors and listen for gossip."

"Where are they?"

"They're in luxury rooms at the three main convention hotels."

"I'll just walk in and follow the noise."

Lyle's phone buzzed. It was Howard. "I gotta take this," he said. "Maybe I'll see you later."

He thought about Kate and wished he'd asked her exactly how she intended to confront Sievers. He walked to what looked like a quiet space where he could talk.

"Howard, have you talked to Kate today?"

"Yes, she's searching our CCTV files, investigating the Russo death."

"Uh-huh. I need to call her. I worry too much."

"Okay. Here's something else to worry about. I just found out from Owings at PAD that one of their ride models is missing, presumed stolen."

"A ride model?"

"Yeah, a big table-top mockup. It was an early one, developed to illustrate how PDE could be applied."

"When did it happen?"

"That's not the right question. The question is, when was the theft discovered? And the answer is today."

"There's more?"

"The missing model was discovered today, but it *could* have been taken any time this week. The finished models are kept in the Conceptularium."

"I know, I've seen it. Uh oh. Hold on." Lyle had stopped in a walkway between exhibits and just as he spoke a door opened and a clown appeared complete with stiff orange hair, red nose, and floppy shoes. He patted Lyle on the back as he scooted by.

"What's the matter?" Howard said.

"Nothing. Just some Bozo. Go ahead."

"Well, they haven't used the model in a long time—or even looked at it in a week. The theft wasn't discovered until today when a designer went looking for it. They have an inventory system and no one moved it or checked it out."

"Someone took it *after* Wyrick turned up missing."

Howard sighed. "Yeah. Son of a bitch. That means there's probably someone *else* involved. Dammit."

"Take it easy, Howard."

"It happened on my watch. Before we had the new security protocols in place. And we still haven't finished the damn perimeter fence."

"It's not your fault. You've been trying to get them to upgrade security for months."

"Too little. Too late."

"Don't beat yourself up. We'll figure it out. Could it have been a break-in?"

"Likely not, but I've got somebody looking at the surveillance video. Even so, we don't have cameras at all the ideal places at PAD yet. All in all, a total f-up. I'm going to have my people re-interview everybody. Got any ideas?"

"Not yet." He explained what he'd been doing canvassing ride vendors. "Hang in there and keep me posted."

*Could Wyrick be alive and calling the shots from somewhere outside the park?*

# CHAPTER 42

L yle? I can't hear you very well," Kate said, "I'm out shopping."

Kate had just walked into a fancy grocery and produce market. Polk locals probably never dreamed they'd see upscale merchants in their small, high-desert town until Max began building Nostalgia City. "I just started buying groceries. Let me put the cart away." She stepped outside and shoved the cart back into the rack. "There, now I can hear better. Where did you say you were?"

"An IAAPA hospitality suite. Actually, I'm outside in a hallway so I could call you. I thought this might be a good place to hear useful gossip since I don't have any leads. How did your talk with Cory go?"

"Not well. I tried to ease into it, to say how it was probably an accident, but he became angry. He called me the B-word."

"Blonde?"

"Bitch."

"Oh."

"He denied everything, *but* I found video evidence of him following Julian out of the park that morning." She explained how she and Drenda had spotted Sievers's car on the CCTV footage. "He told the sheriff's investigators he was at his hotel and in his trailer all morning, but we have him on tape."

"He could claim he was going somewhere else."

"Yes, I know, Mr. Detective, but it might be enough to get a confession out of him." Kate stood away from the market's door, but her last sentence caught the attention of a passerby who stopped, then moved on when Kate glared down at him.

"Are you going to pass this along to Rey?" Lyle asked.

"Yes. And I think I'll have additional evidence that suicide is out of the question. Julian supposedly drank in the Copacetic Bar the night before he died and complained about his life. So when I was in the Control Center today, I also looked at video from the tavern that night. He doesn't look drunk, *or* morose."

"But there's no audio and—"

"I know. I'm coming to that." She stepped away from the shopping cart rack. "I noticed the young bartender who served him. He has a long Beatles haircut. Almost looks like a Beatle. Cute. I called Amanda Updike, who works for me, and asked her if she would mind doing me a favor by going out to a bar tonight."

"You asked Amanda if she would check out the cute guy at the Copacetic Bar?"

"Yes. I told her I'd give her a day off in exchange, but she thought the idea of chatting up a cute bartender for work would be fun. I told her what I wanted to know about Julian, and so she's going out tonight."

"You're covering all bases."

Kate heard an electronic squawking sound. "What was that?"

"An alien of some sort just walked by. You never know who or what you're going to see here. So what are your plans for tomorrow?"

"I need to figure out how I'm going to present the evidence to Rey. He wasn't ecstatic about the video evidence from the canyon I sent him. I'm going to have to persuade him to come out here and look at the CCTV videos himself. What are *you* going to do tomorrow?"

"Unless I get a good lead tonight, I'm thinking of coming home. I've talked to lots of people here and nothing is panning out. And, I have bad news. Hang on a minute. I want to move farther down the hall where I can be alone."

"Okay, I'm waiting." *Please tell me the bad news is not about you.*

"I think it's safe now," Lyle said. He explained what Howard told him about the missing ride model.

"Max won't like that. Did Howard tell him?"

"I don't know, but Howard is really bummed. He feels responsible."

"We all have our hands full. What else is new?"

"I'm going to fade into the woodwork here and listen. I'll call you later tonight or tomorrow and let you know if I'm going to be flying out of here. And please, watch out for Psycho Sievers."

When she hung up, Kate pulled out another shopping cart and walked back into the store. She wanted fresh vegetables and maybe fish for dinner. But she hadn't put one item in her cart when her phone chimed again. Max.

"How are you this Saturday afternoon?" she asked.

"How am I? A little upset, that's how. Just heard that the star of this movie they're doing here says you're trying to blame him for murder. That guy who jumped off the cliff."

*It's Saturday. I'm in the grocery store. I got nowhere with Psycho Sievers. Can I please get my dinner?* "Who's complaining?" *Damn.* Kate wheeled her cart back to the entrance and walked outside again.

"Someone called Guest Relations, so the manager there called someone else and it worked its way up the ladder. You know how that goes. Yes, it's Saturday. I was planning to go out to dinner. So please tell me what's going on."

She didn't want to explain the whole story, certainly not in the store parking lot. How to make this sound palatable to Max? "You see the actor Julian Russo was killed. The cause of death has not been certified. My friend Stephanie Tyler is an assistant director on the film and she asked me to see if someone murdered Russo."

"So you think this Sievers character killed him? I thought the sheriff said it was suicide."

"That's not true. Cory Sievers was recently released from mental health rehab. Anger issues. He has a temper. I just asked him if he knew what happened to Julian."

"I don't like the sound of this. Could you let the sheriff handle it? You need to focus on two things: One, a murder at the park is bad for our image. Two, I don't want to piss off this movie company or the actors. We're under contract, and people are coming here to see stars."

"Now boss."

"And damn it, Kate, we have enough trouble already with our high-tech secrets gone. Do you know about that? Of course you do."

"I've heard rumors."

"Alright. You know the score. I don't want any more yahoos raising hell around here, especially on Saturday. Keep it quiet."

As Max's reprimands go, this one was only a moderate tremor. She'd be careful. And she had an idea who blew the whistle on her. It wasn't Sievers.

# CHAPTER 43

Clinking glasses, the hum of voices, and low music floated through the eighth-floor hotel suite. A temporary bar sat in a corner below a "Welcome to Gastrell Engineering Corp." sign. Lyle stood in line for a drink. Like most of the guests, he wore his IAAPA badge, albeit the counterfeit version.

The guy waiting in front of him turned around. "Say, how ya doin'." It was the margarita drinker from the gondola exhibit. His light brown suit bore a few wrinkles from the gondola seats.

Lyle smiled and nodded. When he met the guy early that morning, he'd been wearing his Nostalgia City badge. He wondered how his change of name and cover story might play out on the cocktail circuit. Now he'd find out.

"Did you ever find yur buddy, ah Mister…" the man looked at Lyle's badge. "Mr. Gallagher?"

"Yes. Just a misunderstanding. I'm enjoying the convention."

"Yeah. Fur sure. 'Cept…" He gave Lyle a wistful look. "I haven't sold any gondolas yet."

*What did this guy have to eat since his margarita breakfast, piña colada lunch? No wonder he didn't sell anything.*

Lyle picked up a drink and proceeded to circulate, listening for stray intelligence that might—even remotely—be useful. A few people smiled, recognizing him from their encounters in the exhibit hall. No one stopped him to offer sea-change technology.

Men and women in everything from casual sports clothes to suits stood in small groups of desultory conversation. For an industry representing amusements, few people seemed amused. Maybe the mood would liven up as the evening progressed.

Across the room, he noticed Larry Michaels from PAD talking to an intense-looking Asian man in a dark suit. He made eye contact and started over. After two steps he remembered his badge, and ostensibly adjusting it, he turned it over. Just in time.

"Larry Michaels," he said, walking up. "I'm Lyle Deming."

"Yes, good to see you." Michaels paused and introduced him to the other man who represented a small firm that did occasional business with Nostalgia City.

Lyle was more interested in Michaels. "How long have you been here?"

"Just a few minutes."

"I mean in Florida."

"I flew in yesterday."

Lyle knew Michaels must know why *he* was there and obviously couldn't discuss it in front of someone else—not that he'd take Michaels into his confidence. He needed to change the subject.

"How do you like the humidity?" *That was original, Deming.*

"Not too bad, but it is different from Arizona." Michaels looked at him as if he were a priest at the Playboy Mansion.

After a further, equally banal exchange, Lyle made his escape saying he was supposed to visit another company's party that offered great food.

• • •

As it turned out, Meng Industries had taken over a restaurant on the hotel's lobby level. Lyle remembered the smell of hot barbeque, so he followed his nose downstairs. Two people in menacing transformers costumes stood on either side of the restaurant entrance like statues guarding an Egyptian temple. Lyle waved to one who looked vaguely female, and she made a move that was either a slight bow or she was reaching for a weapon. He made it through unscathed and wandered into an open bar area where maybe fifty people mingled. Definitely more upbeat here.

Lyle found a barmaid who mixed him a drink, and he was ready to party, or more accurately, to sleuth. Across the room, he noticed Tracy Galvan from Atlantic Adventures sipping a glass of white wine. He walked over.

"Any luck finding what—or who—you're looking for?" She wore a flowery teal dress with a sash. Did she wear that as she explored the IAAPA aisles?

"No, sad to say. I had a promising presentation by one ride company. They told me they were completing work on ground-breaking developments, but they didn't break any ground in Arizona to get it."

"I see you're still Brent Gallagher."

"I'm hoping to drum up business for him in exchange for using his business cards."

"I hope you're successful." She smiled and her eyes shone. "I mean at finding out who stole your ideas—in addition to finding your missing employee."

"He had to be stealing it for someone else. What's he going to do, open his own theme park?"

One of the transformers moved mechanically through the crowd. A large "Meng Industries" sign covered most of his or her back. Was this a bionic version of a sandwich board?

Galvan moved a little in his direction as the tall transformer passed them. "I heard something today you might be interested in. It's just a rumor, but the person who told me didn't know about your theft."

"At this point, I'm all ears."

"Something's going on at Premier Studios Backstage. Supposedly the park was or is looking to borrow ideas that could get high-tech rides up and running in a few months. And here you might interpret borrow to mean *steal*. Maybe the old film studio tours are getting tame, or they're disappointed with the theme park's attendance."

Lyle glanced around to see if anyone was listening. "Go on."

"There's not much more to it." She paused and took a thoughtful drink of her wine. "I might not have bothered to pass this along, except I heard about Premier Backstage looking for new technology from someone else, too. So, I don't know. Maybe there's something to this."

He was about to ask her a question when over her shoulder he saw Rob making his way through the crowd. Lyle made eye contact, frowned, and darted his glance to the side. If Rob wanted to continue examining Atlantic Adventures, it wouldn't be helpful if Lyle introduced him to their executive VP. The eager NC engineer got the message and moved off. Lyle raised a hand to his forehead and accentuated his frown. "I'm thinking. Would Premier Studios Backstage have people here at the show?"

"Maybe," she said, "unless they have your secrets and don't need any more help." She smiled. "But you can find a list of attendees on the IAAPA website."

Lyle thanked her and turned to go.

"One more thing," she said. "If I can help, call me. We're sort of competitors, but I want you to find out who stole your secrets. If they can steal your ideas, they can steal ours. Get the bastards if you can."

# CHAPTER 44

The barbeque aroma lured Lyle to a sandwich bar, and he piled pulled pork on a bun. He sat at a table of eight listening to conversations that, to his disappointment, focused only on sports or which convention booth locations received the most foot traffic. After he ate, he circulated and noticed several people wearing Meng name tags standing around a high table.

"Excuse me," he said. "I was told that Meng Industries might have breakthrough ride technology that a client of mine is looking for."

The three men looked at each other, apparently trying to decide who would speak first. "Maybe I can help you," said a youngish Asian man in a Meng golf shirt.

He and Lyle moved down to an open spot at the end of the bar. Lyle gave him his attorney spiel and explained he was looking for one-of-a-kind ride ideas.

"Well, we use the latest technology in several rides. I don't think you will find anything more advanced."

He wasn't getting the message. Maybe this was another dead end. While Lyle was trying to think of a proper euphemism for stolen goods, Rob appeared at his elbow. Lyle instinctively looked for his badge. He wasn't wearing one.

"Ahh," Lyle said. "This is Fred. He works for my client. Perhaps he can explain to you what we're looking for."

As if he'd been privy to the entire conversation, Rob rattled off a confusing stream of engineering jargon as the Meng representative listened and nodded. "I think I understand what you're looking for," he said to Lyle. "We're constantly improving our AI capability. If you give us some precise specs, we can develop something for you."

Rob shook his head, so Lyle took the cue. "Thanks anyway. We'll keep looking."

As they turned to go, Lyle noticed a man had inched his way along the bar and was staring at him. When he and Rob reached the restaurant exit, the man caught up with them.

"Excuse me. I didn't mean to eavesdrop, but I heard you were looking for advanced XR tech, maybe with a unique ride configuration." He wore a shirt and tie and his badge said Concanon Ride Development.

"We're looking for something that's newer than new," Lyle said, sounding to himself like a TV commercial.

"I'd like to show you what we have." He introduced himself as Marty Jantzen. A smattering of shallow acne scars dotted his face, but his bright smile outshone the blemishes.

Lyle repeated his cover story and introduced Rob as Rob this time, an engineer from the client company.

"Our simulation can show you the capabilities. Our suite is in the Southeast Plaza Hotel next door."

Lyle looked at Rob. "Do you have time?"

"Sure. Let's take a look."

"You go ahead, Rob," Lyle said. "I have one thing to do. It won't take but a few minutes. I'll catch up with you."

"Great. We'll see you soon then," Marty said. "We're in suite 620." He shook hands with Lyle and led Rob toward the hotel door.

Lyle found Galvan standing with a group and asked if she had a moment.

"People are interested," he said. "At least I'm getting a little activity. I talked to Meng, but they didn't offer anything like our missing ideas."

"Meng is one of the biggest Chinese ride manufacturers. They have a vast market in China, but they've found buyers here and in Europe, Indonesia, and elsewhere."

"I'm going to go see a presentation by Concanon Ride Development."

Galvan made a face. "Concanon? Are they still around? We contracted with them once, but never again. They're liars. They make promises, then disappear for months. I doubt they're your thieves, too disorganized."

"They're all talk?"

"They were sued for patent infringement. I thought they'd gone out of business. Probably a waste of your time."

"Thanks for the information. I'll keep that in mind."

As he walked over to the other hotel, Lyle thought Concanon sounded *exactly* like the kind of people who could have stolen their secrets.

# CHAPTER 45

About a dozen people stood around the Concanon suite drinking and talking. A more or less human-looking, blue-skinned figure stood motionless next to the bar. Lyle saw Rob in a corner looking over sheets of paper. Behind him was a twin of the blue figure at the bar.

"Who's your pal?"

"Concanon makes these figures to put in dark rides," Rob said.

Lyle stepped over to touch the blue man. It looked like a stocky, blue store mannequin wearing a baggy outfit. Its skin felt like latex over foam.

"I saw a preview video," Rob said. "It could be what we're looking for, but I need more information. Marty said they have plans and another animation to show us."

"You're the tech expert. I'll count on you to recognize the concept."

"I've been wondering. What do we do if it's authentic? Just tell them we need to think about it, then call the FBI?"

"We could ask them about a price, or just say I have to consult with my client. I'll figure it out. But yes, we call the feds right away."

Rob showed him papers he was holding: technical drawings of

theme park cars and what looked like projectors or lasers. "This looks *vaguely* familiar," he said.

Marty appeared a few moments later. "Pretty impressive, huh? Now to give you the *best* experience of this, I gotta show you our *latest* unique ride technology. I need to show you on a desktop at our office. We route it through a big screen. You get the full effect. Then we can answer any questions you have. We could do it tomorrow, but the office is close by. We're right here in Orlando. Would you like to see it?"

Lyle wanted to confirm or reject this right away. If Concanon proved to be in league with Wyrick, he and Rob would have a good opportunity to tell Marty they'd meet him the next day to discuss details. And the local feds and/or cops could be waiting. If Marty was just a good salesman without stolen technology, Lyle could be on his way home the next day. He looked at his partner.

"Let's take a look," Rob said.

After a short drive in Marty's German sedan, they arrived at a single-story industrial building. Lyle noticed them passing bodies of water on the way but otherwise didn't know where they were. Marty kept up small talk, making comments about the theme park industry in general. Rob was circumspect.

A small Concanon sign advertised the entrance to an office at the corner of the sprawling structure. Even long after the sun had set, the weather had not moderated. As they walked toward the office, Lyle took off his coat and loosened his tie. The dry heat back in Arizona did feel like a pizza oven at times, but with its high temps and higher humidity Florida was like a deep fryer.

They walked through the silent office and Marty nodded to a casually dressed man at a computer desk, seemingly the only other person around. "It's right in here," Marty said, leading Lyle and Rob into a conference room with computer tables and a large LED TV screen on the far wall.

"You've never seen anything like this," Marty said. "Have a seat and prepare for *awesome*."

Lyle hated *awesome* as much as he did *in regards to*, but he wasn't there to give English lessons. He tried to relax. They sat in conference room chairs near a desktop computer and faced the big-screen TV. He hoped it was not another dead end, and he pondered how they'd make a graceful exit if it wasn't.

Marty touched a mouse and the wide screen jumped to life, showing a futuristic landscape of thin, towering buildings, serpentine greenbelts, and rows of dome-shaped cottages.

"Your guests will love this voyage. You can travel to the future or sail back to the past." Marty sounded like he was selling time-shares. He spoke in hushed tones and gestured at the screen as the animation revealed colorful, diverse scenes.

After about five minutes Rob asked a question. "Is this how you simulate the horizon? Is it holographic?"

"It's great, isn't it? So lifelike," he said. "You can be the only park to have our totally unique innovation. We just developed this. Now watch this next part."

Rob started slowly shaking his head. "Wait please," he said. "Can you explain how the guests see this scene from the cars? And how are they actuated?"

"Technical. That's good. Let me try to explain." He flipped open the lid to a laptop and was soon scrolling through page after page of text, supplemented with drawings. He started reading a jargon-laden description of how the ride simulated a controlled reality.

Rob listened, and Lyle studied his face for a sign that Marty was describing PDE. Then another man walked into the room.

"Marty. Can I talk to you for a minute?"

Marty walked out, leaving Lyle and Rob alone. "This is not your ordinary dark ride," the Nostalgia City engineer said. "Nice, but it's not our technology. This simulation is impressive, but Marty obviously doesn't know much about the science behind it. It looks vaguely familiar. I think they developed this and sold it to somebody else already. Or maybe it's stolen. But if this *is* stolen tech, at least it's not ours."

"And now," Lyle said, "they're offering it to us *exclusively*."

Marty walked back into the room with the other man. "Guys, this is Frank. He has a problem." Frank held a gun.

# CHAPTER 46

"Yes, I know what time it is."

"Then why the hell are you calling me this early on a Sunday morning?" Kate said. "And how d'you get my number?" Restless through much of the night, she'd actually been up for a half hour, but Wyatt Lewis's call still rankled. "Did you call the park and complain about my talk with Sievers? My boss called me up yesterday at home." *Actually at the market* "Do you know who my boss is? Archibald Maxwell, the founder and CEO of this whole damn place."

"I have some good news if you just quiet down a little."

"Quiet down? I didn't call *you* this early. You complained, didn't you, because I had a little talk with your out-of-control client?" Kate tightened the belt of her robe and reached for her coffee.

"It's ridiculous to call Cory a murderer. Russo's death was suicide. Do you read the news?"

Kate set her coffee cup down with a bang and took a breath.

"Now before you say anything," he said, "I know that Cory was a little abrupt with you yesterday. That's why I'm calling."

"It doesn't matter what he calls me, Mister Lewis. It's—"

"He wants to apologize."

"What?" *Lewis or Sievers thinks some apology is going to put me off or stop him from going to jail? Wait until I hit him with the videotape—and share that with the sheriff.*

"Cory wants to reach out to you. To say he's sorry for yesterday. You don't understand, Kate. He's really sensitive. Would you have time to talk with him today?"

*Sievers sensitive? To what, not getting his own way?* She would not tell him what Sievers could do with his apology, although it did occur to her. She had a better idea. She'd wondered how she could confront him with the new evidence, and now Lewis presented the opportunity. What sort of expression did Lewis have on his face right now? Was he gritting his teeth or treating himself to a smug smile?

"I can talk with him today. Would he like to come up to my office?"

"He suggested you visit his trailer so he can make amends."

*I'm sure he told you he wanted to "make amends." Is that in his vocabulary? But I'd love to have another go at him. If he thought I was a bitch before....* "Okay, how about this morning? Right away." *Let's get this over with.* "Would he be ready?"

"Yes. I think so. He gets up early to rehearse his lines."

*Rehearse his lines? For the movie or his alibi?* "So how *did* you get my number?"

"Easy. You want to be reachable by the news media, so your number is out there."

Kate set her phone down on her kitchen counter, poured more coffee, then felt exhilarated. You're not usually granted a *do-over*, but now she had one. And she had evidence to back her up. She let the excitement crowd out the uncertainty that would accompany a return visit with a murderer. She was back on the college basketball court again in a pressure situation. Excitement could be the drive she needed to score, or in this case, exact a confession from the killer of Steph's friend.

Should she record their conversation? Take someone with her as a witness? Call Rey on a Sunday?

As she showered and dressed, she reviewed what she would do differently this time. Hitting him with the video evidence might push him to confess if she were confident. Or it might push him over the edge, a place he'd been before. She considered having Drenda come with her, but if Sievers started a rampage, the presence of a 110-pound woman would only give him another target for his rage. Her voice recorder would be her corroboration. She owned a SIG P226 and knew how to use it, although she hadn't been on a range in a while. If she had it in her purse, would she be able to get to it quickly enough? Although it had been more than 20 years since she'd been on the court, she worked out, kept in shape, and would be ready for Sievers.

# CHAPTER 47

The park hummed even in the early morning. Tourists wouldn't see filming on a Sunday, but just the idea of movie stars at the park brought in waves of guests. Before Kate knocked on the trailer door, she heard Sievers reciting lines from the movie. And she heard another voice. Lewis. Sievers was lucky to have his agent handy to clean up his messes, but even Robert Duvall, as the fixer in *The Godfather*, couldn't help Sievers.

Cory Sievers opened the door when she knocked. "Kate, please come in," he said, his voice soft.

Kate took the two steps up easily. She'd dressed in jeans and running shoes. Lewis sat in the far corner of the room holding a script. He got up and moved forward. "Thanks for coming, Kate. We're just rehearsing a scene."

Sievers motioned to a chair. Kate sat near the door in the same place she had the day before. She set her purse next to her on the seat. "Can I get you something to drink?" Sievers asked.

Lewis stepped forward. "We can get you anything, coffee, wine or sodas, stuff like that."

She declined anything this time. Lewis and Sievers stood in front of her as if deciding who would take the opposite chair. Finally, Sievers sat down, but Lewis spoke.

"The reason we asked you here, and thanks again for coming, is that Cory really wants to—"

"Wyatt," Sievers said, "drop the agent talk, okay? Sorry, *I* want to do this." He looked at Kate with a plaintive expression.

"Do you want me to…" Lewis said.

"Please. We can rehearse later. I have this down."

Lewis didn't step out of the trailer until he'd thanked Kate *again* for coming over.

"Okay, I admit Wyatt set this up," Sievers said when they were alone. "I could apologize, but you accused me of murder, and I can't take that. I know you're wrong, and I know you're doing this for some reason. You just need to know you have the wrong man. I think it was suicide, and it's sad. I really respected Julian as an actor, even though he got on my nerves."

"I know the sheriff here personally and I can intercede for you, but you have to tell me the truth." No small talk this time.

Sievers put his head back slowly and looked at the ceiling. After a deep breath, he locked eyes with her. "I *am* telling you the truth. Why would I kill him, because we had an argument?" He slammed his fist on the arm of his chair. "Really? There's no evidence. He drove out there and jumped off the cliff."

"You followed him out. You trailed him to the canyon."

He shook his head and made a face.

"Yesterday I watched video of the day Julian was killed," she said. "I saw him driving his car out of the hotel complex about eight thirty. You followed right after him in your Corvette."

The movie star faltered for a moment as if he'd forgotten his lines again. "No." He rapped the arm of the chair. "That's not, uh —I didn't."

"We have CCTV just about everywhere in the park and we have you on tape following Julian. A security agent has it," she lied, "and is ready to deliver it to the Sheriff's Office."

He kept a fist clenched—a signal he might be ready to do something—but he slumped back in his chair. He glanced at Kate and she returned his stare with a furrowed brow and tight lips.

Kate said, "We know—"

"Shut up," he said. "Look, I was upset, okay? I wanted to talk to him. He was such a wuss, but I didn't want to fuck up the picture. It was my fault, okay? I wanted to tell him that. I dialed his room that night, but he hung up on me. So the next morning I was going to go to his room. But as I walked across the parking lot, I saw him getting into his car. So I followed him. I just wanted to talk. To cool things down."

"So you followed him to the canyon."

"No, I didn't. It was stupid. He woulda been pissed if I waved him down. And he wouldn't listen to reason. I was pissed too, so I just drove off, fast. I cut across some desert road going west. It ran toward the interstate and got real twisty."

"San Navarro Highway?"

"Yeah, that might've been it. I got tired after a while and cooled down. I needed to get back to the set, so I drove back here."

Making up an excuse on the fly, Sievers was a better actor than she thought. Yet there was a genuineness in his tone. "How long were you gone?"

"Not very long. I almost lost it on one of the curves." He picked up his hands momentarily, then let them fall into his lap. "I slowed down and came back. I was gone a half hour, maybe forty-five minutes."

"And you didn't see Julian after that?"

"No."

She leaned back in her chair, resting an arm on her purse. It sounded like a believable story. Sievers was an actor, but maybe he wasn't acting. She could find out. "Okay, if that's your story. Was anyone here in the trailer when you got back?"

"My assistant." He sighed. "But she didn't get here until later."

Sievers seemed worn out from the confession, truthful or not. She told him she'd consider his story and left. When she was only a few steps outside the trailer, she heard the door open.

"Ms. Sorensen," he said, "if you have all that surveillance video, you could see me coming back here when I said."

# CHAPTER 48

Lyle was too old to sleep on the floor, and after one night he was almost ready to take on Marty and Frank barehanded. He and Rob could find no way out of the tiny, windowless office storeroom they'd been locked in overnight—no way that wouldn't alert the guys with guns outside. He thought about using a chair leg to break through the ceiling. They tried squeezing into an A/C duct that would have been too small for Twiggy. But a night of imprisonment had sure beat getting shot.

Hours before, when the Concanon thug named Frank had walked into the conference room, Lyle and Rob had been stunned. Lyle hadn't liked the set-up, going out to a distant office, but he expected at worst a hard sell, not an ambush. As soon as he saw Frank's gun, he remembered the android. Rob was standing near the blue android when they'd discussed what they would do if Concanon turned out to be their thieves. The android had squealed. But of course, Marty and his buddies had misinterpreted Rob's remarks.

Frank wanted to kill Lyle and Rob on the spot because they weren't serious buyers and they planned to turn them over to the FBI. They should be dealt with, permanently.

Marty had saved them. For the time being.

"Okay Marty," Lyle said. "You're thinking we're here to pull some kind of scam on you. Not true." It looked more like Marty and Frank were intent on fleecing *them,* or someone else. But that was beside the point by then.

"We gotta dump 'em," Frank said. He stood more than six feet tall with thick dark hair combed straight back and a scar in the middle of his lower lip. He pointed a 9mm Glock at Lyle.

"Now Marty," Lyle said, "listen to me a minute. You don't know who we are. We're from Nostalgia City. We're looking around IAAPA for dark ride technology stolen from *us.* Obviously what you're demonstrating has nothing to do with our ride software. Just a misunderstanding. Sorry for the confusion. We'll catch a cab back to our hotel."

Marty responded by pulling out a pistol of his own. Lyle judged his odds at grabbing one of the guns at near zero, even though Marty held his weapon in a way that said he had little familiarity with firearms. And Lyle didn't want to risk Rob getting hurt.

"You're not leaving," Frank said, waving his pistol. "We want to know what you're doin' here."

"Now let's just calm down." Lyle held up a hand, palm out, toward Frank. "If we had some kind of connection with authorities, they'd be outside right now."

Frank froze. Lyle could see he'd scored a point. Frank's brows drew together as he appeared to process the information. Finally, he barked at Marty to have a look outside. Now Lyle's odds of grabbing a gun had moved from zero to "are you crazy?" He glanced at Rob, who looked calmer than he expected. He'd probably never had someone point a gun at him. He wasn't stiff or in the grips of an automatic fight-or-flight response. Maybe together they *could* overpower the lone gunman. Then Marty returned.

"The parking lot's empty, Frank. There's no one out there anywheres."

Frank seemed to be encouraged. Perhaps he'd pop both of them right now.

"Look at our IDs," Lyle urged. "You'll see we're from the garden spot of the Southwest, Polk, Arizona. We work at Nostalgia City. Put the guns down and go on about your business. We won't bother you. We're interested in *our* technology, not yours."

That approach seemed as effective as if he'd suggested they call out for pizza and watch the video again. Frank looked around, perhaps judging how much noise his 9mm would make in the small room.

"Cool it Frank. Why don't we see who these guys are? We got another client, I mean a real client, who's interested in a demo tomorrow morning."

Frank agreed, and while he held his gun on the captives, Lyle and Rob emptied their pockets. They set their wallets, cell phones, keys, and IAAPA badges on the table. Marty looked at their driver's licenses. They're right," he said. "They're both from Arizona. Maybe they do work at that park."

Frank told Lyle and Rob to step back. He still trained the gun on them, but with his other hand he picked up their badges. Several Brent Gallagher business cards had spilled out on the table. Frank looked at the cards, then glanced at Lyle's IAAPA badge.

"Wait a minute. This guy's a Florida attorney. What's going on?"

Marty picked up the wallets and looked at Lyle. "Are you Deming?"

"Uh-huh."

"Then who's Gallagher?"

"I borrowed Brent's badge so I could get into the convention center. I forgot mine at my hotel."

"What about the business cards?" Frank said. "I don't get it. I'm confused." *It didn't seem to take much.*

"Gallagher specializes in theme park law," Rob volunteered. "We use him as a reference when we're trying to show companies that we're on the level."

Rob's explanation made little more sense than Lyle's, and the "on the level" line sounded like crime show dialog, but they weren't dealing with masterminds. The pair of geniuses obviously didn't create the ride technology, just peddled it.

Frank motioned at the captives with the barrel of his gun. "These guys are full of it. Who knows what they're doing? Maybe they have a better deal going than we do."

"Tell the truth," Marty said. "What th' hell kinda con are you running?"

Lyle debated telling them the whole story, but even Rob's shaky tale sounded more believable. "We told you, we're from Arizona."

"What the hell are we going to do with them, Marty? When do we talk with that overseas park of yours?"

"I have t' call 'em again. They said they'd come by tomorrow." Marty's voice had lost its polished salesman's tone.

"We need to talk about this," Frank said. "Let's stick them in the storeroom."

"This way gents," Marty said.

As they left the room, Lyle tried to pocket his cell phone.

"Nuh ah," Marty said. "Leave that here."

The gunmen marched them down the hall and into a small room. Metal storage shelves along one wall held office supplies, boxes of coffee and creamer, several computer monitors, keyboards, and cardboard boxes. A counter contained a sink, coffee pot, cups, plates, and glasses. Three chairs sat around a table. The storeroom appeared to double as a tiny break room. Marty picked up a laptop and telephone and took them out of the room. Frank forced the captives into a corner as he rifled through the storage boxes on the shelves. Satisfied with the improvised lockup, the gunmen left. Lyle heard a key in the lock and a dead-bolt click.

"What do you think they're going to do?" Rob asked in a remarkably calm voice.

"Nothing good."

The two captives roamed around the small room looking for a way out, something they could use as a weapon, a key to the door, anything.

"I'm sorry I got you into this, Rob."

"I volunteered."

*You thought this was going to be exciting. It is now, isn't it?* "I forgot to ask you about your son. Where is he?"

"We're staying with my sister. She lives near Lakeland. He's with them right now."

...

They spent a restless night, marked by a hard floor for a bed and the need to relieve themselves in an empty plastic gallon water jug they found on the shelves. Lyle slept fitfully. He awoke once and heard voices outside. When he finally got up, it was later than his normal routine. They had no windows to tell them the sun had been up for hours. Breakfast comprised health food snacks Rob found in a box: hemp blend granola, kale chips, and dried turkey nuggets that tasted something like turkey.

Frank and Marty had been silent or out of earshot for some time until Frank's voice boomed down the hall. "Are those big clients of yours going to show?"

"I don't know. I have to call them again."

"They better get here or we're screwed. The boss didn't bail out Concanon so he could get a free pass to a theme park. We have to keep selling this new technology crap. The convention is going to be over in a couple of days, then what?"

"We'll have enough commitments by then. I pitched some park bigwigs who were sold on it."

"I'm gonna go talk to the boss," Frank said, "about our friends back there."

Lyle could imagine Frank pointing down the hall at the storeroom door.

# CHAPTER 49

K ate *had* to verify Sievers's story.

A call to the Control Center told her that Krystol Robinson was the supervisor on duty. She asked her if she would locate the videos for the same day she had reviewed before.

Without Drenda's help, she had to monitor video from several driveway cameras by herself. It went quickly, however, because traffic *into* the hotel complex was relatively light. When she didn't see the blue Corvette right away, Kate wondered if Sievers had made up his alibi. Did he think she wouldn't or couldn't check it?

Her perseverance rewarded her when she saw Sievers pull into the lot thirty-nine minutes after he'd left. He could not have driven to the canyon and back in that time. Nor could he have left again shortly after he returned and made it to the canyon—even if he *knew* where Julian was going—in time to push him over the edge when the witnesses saw him. She didn't need to look at any more video. She'd cleared Sievers. Now she had to tell Stephanie.

• • •

Kate had hoped for a quiet place to talk, but when she called Stephanie, she heard background noises from the NC Fun Zone.

Her friend told her she'd wanted to take in a few rides on her day off to distract herself from everything going on.

"But we need to talk, Steph. Where are you?"

"I'm in the main plaza in front of the LAPD Chase."

"Okay stay there. I'll leave now and get there as soon as I can."

Kate arrived and saw her friend sitting beside a replica police car marking the entrance to a suspenseful dark ride modeled after LAPD cop shows of the 1970s. Stephanie saw her and got up. They met in the center of the square.

"Let's go on the monorail," Stephanie said.

"I need to talk to you about—"

"I know. Let's go for a ride. Seriously. We can talk in there."

Stephanie might have guessed what Kate had to say and didn't want to hear it. Did a weekend of grief or anger drive her out of her hotel room?

After a brief wait, they boarded at the end of the train and had the last car to themselves. Stephanie sat next to a window looking out.

"Let me tell you what I've been doing. Okay?" Kate said. "You need to know."

Stephanie turned and looked at her as the monorail started to move.

Kate first explained everything she'd done to disprove the suicide theory, including a conversation she'd had that morning with Amanda, who had visited the Centerville bar the night before. The bartender had remembered Julian and said the actor had not been despondent. He'd had but one beer, chatted with customers who recognized him, and complained about missing LA Dodgers games. Kate said Amanda learned the Sheriff's detective talked to a server, not the bartender who waited on Julian.

Stephanie moved an arm from the window ledge to her lap where she clasped her hands.

Kate explained her encounters with Sievers. "I didn't believe his story one hundred percent," she said, "until I watched the video. Sievers and his Corvette returned to the park in less than forty minutes. He couldn't have driven to the canyon and back again—no matter how fast he drove. This clears him."

Stephanie's shoulders slumped, and she looked away. "I can't believe it."

The monorail banked into a turn and accelerated across one side of the park. "It's true. Whatever you think of Cory Sievers, he didn't kill Julian. I'm positive."

Stephanie shook her head, then turned toward her friend. "I'm crazy today. It's a nightmare. But thank you *so* much for doing all this. I don't know what to say."

Kate squeezed her shoulder.

Stephanie's lips almost formed a smile. "You did so much. You're amazing."

Kate had invested time and emotional energy and come away with little except letting her friend down. "I'm sorry it didn't work."

Stephanie returned to silence until the end of the ride. "You didn't prove Cory Sievers murdered Julian," she said. "But you did prove that *somebody* killed him. Would you find him? I mean, *can* you find him?" She closed her eyes and gripped Kate's arm. "I'm sorry. It's too much, isn't it? I shouldn't ask."

Kate had pondered the question of another suspect ever since she started believing the tone of Sievers's voice earlier in his trailer. By the time she'd seen the exculpatory video, she'd started to make a mental list. A short list because she didn't know why someone would push Julian over the cliff. She'd start with relatives or others with an emotional connection.

"Do you know who is going to claim Julian's body? Will his son be coming here?"

"Gary is here. I haven't talked to him, but Julian's agent told me."

"Where does he live?"

"Oro Valley. Is that close by?"

"Oro Valley, *Arizona*? That's just north of Tucson. Did he come up to visit his dad while he was here?"

Stephanie shook her head.

"Hmm. Is there going to be a memorial service?"

"In Southern California."

"Do you know where Gary's staying?"

"Yes, at the Rockin' to Sleep Motel in Polk. Are you…going to talk to him? Really?"

"The son is a place to start. You said you didn't know what kind of relationship he had with his father. I'll find out."

The monorail car shook as the train decelerated coming into the station.

"I can help," Stephanie said. "I'll ask—"

"Don't do that. Don't stir things up. Just put up with Sievers and do the work you love. Asking questions could jeopardize your job."

*And maybe your life.* A murderer was among them. Somewhere.

On the way back to her apartment, Kate called Lyle. She'd tried before. The call when straight to voicemail. He was probably on a plane home.

# CHAPTER 50

After not hearing Marty and Frank for ten minutes, Lyle banged on the door. "Marty, Marty, can you hear me? We've got a deal for you. I can help you sell your ride to another park."

"What?" Marty's voice came from a distance.

"Rob," Lyle whispered, "It sounds as if Frank is gone. This may be our chance. If you can explain to Marty how you can make his sales pitch better—maybe with some technical details—I'll try to get the gun away from him. It could be dangerous."

"It's okay. Let's do it."

"I don't really think Marty would shoot us."

Rob put a hand on Lyle's shoulder. "It's alright. Let's go"

"Marty," Lyle shouted. "Do you want to sell to another park or not? Rob has some inside information. He's an engineer."

After a minute, Marty opened the door. He stood in the doorway pointing a gun at them. "Back up."

Lyle and Rob stepped back from the doorway.

Marty began to speak, then had to suppress a yawn.

"You here all night?" Lyle asked, then he noticed Marty had changed clothes and shaved. "Where's Frank?"

"He'll be back. What do you want?"

"You have a presentation coming up. Rob is a ride engineer with Nostalgia City. He can help."

Marty took a step into the storeroom and motioned for his captives to back up farther. He glanced down at the remnants of their breakfast. Lyle took a small step to the side.

"Your video simulations show lots of possibilities," Rob said.

Marty looked up at him.

"But you should emphasize the interactivity. That's an important selling point. And I think customers need some more specifics. Engineers would want to know—"

"I don't go into many details," Marty said. "Just an overview. All I need to do is get prospects hooked, then the Concanon designers and engineers explain the technical side. It really works."

And, Lyle thought, where do the brilliant Concanon ideas come from in the first place? He took another small step.

Rob spoke up. "One thing that's really important is—"

Lyle lunged at Marty, bringing a fist down on his right hand. Marty's grip was not firm, and the gun dropped to the floor. Lyle pushed him against the wall, and Rob picked up the gun.

"You bastards," Marty said, straining against Lyle's hold. Then he slumped back and relaxed. "Ok. I told Frank we should have let you go right away."

The thought of Frank spurred Lyle into action. Rob stood holding Marty's gun pointing at the ground.

"Set it on the table," Lyle said. He pushed Marty into a chair. "Hand me that wire." He pointed to a spool of electrical cord on a shelf.

When he'd secured Marty to the chair, he picked up the gun and pulled out the magazine. Marty hadn't even chambered a round. He couldn't have fired. They locked him in the storeroom and found their belongings still sitting on a table in the conference room. Lyle headed to the office door.

"Keys?" Rob said.

"Good thinking." Lyle went back to the storeroom, went

through Marty's pockets, and extracted the key fob to the BMW sedan.

They jumped in the car, and Lyle fired up the powerful engine. He threw the car in reverse and sped backward into the empty lot. He trod on the brake, twisted the steering wheel, and accelerated toward the exit. Hesitating only a moment to look both ways, he turned left down a narrow road. He could see traffic one hundred yards ahead on a cross street. Before the BMW reached the intersection, two men in a dark Chrysler passed them going the other way. Frank sat in the driver's seat. He locked eyes with Lyle as they passed.

In the rearview, Lyle glimpsed the Chrysler doing a controlled spin into a U-turn. At the next street, Lyle turned right and hit the gas. With light traffic on the two-lane road, he made the BMW fly.

"Should I call the cops?" Rob held his phone.

Lyle glanced in the mirror and saw Frank's car make the last turn and speed toward them. "Wait just a minute," he said, then wondered if Frank would start shooting if he got close. The BMW responded to more pedal pressure and soon the speedometer moved past seventy miles per hour.

A small lake bordered the road on the right. After a half mile, Lyle saw a T intersection ahead. To the right, the road followed the lakeshore. Lyle stomped on the brakes yet still entered the intersection too fast. As he turned to the right, the rear of the car slipped out of its lane. Lyle gripped the wheel and fought the skid. The car responded and in seconds they were tearing down the road. Water now bordered the street on both sides.

Soon Lyle saw the Chrysler attempt the turn. It too threatened to spin out. Then Frank overcorrected, and the car veered off the road into the berm. It fishtailed as the driver tried to get back on solid pavement. Lyle didn't wait to see what happened and crushed the BMW's gas pedal.

"Now you can call the cops," he said.

After a series of abrupt turns, they were in a quiet residential area with no one in the rearview mirror.

# CHAPTER 51

I 'll try to catch a plane today," Lyle said. "We've already looked at mug shots and told the police our sordid tale, twice. It depends on the local cops here."

Kate set her cell phone on her desk. Relieved to hear his voice on the phone, Kate had a feeling Lyle was not telling her the whole story about Orlando, but it could wait. Now that he was on his way back, she would focus fully on suspects. She picked up her phone again and dialed Gary Russo at his motel. He agreed to meet with her in the lobby. On the way out, she stopped at Joann's desk to fill her in on her unofficial Julian Russo investigation. Her secretary had worked at the park longer than Kate had—even before it opened—and had contacts all over Nostalgia City. If she knew what Kate was up to, she'd be in a better position to run interference and to listen for useful intelligence on the park grapevine.

. . .

Built after Nostalgia City opened, the Rockin' to Sleep Motel, like many Polk enterprises, tried to capitalize on the retro mood. The motel's adjoining restaurant, Sandra's Shakes, featured a jukebox and black-and-white checkered décor. Was that bacon Kate smelled? The spacious motel lobby held a coffee bar and contemporary furnishings. A young man stood when she walked in. He wore khaki slacks and a button-down shirt.

"Gary? Thanks for meeting me. Please accept my condolences. I'm sorry about your father."

"Thanks. We can sit over here."

Gary must have inherited his height, or lack of it, from his father. He stood probably five-six in shoes. His light skin and ginger hair likely came from his mother. He led Kate to a corner seating arrangement where two couches met at a right angle at a coffee table. He sat on one side of the table, she the other.

"How long have you been here?" Kate asked.

"They called me Friday. I got in Saturday."

*He got a call* two days *after his father's death on Wednesday? The sheriff must have had a hard time contacting him.* "I understand the services are going to be in Southern California."

"Yes. Dad has a place at Forest Lawn, next to mother." He said it in matter-of-fact tones that gave Kate little clue to how he felt.

"He was filming a crime drama about the Vietnam era at our park. I had a chance to meet him. I've seen many of his pictures."

A man carrying a newspaper and a cup of coffee walked by. Gary waited until he had passed them to respond.

"If you're here to express condolences for Nostalgia City, thanks. It's appreciated."

"I am, of course, but I wanted to talk to you about your father and his death."

"About his suicide?"

"Your father didn't commit suicide."

"That's what the Sheriff's Office said."

"Do you think he would do that?"

He held up his hands. "I was surprised, yes, but it happens." He made eye contact. "Why are you asking? What's going on?"

"A friend of your father's doesn't think he committed suicide either and asked me to look into it."

"You said you were in PR."

"That's right. This is unofficial."

He narrowed his eyes. "Pardon me, but in that case I'll—"

"Gary, don't you want to know exactly what happened to your father?"

"Sheriff's detectives already talked to me. Said he jumped from a cliff."

"I don't think that happened. Do you know anyone who would have wanted to harm your father?"

"My father hasn't spoken to me more than two or three times since my mother died two years ago."

"I'm sorry."

"Look, we weren't close." Leaning with hands on his knees, he looked as if he'd get up and leave any moment. "This is my family's business, not anyone else's."

"I don't see my father very much, either," she said. "He lives out of state. My mother died several years ago. I miss her." She stretched an arm across the table toward him, not to touch him, but as a sympathetic gesture. She glanced at the serve-yourself coffee stand. "Can I get you a cup of coffee?"

He shook his head.

"Mind if I get one?" She smiled and stood up. *He wouldn't walk out on me while I'm getting coffee, would he?*

"Okay, I'll take a cup. Black."

As she poured the coffee, she marshaled a sympathetic expression, even though she was trying to find out if *he* killed Julian.

She set his coffee cup on a paper coaster printed to look like a miniature LP record. He mumbled thanks.

"You live just north of Tucson. Did you know your father was working this close by?"

"No."

She would have to ask Steph if Julian had said anything about that. She held her coffee and sipped slowly, letting the silence between them become a bridge.

Gary held his cup close and stared into it. "I was an only child in a show business family."

"Yes. I know your mother was a costume designer."

"It's not glamorous when you're a kid. They were always busy. Both of them. The next picture..." he sighed, "the next party."

"Did you want to go into show business?"

"Hell no. I went in the Army. My dad said I was stupid. Maybe I was. I wound up in the Middle East. That was a sick mess. I was almost glad to get home."

"When your mother died, you didn't become closer to your father?"

"You'd think so, huh?" He looked at her and she saw a reflection of his father in a sorrowful, troubled mood. "She was sick. She had cancer for a long time. I wanted a quiet funeral. He let people tell him what to do. I don't know. Losing my mom upset him, yeah, but he just got strange. We couldn't agree on anything. He didn't want to talk, so I left California."

Emotionally scarred, but did he really not know his father was in Arizona? If Julian had contacted him, would that have precipitated a fight? "Will you inherit your father's estate?"

He looked at her and Kate feared she'd broken the reverie. "I suppose."

"Do you know of any conflicts your father had with anyone, any show business grudges?"

He shook his head and made a weak gesture with his hands.

She finished the interview by asking him about his job, family, and anything Julian might have mentioned in their last conversation. Nothing Gary said sounded relevant.

She set her coffee cup down, then looked up at him. "So, you were in the Tucson area until Saturday?"

"Uh-huh."

"How long are you going to be staying here?"

"Not long. I'll have to go back to California for the funeral."

Kate thanked him and handed him a business card. If she hadn't sounded too much like a detective, maybe he'd call if he remembered something.

He stood up.

"I need to check messages." She pulled out her phone. "I'll just stay here a few minutes."

She waited until he left the lobby, then she walked up to the front desk. A young man in a red vest looked up from his computer.

"My brother and I were just talking about his bill." She motioned to where she and Gary had been sitting. "He said you're going to bill him for Wednesday, Thursday, and Friday of last week."

"What's the name?"

"Russo, Gary Russo."

The young man tapped on the computer, looked up briefly to take in Kate's smile, then back at the screen.

"Mr. Russo checked in Saturday. I don't show any charges for those other days."

*If he was up here earlier, at least he didn't stay at this motel.*

She didn't cross him off her list because she didn't *have* a list, a written one anyway.

# CHAPTER 52

She wore a navy dress, her jacket draped over the back of her chair. Even dressed for work, she could still stop traffic. Lyle's friend and ex-partner at the Phoenix PD called Kate the blonde bombshell. It fit.

"Good afternoon, beautiful," Lyle said, his head peeking into her office.

"You don't usually call me that."

"But I think it all the time." He walked around her desk, and she stood so they could fling their arms around each other.

"I didn't expect you until tomorrow," she said, her nose an inch from his.

"With the time difference, a flight from Orlando to Phoenix is only an hour and a half." *Mmm feels good.*

"You going to tell me what happened?" Lyle recognized her office voice, so with a quick squeeze, he retreated to the front of her desk and sat down.

"So, you said you found a company that could have stolen our secrets. But it didn't pan out. Then you spent the night locked in an office storeroom, ate kale chips for breakfast, and escaped in a BMW. Is there any *more* to this tale?"

"It's a *little* more complicated. I can tell you the whole thing tonight. But tell me, did you catch Sievers?"

"The opposite. I proved his innocence. That's a long story, too."

"*Psycho Sievers*?"

"Psycho yes, but he didn't kill Julian. And he didn't threaten me either. Except the 'bitch' thing. And, I learned a lot about the park's CCTV capabilities. So, did you enjoy IAAPA?"

"*Enjoy* is too strong a word. But it's an *experience*. It's more like a theme park itself, only instead of just offering you a ride on a roller coaster, they want you to *buy* the roller coaster. Rob tried to get me on one. You know how I feel about them."

"I do. Who's Rob?"

"Rob Napier. He's an NC engineer. I ran into him by accident. He helped me with the details of our stolen technology. And to thank him, I got him kidnapped with me."

"*Kidnapped*?" She leaned forward across her desk. "You didn't say anything about being kidnapped. You said you spent the night in a storeroom."

"Not voluntarily. Unfortunately, our captors got away before the police arrived. That's why I talked to the Orlando PD yesterday and this morning."

"Are you okay?"

"Fine. Except the bottom line, as they say, is that we talked to the major ride companies, and no one is offering anything like what was stolen."

"No clues to Wyrick?"

"None."

"What happens now?"

"I don't know. I'd like to talk to Howard this afternoon before he leaves."

"I guess the stolen model means there's still a spy or thief in our midst."

Lyle nodded his head vigorously. *And I don't know how in hell to find him.*

"Wait a minute," Lyle said. "If you proved Sievers didn't kill Julian…"

"Then someone else did."

"Are you going to find out who did it," he asked, "or did ruling out Sievers satisfy your obligation."

"I'm not obligated, but Steph needs help, and now I just want to finish it. You've felt that way."

Lyle nodded again. *And I'm still trying to get over those feelings.*

"I talked to Julian's estranged son this morning. He resented his Hollywood upbringing, and when his mother died, he and his father drifted apart. Did he do it? I'm reserving judgment."

"Anyone else on your list?"

"A list. That's just it. I want to do one of your yellow-pad lists, but I don't know who to put on it."

"You got a good start with family. Showbiz feuds and jealousies might fill in the rest."

"And there's one other piece of evidence I want to confirm." She explained how she and Drenda decided Julian was flying a drone at the canyon, but that they didn't know if deputies found a controller. "I was hoping Howard might know."

"Why don't you just ask Rey?"

"I'm trying to rehabilitate my professional relationship with the undersheriff. He was upset with you last week and somehow that rubbed off. He shared his list with me, but I don't want to bug him too much."

*I'm glad that worked out. Am I going to have to revisit my illegal trip to Wyrick's condo with Rey?*

As if she were reading his mind or just his expression, she said, "You're not wearing your rubber band. Have you—"

"Have I given it up? No, it broke before I went to Florida, and I haven't replaced it yet. It does work, you know. One snap brings you back."

"To our wonderful reality?"

# CHAPTER 53

L yle met Howard at the PAD employee patio. They sat under an umbrella apart from the few other employees chatting at scattered tables. Howard's expression said it was Miller time. "How'd it go in Florida?"

"I had an excellent fish dinner."

"That was the high point?"

"Pretty much. That and getting decked by a martial arts expert, bagged for impersonating an attorney, and kidnapped by a couple of conmen."

"Uneventful then."

"The bad news is, I couldn't find anyone who knew anything about our spectacular tech or our missing employee. And then I came across the Concanon goons I told you about when I called you from the Orlando PD. They had stolen technology alright, but it wasn't ours."

"That's too bad. And sounds like you used some of your unconventional methods of investigation."

"The only time I have any luck is when I don't act like a cop. Except this time. Things quiet around here?"

"Keeping the stolen ride model a secret was easy. If you're not a park employee or one of the thousands of San Navarro County residents, then you probably never heard of it. And as a result, everyone at PAD was immediately suspect—by everyone *else* here. Max is steamed, and I can't seem to get a handle on it." He loosened his tie and glowered.

"Don't blame yourself. We'll catch the guys who did this." *Maybe.* "And I'm the one who's come up empty. From what you told me, the odds are that someone at PAD stole the model. Probably the same person who worked with Wyrick. I'm hoping if we find the person who stole the model, he'll lead us to Wyrick and his partners."

"You think Wyrick's still alive?"

"Maybe not, but whoever got him to steal the secrets, or whoever he sold them to, certainly is."

"We've narrowed it down a little. Anyone who works—worked—with Wyrick or knows him is most likely his accomplice. But all in all, that's thirty-five or more people."

"Anything happening with the patents?"

"Not good there either. Legal and Owings's office are still going at it."

*So we're no better off than we were last week. Maybe worse.*

"I'm having my people talk to PAD employees again. I've got interviews myself. So far nothing conclusive."

They stopped talking when two men at a table thirty feet away started arguing. Lyle and Howard looked at them, and the men lowered their voices.

Howard turned back around. "You know the FBI is still chasing the idea that China is involved. I did some research on theme parks in China, and there's a ton of 'em. One is building a full-scale model of the Titanic. Full size. And there's a theme park chain with parks in seven major cities in China. It's like you put Disneyland in New York, Chicago, Houston, San Francisco, Phoenix—"

"Wait. Not Phoenix. Too close to us."

"But you get the idea. There are more big theme parks in China than anywhere in the world."

"I was thinking about our agent Peng when I was at the theme park trade show. Many of the ride manufacturers were Chinese companies. Big companies. I asked one of their reps if they'd ever steal ride ideas from the US. You know what he told me? He said, 'we don't want to steal *your* rides, we want you to *buy* ours.' Does that make sense?"

Before Howard could answer, a chair toppled over followed by, "You son of a bitch. You have more access than I do."

"I'm not the fucking hacker," shouted the other man.

One man took a swing at the other guy. Then both men were on their feet swearing and throwing ineffective punches. Howard and Lyle reached them at the same time. The bigger guy swung a haymaker that fanned the air. Howard grabbed him from behind and pinned his arms back. The other man seemed to object to the fight being broken up, so he took a swing at Lyle. He ducked the punch, grabbed the man's arm, and twisted it until he stopped fighting.

Howard shook his captive until he stood still. "What's going on?"

"He thinks I'm working with Tom Wyrick," he said.

"That's bullshit," said the other. "I just asked him about why he has such unlimited access."

Lyle recognized one of the men but didn't know his name. "Calm down you guys."

"I'm going to call for a security car," Howard said. "We can let them debate this in the office."

"I'm okay. Please stop," said the man Lyle held. "Please, it's my fault and I apologize. Can't we let it go at that?"

The other man lowered his eyebrows and glared. "Alright," he said with a sour expression. "It's okay. We just got a little hot. It's frustrating to think someone here is responsible for the break-in."

"What do you think, Howard? Shall we let them go back to work?"

"You guys calm enough?" Howard shook his man again to get his attention and he finally relaxed his shoulders. "Okay, we'll let you go. But you know who I am. Do this again and your supervisors will have to adjudicate. Tell me your names."

"I'm Paul Vang," said the man Howard had been holding.

"Ryan Smith," said the other.

As he and Howard returned to their chairs, Lyle said, "When was the last time you broke up a fight?"

"A lotta years ago. How about you?"

"Not *that* long ago. It was a fight in the homicide section between two detectives. One of them was me."

Howard gave Lyle a look as if he thought he was kidding. Lyle left it at that.

"See what I mean about animosity and suspicion around here. That's the first fight—that I know of—but it's getting tense."

When they sat down, Lyle asked Howard about Julian Russo's drone controller. "Has Rey mentioned it to you?"

"As a matter of fact, he did. They found a controller on the cliff edge. I think they were going to look for the drone, but finding it out in the canyon would be a long shot. Why do you ask?" He held up a hand. "Wait, Kate's nosing around the death, isn't she?"

"Uh-huh. She's pretty sure it wasn't suicide."

"Does she think Cory Sievers was involved?"

"No. He's got a tight alibi."

"So what's she going to do?"

"I'm not sure."

They sat in silence for a minute, then Howard said, "I think I'll head home. Come back tomorrow and try again."

"Me too."

As they stood, Howard paused. "If only we had someone who worked in PAD, aside from the top people, who we could trust to nose around without attracting attention."

Lyle grinned.

"No, I don't think you could pass as a programmer or engineer

Lyle, besides a bunch of people at PAD know who you are. I thought about putting one of my guys in there too, but it wouldn't work. We need somebody tech savvy."

"I have a suggestion for you."

# CHAPTER 54

"Tori, were you related to Julian Russo?"

"No."

"Not even by marriage?" Kate asked.

"He was married to my husband's sister. How did you know? Why do you ask?" Malcolm's sentences flowed together without pause.

Kate sat in front of a wide folding table that served as the movie publicist's desk. Tori Malcolm shared office space in a small NC hotel meeting room with the assistant location manager and the associate producer. Kate lucked out and found Malcolm at work and alone first thing in the morning.

The night before had been uneven. Lyle spent the night and their urgent lovemaking filled a void, but she remained restless. Although Lyle's presence comforted her, thinking about the murder kept her awake, again. She was happy with their relationship, but another relationship weighed on her.

She'd planned to continue her investigation of Julian's death before Stephanie asked. But how far did her commitment go?

What are the bounds of the social contract when murder is involved? She would find out.

"So Julian was your brother-in-law," Kate said.

"Uh-huh."

Judging by Tori's expression, Kate almost expected her next comment to be, "what's it to ya?" Tori wore a short-sleeved blouse that exposed her thin, wiry arms. She always looked distracted.

"After Julian died," Kate said, "I read stories about him and his wife and noticed the name Malcolm. I wondered if you were related. I'm sorry you lost him."

"Uh-huh." Tori looked down at the phone next to her laptop and thumbed the screen.

"I was wondering if you know of anyone who might have wanted to hurt Julian."

A cell phone sounded, but it wasn't the one on the table. Tori picked up her purse and pulled out the chiming device. "Hello, Tori Malcolm. Yes, that's exactly what I was proposing. When?" She scratched the top of her head, then absently tried to straighten her short blonde-streaked brown hair. "I can have him available for an interview tomorrow afternoon." She hung up and dropped the phone back in her purse.

"So, did you want something? I'm kinda busy."

"Yes," Kate said. "I want to know if you think anyone might have wanted to hurt Julian, to kill him."

"Kill him? He committed suicide."

"I don't believe he did. And I'd like to find out who killed him."

"Have you talked to Cory Sievers?"

"After their fight, Cory was an obvious suspect. But he's innocent."

"No offense, but why are you talking to me?"

"As a relative, I thought you might have some insight."

"I knew his wife Eloise well. She was my sister-in-law and a friend. I never really got to know *Julian*."

"Why was that?

"He was different."

"Different how?"

"It's a long story. Julian vacillated. You know the word? He did things one way today, but the next day was a different story."

"Movie-star personality?"

"Something like that." Tori glanced at her phone.

"Eloise Russo died of cancer two years ago."

Tori's eyes narrowed for a moment. "Yes, she did."

"Did Julian take it hard?" Kate said. "Do you know how he dealt with it?"

"What, before she died or after?"

Before Kate could pin her down, a man walked in and sat at another table. Kate recognized him as Alan Clappison, the associate producer. He smiled at Kate as if he remembered her.

So much for a private conversation. Kate got up. She could always come back and catch Tori in another mood, if she had one.

Before she reached the door, Kate turned. "Tori, the picture you had taken of the *Murder for No Reason* cast. Why didn't it include Julian?"

. . .

Nothing Tori told her made Kate want to strike her from her suspects list. And since she didn't *have* a list, a yellow pad was her first priority. She had walked to Tori's hotel from her office rather than take her car, so now she would complete the long round trip. She needed the exercise. She hadn't been able to get in her regular run. As she walked out of the hotel, her cell phone chimed with a text. Lyle wrote to say deputies found a drone controller—but no drone—sitting on the ground near the edge of the cliff when they responded to the call of Julian's death.

Good to have the confirmation but no surprise.

"Do we have any yellow pads?" she asked Joann when she got back to her office.

Joann held up a five-by-seven notepad.

"No, I need the full-size one. Lots of room to scribble, make notes, and draw arrows to connect things."

Joann promised to find one, and Kate went back to her desk. Settled in her chair, she stared at her brass paperweight shaped like a basketball backboard and hoop. Her mind went through the *Murder for No Reason* cast and the crew members she'd met. She remembered reading somewhere that Jana Osbourn and Sievers had a romantic connection. Had it survived the past year, and if so, would the movie's co-star want to bump off or scare Julian to settle some score for Sievers? That made little sense. Did she know Julian from before? Regardless, the female actor might know *something* useful.

Stephanie had given Kate phone numbers of some stars and crew members. She dialed Osbourn and talked to an assistant who set up an appointment to see the star that afternoon. Now, how was she going to broach the subject of murder?

# CHAPTER 55

Lyle recognized the Campbell's tomato soup can. It had been a while since he'd seen Max in his office rather than a conference room, but he remembered the Warhol painting. Was it an original?

It hung on a side wall of the CEO's spacious office, occupying a corner of the top floor of the Maxwell building. Max invited Lyle to join him at a small table next to a floor-to-ceiling window overlooking Centerville. Lyle had bad news, and Max knew it.

It took him a few minutes to expand on the details about Atlantic Adventures that he hadn't told Max about on the phone. Then he launched into his exploration of IAAPA, saying he found no companies with technology as sophisticated as PDE.

"And that includes those Concanon yokels, right?" Max asked.

"Yeah. I guess Howard filled you in on that mess. Rob Napier, a PAD engineer, helped me immensely as we sorted through all the competing technologies out there and he got waylaid with me at Concanon."

"What do you hear from the police there?"

"Nothing yet. They're still looking for the yokels."

"This is looking hopeless with every damn day that passes."

He held up a hand. "Not your fault. Done a lot already. I appreciate it. Just frustrating."

Max got up and walked along the window. "I was sure it was Jack Danneman, but it *could* be someone else. You see, it's kind of a personal thing. Building an image, attracting more guests, having leading-edge attractions. That's what I want. That's what Jack Danneman wants. We're all after the same thing."

*And money?*

"Technology is expanding," Max continued as he paced. "Everyone, every park wants to offer the latest. Guests expect more." He raised both hands and shook them. "They want more 'holy moly' experiences. And so my boy…"

Lyle knew this was coming, but he'd hoped he could hang around home to help ferret out the local miscreant. And where did the "my boy" come from?

"How about the FBI?" Lyle said before Max could finish his thought. "Have they reported anything?"

"Howard's dealing with them. I've talked to agents, but they're not saying much now. They don't know this business. Their focus is international trade. We need someone on the ground investigating who knows theme parks."

*Let me guess.*

"I want you to look at Premier Studios Backstage, the movie studio park. I've heard they want to expand their market share any way they can. They're shady. Check them out."

"Premier Studios Backstage, huh?"

"Tell my assistant Marion to help you with anything you need. Find out what's going on out there."

And how was he going to accomplish that? Dodge security, sneak into locked buildings? Flash Wyrick's picture around? No. He wouldn't skulk and he wouldn't act like a cop. He needed to find another way. He'd go nuts with the same routine *again*.

# CHAPTER 56

Attending to her neglected publicity work, Kate arranged a luncheon with a magazine feature writer and they agreed to meet at a roadhouse about halfway between Polk and Phoenix. As she pulled out of the NC parking lot and drove south, she thought about Steph and Julian and replayed her interview with Tori. She drove along a hilly two-lane highway and didn't pay attention to the dark SUV with tinted windows that grew rapidly larger in her rearview mirror until it was two car lengths behind her at nearly 60 mph.

She sped up. The SUV grew close, then closer. After traffic in the other direction opened up, Kate slowed so the driver could pass. The SUV sped up but didn't pass. Tires screeched as the car braked, just avoiding rear-ending her. She resumed speed and the dark vehicle finally jerked out into the other lane and accelerated. The driver—it could have been a man—passed Kate, then veered back right in front of her.

Kate swerved to avoid him and didn't have time to jam on the brakes. Her car's emergency collision system did it for her, bringing her to a stop as she steered to the side of the road near a ravine.

She looked up and saw the SUV as a distant black speck. Was

this some crazed tourist in a hurry or someone trying to run her off the road? It happened so fast she didn't have time to see a license plate or get a good look at the driver. The car? It could have been a Cadillac SUV or maybe some other brand.

Back at her office after lunch, she could still imagine the car racing behind her when her secretary came in to say Wes Moody wanted to see her about an urgent matter. He walked into her office and shut the door.

"Please have a seat," she said. "Something serious?"

He sat down and gripped the chair's arms with his elbows raised as if he were ready to jump up. "You've been interrogating people in the company. Asking questions and making accusations. It's not helpful. You're stirring up the cast and crew."

"I'm not making accusations. I *am* asking questions."

"But why?" the director wore jeans and a *Murder for No Reason* T-shirt and could have been mistaken for a grip, except perhaps for his artfully askew hairstyle.

"One of your stars was murdered, and I thought it would be a good idea to find out who killed him. It's unnerving to have a murderer roaming about Nostalgia City."

"Poor Julian's death already disrupted our filming. Now we're trying to refocus. But he killed himself. There's no murderer roaming around."

*Poor Julian,* such a sympathetic figure. Especially after Wes kicked him off the set for a day to satisfy his volatile leading man. "Yes, I know that's what the sheriff said, but the evidence doesn't bear that out."

"Fine, but keep your theories to yourself and don't disrupt my production. I need everyone to concentrate. We're going to get this film finished on time."

"Getting at the—" Kate said, but Moody interrupted.

"I don't direct *art* films, Ms. Sorensen. I'm a commercial direc-tor. I make movies that fill theatres, movies that people pay to stream. Yes, this film has a Vietnam, futility of war, subtext. I'm okay with that, but it has action, killing, a mystery, and well-known stars. I know who I work for, and I deliver. The scorpion sting was a problem, but we rearranged the shooting schedule. And yes, we're paying tribute to Julian, but we're going to be on time. Do you understand?" He looked like he might be ready to jump up in her face.

*Is he equating Jana Osbourn getting stung with Julian being murdered?* "I want this production to be as trouble-free as you do," she said. "Any problems reflect on us, too."

"You're right. They do. So we all want to be on the same page." He got up and walked to the door. As he gripped the knob, he turned around. "I'm glad we could talk. Arguing over our contract with Nostalgia City would involve Mr. Maxwell and wouldn't help anything. So if you've got plans to talk to anyone, don't."

"Wes," Kate said. "Do you drive a black SUV?"

He flashed a puzzled look. "No." And he shut the door behind him.

*He wouldn't try to run me off the road, then storm into my office to reinforce the message. And now he's threatening to go to Max like that dumb agent of Sievers's. Any argument over the filming contract would hurt Moody. The park could continue as usual. But where would Appropriate Brand Pictures find another Nostalgia City?*

She stared at the door that Moody had just closed. *Where was he the Wednesday morning when Julian died? Was he on the set?*

A moment later, the door opened and Joann appeared. "Sorry it took so long. We were out, and I had to order more from supply." She held out a yellow pad.

"Great. I have names to write down."

Joann gave Kate a knowing look and left.

Kate grabbed a pencil and wrote:

Tori Malcolm
Gary Russo
Wyatt Lewis
Wes Moody

Jana Osbourn?

She wrote Cory Sievers but drew a line through his name.

*Sievers couldn't have done it, but did he get someone to do it for him? Motives. I need to list motives. Something off the wall? I need to call Howard.*

# CHAPTER 57

L ate that afternoon, Kate knocked on Jana Osbourn's hotel room door.

"Kate Sorensen? Please come in."

Kate entered and took in the stunning sweep of desert and distant mountains through the broad windows of Osbourn's suite. "Thanks for letting me visit."

Osbourn wore a linen blouse and tight black jeans. She held a glass of white wine. "This is a light California...something. Perfect for the afternoon." She walked to the bar. "Would you like a glass?"

Kate accepted. "Beautiful suite. This is our top-of-the-line hotel."

"Oh, have you stayed here?"

"No, I have an apartment in Timeless Village, in that direction." She pointed southeast.

They took their wine glasses and sat facing each other on opposite couches separated by a low, glass coffee table. An arrangement of fresh roses and lilies occupied one end of the table.

The blonde movie star had obviously removed her theatrical makeup and replaced it with blush and a few other touches. She was 30, according to Kate's research, but she looked young enough to be carded in a bar if she wasn't recognized as Jana Osbourn. "So you're vice president of publicity?"

"Public relations, yes. How are you enjoying Nostalgia City?" Kate instinctively raised a hand to her mouth. "Oh, sorry. I'm sure you didn't enjoy getting stung. How are you doing?"

"No worries. I'm okay. It hurt like bejesus for the first day and throbbed for a while after that. But see." She raised her right hand and turned it around. "I'm fine now." She picked up her wine glass for a sip.

"But that was a scare," Kate said. "I was near the set when it happened."

"That wasn't good publicity, was it?" she smiled.

"I wasn't concerned about that. Just that you were—"

Osbourn waved away her response. "Just teasing." She chuckled and took another sip.

"You got me," Kate said. "But maintaining good publicity and image *is* what I do. Tori Malcolm is working on publicity for the film, and you probably have your own publicity person."

Jana nodded.

"My job is watching out for *the park,* and now I'm mostly concerned about Julian Russo's death. Did you know him very well?"

"I knew him a little. We did a pilot together for a legal drama. That pretentious redhead from the new sci-fi show was also in it. No names, but you know who I mean. She'd just had a boob job," Osbourn said in a conspiratorial tone, "and she kinda looked like a tall Dolly Parton. The show didn't get picked up, so we moved on." Osbourn smiled, then shrugged."

"So you didn't get to know Julian very well."

"No. That was the first time I'd worked with him. And now it's so sad and he's all over social media. Is that bad news for the park? His death didn't happen here."

"No, but his death is tied to the movie and the park. A tragic story for everyone."

"Tori probably isn't crying any tears over poor Julian."

There was that *poor Julian* again. "Really? Why?"

"Oh, doesn't most everyone know about Julian's wife?"

Kate maintained eye contact and made a nod of encouragement.

"She got ovarian cancer. It was awful. Tori is married to her brother—I think. Anyway, she and Tori were very close. And Tori didn't think Julian was doing all he could for her, getting her the best treatment. I really don't know much more, honest, but Julian's wife died suddenly and Tori kept saying they could have prevented it." Her expression said she should be embarrassed by the grisly gossip, but she wasn't. She finished her wine.

"I knew they were related. I didn't know about the fight over cancer treatment." *Wait 'til I spring this on Tori.*

"Like immensely sad." Osbourn stood up. "Can I get you some more?"

As Osbourn retrieved the bottle from the bar, Kate glanced around. The suite looked bigger than her apartment. She wondered if anyone was in one of the other rooms. Kate's host returned and filled their glasses.

"Tori's not the only one who didn't like Julian a whole lot," Kate said.

"Cory? Well, yeah. But he's had it rough."

"Did I read that you and Cory were seeing each other?"

She shook her head. "That's over. History. It was over before he went into rehab."

*Does this cross her off my suspect list? She sure likes to talk.*

"Yeah me 'n' Cory split. It was mostly physical, y'know. That was back when I was doing' that ocean picture."

"*Mendocino Coastline*? I saw that. You were good as the lonely beachcomber."

"Thanks. You know," she said, leaning forward, elbows on her knees, "One of my costars had a thing for Cory when we did that picture. Cory wasn't in it, he just hung around. But he made her so nervous she was popping Xanax every time she saw him. But you know who really hits the tranks?"

Kate shook her head. *Tranquilizers?*

"Steve McClintock."

"He was scheduled to do this picture."

"Yeah."

"It was a contract dispute. That's what I heard," Kate said. "He had a conflict with another picture."

"That's what they said to cover it. Now I don't know this for sure so, y'know." She waved her hand down as if it were hush-hush. "And I don't want to throw shade, but I heard he freaked out for some reason. How did he get out of his contract?"

Kate fortified herself with a good slug of the sauvignon blanc.

Osbourn leaned back on the couch. "I think Steve would of really freaked if he saw a scorpion."

*Where is this going? Did Sievers really luck into the role in* Murder for No Reason?

Kate set her wine down. She'd had enough. "So what I'm wondering is, is there anyone you think might have wanted to kill poor Julian?"

"Kill him? It was suicide. That's what I saw on the news." She pointed to her cell phone on the table.

"There's good evidence that hasn't been made public yet. I don't think Julian jumped. I think—"

"Someone pushed him? Oh my God. Really? Who would do that?"

Kate waited.

"What? No. Cory didn't like him, but he wouldn't kill him."

"Did Cory's agent, Wyatt Lewis, like Julian?"

"No, I don't think he did."

"Did you happen to see Julian last Wednesday morning?"

"Last Wednesday? No, I don't think so. Oh, I remember. I was in makeup then we had a problem with wardrobe. I didn't get to the set until way late. Did somebody else see him?"

"I don't know."

"Well, what's going on? What are the police doing? Do they have suspects?"

"I don't know what the sheriff is doing. I just wondered if you'd heard anything?"

"Me? No. I hope they find them. That's kind of creepy, isn't it? You know this reminds me of that old slasher movie I did. Well, it wasn't really a slasher flick, more of a mystery…."

Eventually, Kate thanked Jana for her time and told her to have her publicist call if she needed anything. When she stepped into the *down* elevator, she saw Wes Moody walk out of another elevator and head toward Osbourn's room. He looked over his shoulder twice.

# CHAPTER 58

The assistant manager at the Centerville emporium couldn't help. He'd worked at Premier Studios Backstage for three years in retail, hadn't kept in touch with anyone, and hadn't been back to the park since he left two years ago. Lyle thanked him and wandered outside.

He looked down at the list of names. He'd talked to five people who had worked at the California park, from a ride supervisor to a chef. None of them were any help. It had seemed like a good idea at the time. The best way to investigate Premier Studios Backstage would be to find someone with inside connections at the park. But it was proving difficult. None of the former Premier Backstage employees he talked to knew much about park security, nor did they have any current park contacts who might be helpful. Of course he had to be careful. He didn't want to alert the California park that someone was trying to learn its secrets.

He would try one last person. The next name on his list had been a department head and worked at Premier Backstage for eight years before coming to Nostalgia City. *But what did he do here?* The list didn't tell him where he worked at NC. Max's assistant, Marion Keegan, had obtained the list for Lyle from the park's VP of human resources. A short walk took him to the HR office. He lucked out. Pamela Quarrie was in her office and had time to talk.

He had met her once before and she greeted him by name. They sat at a corner table in her office.

"This will just take a minute," he said. "I'm trying to locate an employee." He set his list down and read the employee's name.

Quarrie glanced at the list, so Lyle turned it around so she could read it and pointed to the employee's name.

"This is the list I gave Marion. She was unclear about why she needed it, but the request came from Mr. Maxwell so..." She gestured at the paper. "I cautioned her about the confidentiality of personnel files."

"Yes, I got the message."

Quarrie tilted her head. She had a small mole or beauty mark an inch from the side of her mouth. "Can you tell me why you wanted the list?"

"I have an assignment from Max—Mr. Maxwell—that former Premier Backstage employees may be able to help me with. I haven't been asking them any personal questions."

"Okay…"

He didn't want to explain further. "You probably know the park keeps files on our competition. You could say I'm working on that process."

"I'm aware of that. So you're asking former Premier Studios Backstage employees to tell you about that park? If I recall correctly, you've investigated crime here at the park before."

*Oh hell.* "If you look at my employee file—" *which she'll probably do as soon as I walk out of here—*"you'll find out I used to be a Phoenix police detective."

"I remember." She raised an index finger in front of her nose.

Lyle could see her process everything he'd said. She had to know at least some of what was going on at PAD.

"It's not complicated," he said. "Mr. Maxwell wants me to look into Premier Backstage and I was hoping to find someone here who might have useful background or know someone at the California park who might be willing to talk about…things."

"Would you be interested in talking to a disgruntled Premier Backstage employee who used to work here?"

Lyle tried not to sound too interested. "Possibly."

"Carlos was one of our best trainers. He left to work at Premier Backstage about six weeks ago, and he hates it. Let's just say it wasn't what he expected, and now he feels stuck. He might help you find out about…" She tilted her head again. "Things."

"Sure. I can give him a call."

"Why don't you let me call him first. I can do it right now if you like."

Lyle listened to Quarrie's side of the conversation. She explained Lyle's background and said he was interested in information about Premier Backstage. After several minutes she finished with, "I'll tell him he can call you."

He thanked Quarrie and waited only as long as it took him to find a quiet corner of the HR building to call Carlos. After a twenty-minute conversation, Lyle was ready to tackle Premier Studios Backstage—from the inside.

When he finished the call, he read a text from Rob. He needed to talk. Lyle met him at a small workroom in an outlying PAD building.

"Virtually no one uses this room anymore," Rob said. "We won't be disturbed."

They sat at a polished wood table, and the engineer placed a thin leather case between them.

"I have a suspect," he said.

"That was quick. Did Howard talk to you?"

"Uh-huh. And I think I found someone. His name is Dave Egan."

"Doesn't sound familiar. Tell me about him."

Rob adjusted his glasses. "He's twenty-eight and has been here for less than a year. He joined the park from a San Francisco tech start-up." Rob pulled out papers from his case and glanced at them.

"I did a little research, and the company seemed to have had promise when it started, but the co-founders had a fight and the company lost its attraction for investors."

"So Egan comes here."

"Right. And he's a real social guy for a techy. He's on a local parks and rec sports team, and he hangs out after work with lots of people—including Tom Wyrick. But what makes him a likely suspect is that I've heard people say he's been acting nervous or secretive recently. Maybe the last few weeks."

*Since Wyrick disappeared.*

"As I said, he's usually extremely outgoing but has been quiet recently. I don't know what that's about, but worth looking into, don't you think?"

"Yes. I wonder if Howard's people talked to him."

"I mentioned his name to Mr. Chaffee, but he didn't remember it and said he might not have been considered a suspect." Rob glanced at his notes. "He's married and lives in Polk. I have his address."

"Hmm. Egan, huh? Could be a good lead."

Rob pulled out a photo. "This was taken several weeks ago at a company get-together."

Egan beamed into the camera. With a charming smile and tousled hair, he looked like a life-of-the-party type. "Now if I only knew what his car looked like, I could tail him for a little while, see what he's up to."

"He drives a year-old Subaru wagon. Green."

Lyle leaned back and grinned. "You came prepared. You want to follow him after work?"

"Is that really a good idea? He knows me."

"I'm kidding, Rob. You did an amazing job. I'll do a little follow-up."

# CHAPTER 59

F or excitement, staking out a parking lot ranks just below watching golf on TV. Lyle once spent four days in the Arizona heat sitting in a parking lot. A homicide suspect had parked there and was expected to return. Later Lyle found out the guy had been shot robbing a convenience store in New Mexico while he sat watching the Phoenix lot.

Checking out a Nostalgia City parking lot after work took no time at all. Before five o'clock Lyle found two green Subaru wagons in the PAD employee lot. He picked the newer one and parked several spaces away.

At quitting time, employees filed out in ones and twos. Lyle noticed several employees he recognized, many he didn't. When a thin man in slacks and an open-neck shirt walked with a determined step down his aisle, Lyle glanced at Egan's picture. It was him.

Egan got in his wagon and pulled out.

Many employees leaving at the same time gave Lyle cover to follow him. He left two cars between them as they drove out on the road that connected with the highway to Polk. The Beatles's *Eleanor Rigby* played on the radio as Lyle kept a comfortable distance behind Egan. He didn't expect to learn much, but he wanted at least to check out where Egan lived before he headed off to California and had to hand the investigation to Howard's crew. If he was lucky, maybe Egan would stop somewhere for a drink with coworkers or friends and he could sip a beer and eavesdrop.

Lyle tried not to lose sight of Egan in the rush hour traffic when they reached the outskirts of Polk. Before Nostalgia City was built, Polk didn't have outskirts. You were either in Polk or you weren't. But now the formerly sleepy desert town extended housing tracts in several directions, many still under construction. Before he'd staked out the PAD parking lot, Lyle had checked an online map to see where Egan lived. His home lay across town, but Egan turned east on a new thoroughfare. Lyle followed at a safe distance, mildly intrigued.

They passed a strip mall with a supermarket, laundry, and bank. Egan continued on. They reached a development of new apartments and condos. As traffic flow dropped off, Lyle held back. His silver Mustang convertible was not the most inconspicuous of cars. They passed a two-story apartment complex bordered by a hedge, and Egan turned left at the corner. Lyle let him get ahead a long block. As he nosed his car into the intersection, he saw Egan's green wagon turn left at the next street. Lyle crawled down the street between apartment buildings and crept up to the next intersection. Egan turned left again. He was circling the block.

On impulse, Lyle spun his Mustang around, hit the gas, and raced back the way he had come. After two sliding turns, he headed back in the opposite direction on the main road—and pulled over at the corner. Soon he saw Egan turn the corner at the end of the block and pull into a small parking lot for the apartment complex.

From a distance he could see the man get out of his car and hurry up a walk, straightening his collar as he went. Lyle drove down the block and parked in the street. The hedge bordering the complex blocked much of Lyle's view, but he could just see over it from the driver's seat. Egan headed along a sidewalk and didn't turn around. The path took him to an apartment door.

Lyle saw a woman open the door. She seemed to put an arm around Egan as he walked in, but Lyle was too far away to see clearly.

So what next? Egan could be visiting a friend, a sister, someone from the office. Almost anyone. But sitting and waiting for Egan to come out, and likely drive home, wouldn't tell him anything. He should probably make a few notes and head home himself. He'd be leaving in the morning and he wanted to see Kate.

But why did Egan drive around the block? Parking spaces were open when they passed the lot the first time. Was he lost? Something told Lyle Egan had been there before and was being cautious. Maybe he was lucky Egan hadn't spotted his Mustang.

Not knowing exactly what he was going to do, Lyle got out and walked a wide circle around the building Egan had entered. The individual unit had curtains drawn in the front windows. He circumnavigated the building a second time, glancing at his phone and pretending to be lost. He noticed the ground-floor units had fenced patios at the rear accessed by sliding doors. The row of fenced patios in one building faced the fenced patios of the adjoining building. A narrow greenbelt and decorative dry streambed separated buildings.

Twilight dulled the sky. He took a chance. The grape-stake fencing stood just above his line of sight, but he could see the open drapes in the corner unit where Egan entered. Lyle picked up a large rock from the streambed and set it next to the fence. When he stood on it, he could peer over the top. A flowering plant grew inside next to the fence. Lyle peered through the leaves, hoping to remain unseen. He glanced over his shoulder to see if anyone in the opposite building could see him.

When he looked back, Egan and a young woman walked into the bedroom and embraced. They held each other for a prolonged, athletic kiss. When they separated, he ran his hands through her long dark hair as she undid the buttons on her blouse. She slipped it off, and Lyle saw she wore nothing beneath it. Egan shifted his attention lower.

Lyle felt as exposed as the woman, so he lowered himself off the rock. He bent over slightly and found a place where he could see through the grape stake. Egan had his shirt off and the brunette was on her knees unzipping his pants. She was probably not his sister.

*Is this how professional PIs make a living?* Again, he looked around to see if anyone was watching. That's just what he'd need, to be arrested by San Navarro County deputies as a peeper. Should he take one more look? No need. He was familiar with the story and knew how it ended.

As gracefully as he could, he replaced the rock, extricated himself from the rear of the apartments, and walked back to his car. Egan might still have a connection to the PAD theft; however, Lyle was pretty sure the slinky brunette was the prima facie reason for his suspicious behavior. But he wanted to be sure.

He drove to Egan's home address, walked up to the front door, and knocked. A young woman in a casual dress opened the door.

Lyle smiled, introduced himself using a phony name, and confirmed she was Mrs. Egan. "I work at Nostalgia City. Is Dave here?"

"No. He's working late, but it shouldn't be too long." She sounded hopeful and looked at him with soft blue eyes.

"Yeah, I left a little early. I thought he'd be here. It's no big deal. Maybe I'll call him later this evening." He took a step back and tried to smile. Did this fresh-faced woman do something to drive Egan away, or was he just a womanizer? Regardless, he felt sorry for her. He could have simply telephoned instead of showing up at the door. Now he wished he had.

As he drove away, he remembered days of pain caused by the vagaries of love.

# CHAPTER 60

After almost two glasses of Jana Osbourn's wine, Kate decided on a cup of green tea that evening as she prepared dinner. Stephanie had called late in the afternoon with questions she couldn't answer. Yes, some people didn't like Julian, maybe hated him—but enough for murder? In the middle of putting together a meal from bits and pieces she found in Lyle's refrigerator, she searched for a necessary ingredient.

"Where do you keep the olive oil?" she shouted.

Lyle walked into his kitchen. "In the cabinet, here." He leaned over, pulled open a door, then stood up and kissed her.

She wore one of Lyle's aprons over her slacks and T-shirt. He stood close.

"Mmm," he cooed as he put his arms around her.

He felt good, but she was busy. "Lovely. Now finish your packing. I'll get this in the oven, then we can talk."

"It's really my turn to cook, but I didn't have time. You shouldn't—"

"You have to get ready for your trip. Go."

"I'm almost done. I'm taking casual stuff so I can blend in. But then that's what I usually wear anyway, isn't it?"

"Like the old Magnum PI."

"Were you a *fan*?"

"It was rather ubiquitous when I was a kid."

"I like Hawaiian shirts. Let's leave it at that."

Later, when Kate put a casserole dish in the oven, Lyle walked into the adjoining family room wheeling a suitcase. He stopped at the bar separating the family room from the kitchen and mixed himself a drink.

"You sound a little down this evening," she said. "Dinner won't be ready for a while. Let's sit."

She led him over to his black and white herringbone couch. She patted the rough, tweedy fabric, inviting him to sit. "You were out a little late this afternoon. What's going on?"

He set his drink on the coffee table in front of them, looking like he wanted to guzzle before answering but didn't. "I eliminated one suspect from the PAD employees who might have stolen the ride plans, but it wasn't fun." He explained the case of Dave Egan and his girlfriend.

"Rob suspected Egan because he was being secretive at work. Now I know why."

She was tempted to tease him about being a Peeping Tom, but the look on his face told her not to. He looked the way he sometimes did when he talked about past police work.

"How exactly did you get a job at Premier Studios Backstage?" she asked changing the subject.

Lyle paused before replying, as if clearing his head. She put a hand on his knee and their eyes met.

"Pamela Quarrie introduced me to a guy who works in HR at Premier Backstage. He used to work for her, but he left recently thinking he had a better job lined up. That's not how it turned out. He expected he would be a lead trainer and found himself interviewing applicants for ride attendants."

"So they misled him, and he left Nostalgia City."

"I guess so. What I'm sure of is that Carlos is pissed as hell. I told him I wanted to do a little investigating—undercover if possible—and he was happy to help. I tried to explain, in broad terms, but he stopped me. Said he didn't care, and he'd find a position for me."

"What are you going to be doing?"

"I'm not sure. He emailed me a job application. He said he just wanted a little information and he'd create the rest."

"Fill in the job application for you?"

"Sounds like. He said I'd have to go through a day of orientation and training, then I'd be a bona fide park employee."

*How many theme parks is Max going to make Lyle investigate? Is he getting too stressed? What's the FBI doing?*

"Kate?"

She realized she hadn't heard what Lyle just said. "What? Sorry."

"*I said* I might be able to help Carlos out in return. Pamela said he was a terrific trainer. Maybe she could be persuaded to hire him back."

"I hope this works out. You can find the thieves and call the FBI."

"The park looks like a better prospect than Atlantic Adventures. Max suspects them, apparently for the way they do business. And of course being in California, rather than Florida, makes them a closer competitor. But what cinched it for me was something an executive at Atlantic Adventures told me. She said she'd heard that Premier Studios Backstage was dealing in secrets."

"Sounds promising."

"Did you know Nostalgia City has a file on all the competing theme parks in the country? Our engineers visit the other parks and take notes and pictures. I read our 'book' on Premier Backstage."

"Our department has files, too," she said. "But we focus on advertising, publicity, and industry attendance figures."

"I wish someone had told me about these files before I went to Florida." The corners of his mouth turned down. "At least at Premiere Backstage I'll be an employee working on the *inside*."

# CHAPTER 61

I hope you have better luck than I've had so far with Julian Russo," Kate said. "*I'm* working on the inside here too, and it hasn't helped." She picked up her notepad from the table.

Lyle pointed at the tablet. "Is this your suspects list?"

"Suspects and notes, yes. And down here—no, on the next page—this is a note about when Max called me to complain. He doesn't like me investigating, so I have to keep a low profile."

"You can't exactly do that and still question suspects."

"I realize that, Lyle. And I'm wondering if someone besides Max wants me to cool it." She explained her episode with the SUV. "It could have been some antsy tourist, some idiot."

"Or someone warning you off?"

"Uh-huh."

Lyle grimaced. "Kate, you need to be—"

"I know. I will be careful." *Maybe I shouldn't have told him.*

She tapped her yellow pad. "Look here. Nothing seems to fit."

She pointed to the first name on her list. "Tori Malcolm, she's the publicist for Appropriate Brand Pictures. She's a high-strung LA type. She's related to Julian's deceased wife, but she denied it at first. And she didn't tell me she had a fight with Julian over his wife's cancer treatment. That gives her a grudge."

"Do you think she was mad enough to kill him?"

"I can't tell. I should talk to her again and ask her about her fight with Julian. Our interview was interrupted."

"What about the son?"

"Gary Russo. I don't know much more about him." She pointed to her notes. "He lives in Oro Valley."

"Family members are always—"

"I know. Prime suspects. He only checked into his Polk motel after his father was killed, but he could have come up here earlier. I'd say the jury is still out."

She flipped the pages of her tablet, then sipped her tea. She summarized her talk with Jana Osbourn. "No grudge motives there. She and Sievers broke up before Sievers went into rehab."

As she spoke, Lyle slid closer and slipped an arm around her back.

"That feels good, but c'mon. I want to talk about Julian." She scooted back and turned to face him.

"Sorry. I'll keep hands off." He held his arms in the air. "I just remembered for a moment that you were a woman."

*Can't he see I need to be serious about this?* She stared at him for a moment and he looked contrite. Or was he pouting?

"I couldn't sort out everything Jana Osbourn said. She just talks and talks—doesn't seem to have anything to hide."

"Everyone has something to hide. That's what makes investigation difficult. A dark secret may make someone look nervous, but it might have nothing to do with the crime you're interested in —like the case of Dave Egan today."

*I can figure that out.*

Lyle pointed to lines on Kate's pad.

"My notes after talking with Howard today," she said. "I've been wondering if there's any connection between Julian's death and the theft of our ride secrets."

"You think Julian was involved?"

"I don't know. I asked Howard if Julian's name or the movie filming came up when they questioned PAD employees."

"And?"

"Nobody mentioned him or the movie." She tapped a hand on the yellow pad in her lap. "Last week a security officer confiscated one of Julian's drones when he was flying it near the PAD buildings."

"He was snooping?"

"Didn't look like it. Howard said his videos showed nothing but aerial gyrations. I'm just trying to find persuasive motives—somewhere."

"How about this guy," Lyle said, pointing to another name.

"That's the director of the picture," Kate said. "Wesley Gordon Moody."

"Okay, go on. He's a suspect?"

"Well, he wasn't until he stormed into my office and told me I was interfering with the filming by looking for who killed Julian. Said he'd make trouble with Max if I didn't stop. I don't *know* what his motive might be." She reached for her tea. "Another question mark.

"Then we have this guy, Wyatt Lewis, Sievers's agent." She recounted her early interactions with Lewis. "He seems to have a lot riding on this picture. He's spending all his time here. Doesn't he have other clients? Maybe he thought he was doing Sievers a favor by getting Julian out of the way."

Lyle shook his head. "He murders someone just because he had an argument with his *client*? Really? You said *Sievers* started the fight."

"You don't have to say it like that. I know it sounds crazy. This whole movie crew is a little crazy." She paused for a beat and looked down at her notes. "Lots of people might have had it in for Julian, but nobody—except *maybe* Tori—has an overwhelming motive. Would you push a sixty-eight-year-old guy off a cliff because he has an irritating personality?" *Something like yours tonight.*

She stopped and smelled. "I think dinner's ready."

She headed into the kitchen and pulled supper out of the oven.

She walked to the end of Lyle's family room and placed the large dish in the center of the dining table. Looking up, she saw Lyle set his semi-automatic pistol and holster on his suitcase.

"You're taking a *gun*?"

Lyle sat at the table. "I'm not going there to shoot people. I doubt I'll use it, but since I'm driving instead of flying, it's easy to throw in."

"Well, at least be a little more careful than in Orlando."

Lyle set his empty drink down with a bang.

She hadn't meant it as a dig, just a sign of her concern. She handed Lyle the serving spoon. He didn't speak.

"I just want you to be safe." *We're both on edge tonight. No surprise considering, but solving these issues, these crimes, shouldn't affect our relationship. C'mon Sorensen, where's your Scandinavian detachment and your basketball-court calm?*

She said, "Here, have some fish pie."

# CHAPTER 62

Traveling parched miles along Interstate 40 west took Lyle's Mustang past hardscrabble towns of Kingman, Needles, Barstow. Accompanied by The Eagles, Blondie, and other '70s stars he drove across the sandy expanse where the Sonoran Desert met the Mojave, covering a similar path worn by Steinbeck's Joad family and the thousands who traveled Route 66 to flee the dust bowl of the 1930s. After hundreds of arid miles, he approached Los Angeles, the city recognized as much as anything by its movie and entertainment business.

He by-passed downtown and took the Ventura Freeway west across the San Fernando Valley. He got off at Warner Center and drove north to Chatsworth, where he'd reserved a hotel near the studio and theme park.

Nestled against the hills in the northwest corner of the valley, Premier Studios arrived later in the history of motion pictures, after movies had begun to talk. The rural, farming location, a half day's drive to downtown Los Angeles at the time, provided plenty of rugged background for westerns and adventure serials.

Premier built massive sound stages that attracted the most famous stars of the 1930s and 1940s.

Gradually suburban neighborhoods replaced valley farms and by the 1970s the studio was no longer isolated, but still maintained a reserve of open land that soon became the Premier Studios Backstage theme park. While the studio itself and independent production companies continued to roll out films and TV shows, the theme park capitalized on Hollywood-style glamour with tours of the movie sets and later, roller coasters and dark rides.

The park's human resources department occupied a two-story building away from the rides and attractions. By leaving Nostalgia City before dawn and scheduling a late afternoon meeting, Lyle was able to see Carlos Betancourt the same day he arrived at the park. Following signs, he walked upstairs to a reception area that fronted a collection of cubicles.

"Lyle?" said the young man who came out to greet him.

Trim and slightly shorter than Lyle, Carlos had an easy smile and relaxed manner. He held a tan folder. "Why don't we go into a room over here," he said after they shook hands.

He led Lyle to a small conference room presumably used for interviewing applicants. Carlos sat in a swivel chair on one side of a table.

"Do you mind if I stand for a few minutes?" Lyle asked.

"Did you drive in from Arizona today? Sure."

Judging by Carlos's age—he looked barely 30—and his build, he probably never had a problem with sitting in a car for hours on end. Lyle stood behind his chair facing Carlos. He leaned on the chair back and extended one of his legs behind him, then the other. "Thank you for getting me a job. I didn't expect this much help. I appreciate it."

"No problem." Carlos looked out the interior window that faced the cubicle farm. "How long have you been at Nostalgia City?"

"I started there about six months after the park opened."

"You like it?"

"I like my job driving a cab, talking to tourists, helping people on vacation. And I have friends at the park."

"I liked it there, too. That's another story." He leaned back in his chair, showed a wry smile, then opened the folder in front of him.

"Ms. Quarrie said you used to be a cop."

"I was a Phoenix PD detective."

"Well, we won't put that down on your application. She said you helped the park when it was in trouble. And the chief of security there gives you five stars."

*Pamela must have read my personnel file and given Carlos Howard's number. Thorough.*

"So what is it you want to do here?"

Lyle finished stretching and sat down opposite Carlos. "I need to investigate. I'm looking for—"

Carlos leaned forward. "Don't go there. I get it that you're investigating. I don't need to know any more. I'm just wondering, do you want to explore the rides? Are you interested in employee areas, our warehouses?"

"I see. I'm particularly interested in ride development, engineering. Technical behind-the-scenes places."

"You want to be able to move around. Come and go."

"Right."

"That's kinda what I thought from what you told me on the phone. We have openings in maintenance. That means you could work anywhere in the park and you wouldn't seem out of place."

*Perfect.* "Will I have to wear a uniform?"

"Yeah. Just about everybody here goes to costume. Maintenance guys wear dark khaki slacks and a uniform blouse. You can pick them up and take 'em home or change in one of the locker rooms. It's up to you. But if you want to do any snooping behind the scenes—employee-only areas—you'll need the uniform, a name badge, and your prox card ID." He gave a quick glance out the window again. "I'll request a higher access for you than a maintenance worker would normally have. If it goes through, it won't get you in everywhere, but you'll be able to see most of the areas you might be interested in. "I'll explain in a minute. Let's finish your job app."

Dark eyebrows were the most prominent feature on his square, handsome face. He wasn't wearing a wedding ring. Lyle wondered if he'd landed a girlfriend in the park yet.

"I filled out the application with the minimum of information," Carlos said. "I gave you a local address and used your cell phone number. Here's a copy in case you get any questions. You said you won't need to be here for more than, like a week?"

"If I can't find what I'm looking for by then, I'm out of here. I hope it will take only a day or two."

"That's good. You have orientation tomorrow, then you can get to work. I fixed it so your boss won't be expecting you for a couple of days. You can check things out on your own without having to do any actual work. Can you repair anything?"

"Change light bulbs without help."

Carlos smiled. Lyle could imagine him relaxed at the front of a classroom, educating *and* entertaining new hires.

"Will this get you in any trouble, Carlos?"

"No worries. It won't be a problem—not that I care. When you're finished here we'll just say you were a flake and quit without notice. Something like that. I'll delete your file, toss any paperwork, and no one will follow up."

"I'm sorry your job here is not what you expected."

"Yeah, I feel kinda trapped. But most of the people I work with are nice. Except my boss is a lying asshole. Now, let me show you how to get into locked doors."

# CHAPTER 63

If only Kate could spend all her time searching for Julian's killer, but she did have a job. Equally frustrating, no one else but Steph seemed concerned about the actor's death. Kate remained steadfast. There had to be more to it.

Lyle had called the night before. He was eager to accomplish *something*. So was she. She ignored a report on her screen tracking Nostalgia City's weekly media hits and reached across her desk for her yellow pad. As she flipped through the notes, she stopped at Wyatt Lewis. Show business connections came and went. Lewis could have multiple links to Julian, however remote. Had he ever represented Julian? It was worth a phone call. The agent for the deceased star, however, was out of the office. She left a message.

Why not ask Lewis himself? She'd probably find him near the set.

Filming had shifted to the Centerville Bowling Lanes, where an assortment of period automobiles sat in the parking lot. Nostalgia City provided the film company with the old cars at a reduced rental rate. Rental of period cars contributed significantly to NC's bottom line. Visitors couldn't drive their own cars on Centerville streets, but they could rent fully restored, brand-new looking 1960s or 1970s cars for about the same price you could rent a Lamborghini from Avis, if Avis rented Lamborghinis.

A café formed part of the facade of the bowling alley, and the film crew was arrayed around the restaurant's outdoor patio. Cameras, reflectors, control panels, cables, and stacked storage containers dotted the pavement. Behind the café's outdoor seating area, sliding doors stood open, exposing the shaded interior of the restaurant. Kate spotted Lewis's shiny head. He stood just outside the roped-off viewing area where tourists waited for something to happen.

"Wyatt, did you ever represent Julian Russo?"

He paused for a moment, either startled by Kate's directness or fishing for a safe answer.

"Why no. I never did. What makes you ask?"

"Cory proved his innocence. But that means someone else pushed Julian."

"Who, me? That's nonsense. He was a nice old guy."

"That's not how Cory described him."

"Look, Cory had issues, okay? We resolved all this. Why don't you leave it alone?"

"You don't think anyone should try to find out who killed him?"

"Well, yes, if it was murder, but—"

"Can you think of anyone who would have wanted to kill Julian?"

"Ah, no, not at all."

"Can you tell me where you were on that Wednesday morning?"

"Yes, because—" Lewis looked away. Cory Sievers had just walked out of the bowling alley, his suit coat off, a gun on his hip. Lewis waved at him and pointed to a corner of the set. "Excuse me," he said, and walked off.

"Can I have your attention," Stephanie shouted. She faced the guests in the parking lot. "In a few minutes we're going to have some gunshots. There's nothing to worry about. They're all blanks, but if you're sensitive to sharp sounds, you might want to back away."

Actors stood at the edge of the patio with semi-auto pistols in their hands. One of them pointed his weapon at a wall and sighted down the barrel. He held the weapon in both hands with his left thumb hooked around the end of the gun.

Kate walked toward the actor just as she heard, "Quiet on the set." She dashed up and gripped the man's wrist.

Wes Moody appeared immediately behind her. "What are you doing now?"

Kate turned. "Well, unless you want him to rip his thumb off, you'd better show him how to hold a pistol. I don't know how these movie guns work, but if it's real, that's what would happen."

"Damn," Moody said to the actor. "What are you doing? You've handled guns before. Did Brandon review this scene with you?" He turned and scanned the set. "Where the hell is—" He stopped and sprinted across the set, waving at Stephanie to follow him. The two stopped a guy in shorts and a movie T-shirt—presumably Brandon, the weapons master. Kate couldn't hear what the director was saying, but judging by how he waved his hands at Stephanie and Brandon, the conversation was X-rated.

Kate reminded the actor next to her about the safe way to hold his gun, keeping his hand out of the way of the slide when it fired. He thanked her, and she stepped back from the set. With Moody overseeing, Brandon and Stephanie talked with the actors holding guns and walked them through the scene twice.

The crowd had thinned out after Stephanie's noise warning. Kate moved into the parking lot and found a spot from where she could see the action. She leaned against the cab of a vintage yellow pickup truck and watched the scene begin.

Blam. The sound of the actors' blanks ricocheted off the bowling alley wall. Simultaneously, Kate heard the crack of the pickup truck's windshield fracturing. A small spray of glass erupted a few inches from her chest.

# CHAPTER 64

"Now you need to be familiar with our new VIP passes and wristbands," said the instructor. "These identify special guests or season pass holders."

Lyle sat at a desk, not unlike those he'd occupied in college, listening to a Premier Studios Backstage instructor. This part of the new-employee orientation program didn't concern him. Maintenance workers didn't deal with guests.

"Those of you going into maintenance and custodial, you need to pay attention, too," the instructor said. "Everyone here is part of the cast and needs to be ready to assist our guests."

*Oops. VIP passes and wristbands. Check.*

The instructor, a middle-aged woman with serious overbite, droned on for hours in a continuously rising and falling tone. She explained the rationale behind each of the park's signature rides, recited what possessions guests were not allowed to bring into the park, and cautioned everyone to be on the lookout for lost children. Lyle looked at his watch. Why did people think that a singsong voice kept a presentation interesting? How could this woman be a better trainer than Carlos?

Finally, Lyle heard, "Okay, we'll break for lunch. Those of you who already had your pictures taken can pick up your proximity card IDs in the office. We'll meet back here at one thirty."

Lyle picked up his card and name badge, then followed other students to an employee cafeteria. Italian was the flavor of the day. He helped himself to a little spaghetti and lasagna, grabbed some garlic bread and a drink, and looked for a place to sit.

People dressed as tour guides shared round tables with space aliens, jungle explorers, gangsters, sailors, and train conductors. Lyle saw an empty seat between a woman dressed as a fuzzy animal and a guy who was probably a security officer, if not a movie cop.

"May I join you?"

The security officer waved him into the empty seat. "Are you a new hire?"

"Guilty. I'm in training today. Going to be in maintenance." Lyle introduced himself.

"You don't look like maintenance," said the woman next to him.

"And you look like a mountain lion, except you don't have any cat makeup."

"Oh, the rest of me is over there." She pointed to an open cabinet with various parts of costumes on hangers and shelves. "I'm Bonnie the Bobcat."

"Nice to meet you, Bonnie."

"My real name's Lauren."

"Did I hear you had a code 26 today?" someone asked the security officer next to Lyle.

"Yeah, a big surprise. I was standing by Sunken Island when a private tour group comes by. And there she is, listening to the presentation like she was going to critique the guide."

Lauren must have seen Lyle's puzzled look. "Even *I* know what that means. Code 26 means Mrs. Z."

"Who?"

"You'll find out. She's the boss."

"Executive VP," said the security officer."

"Her word is law around here," Lauren said. "Everybody knows who she is. She's not on the grounds too often, but when you see her, better have your costume straight and be smiling at guests."

"Ah ha. Code 26 means watch your back," Lyle said.

"Pretty much," the officer mumbled through a mouthful of spaghetti. He swallowed, then asked Lyle, "What did you do before coming here?"

"I drove a cab."

"That must have been interesting."

He gave a noncommittal grunt in response.

"Here in LA?"

"No, not here." Lyle made small talk and hurried through his lunch so he wouldn't have to answer more questions. He nodded to Bonnie the Bobcat as he bailed out of the lunchroom and headed for costuming.

Unlike the Nostalgia City costume shop, which specialized in retro-style street clothes, the massive Premier Studios Backstage wardrobe department covered most periods in world history and that of other galaxies. Lyle wandered the aisles. Each costume had multiple copies in sizes to fit anyone from Shaq to Danny DeVito. The maintenance uniforms were nondescript khaki and light blue. A clerk told him employees had to provide their own shoes, black oxfords with non-slip soles or black athletic shoes.

He tried on his uniform and looked in the mirror. "May I fix that toilet for you?" he said to his reflection. "Is your Ferris wheel on the fritz?"

With time left before class, and dressed as an official maintenance man, he decided to get a head start on snooping by exploring part of the engineering and mechanical areas of the park. Thanks to orientation, he knew where they were.

To cut across the park, he chose a nearby employee door and found himself in a forest of spooky, distorted trees. Guests wandered around, some looking at small maps. Lyle searched for a way out and realized he was in a tree maze. The farther he walked, the darker the forest became. Some trees took on human features. Were some moving? After many steps forward and a number back, he thought he'd found an opening into the rest of the park when a hairy creature swept down upon him from the treetops—a huge flying monkey. Lyle threw his arm up to shield his head. The creature hovered above him, then sprang up another tree with a sound between a growl and a shriek.

A boy of nine or ten happened by, gave but a cursory glance at the attacking monkey then looked down at his map.

"May I see that?" Lyle asked.

The boy clutched the map to his chest, then reluctantly held it out.

"Oh, this is the forest from the Wizard of Oz," Lyle said. "That explains it."

"Duh," the young man said. He pointed down. They stood on yellow pavers.

With the help of the map, Lyle was finally out of the woods. He walked diagonally across the park toward a series of industrial buildings. He found an exit and used his prox card to enter the employee area.

Here, as at Nostalgia City, the buildings were labeled with numbers and letters. Using what he'd learned in class, however, and the notes he'd read before he left Arizona, Lyle could make a reasonable guess where he wanted to go. He walked past a row of offices housed in portable buildings and turned a corner where a forklift unloaded the back of a semi-truck. The next building stretched for a block. An unassuming door marked the corner. Lyle could see no windows, just the one metal door, a pass card panel, and CCTV cameras. He waved his card at the panel and nothing happened. He waved it again and tried the door. Locked.

"Excuse me there. This area is out of bounds."

Lyle turned and saw an armed, uniformed security officer. Where'd he come from? The man's eyes were close together, his nose long and pointed, reminding Lyle of a rat, minus the whiskers.

"I'm with maintenance," he said, as if the guy couldn't recognize his uniform. "This access pad doesn't seem to work."

"Lemme see your card."

Lyle held it out.

"You're not authorized here. Can't you tell? Look at your code letter." The officer started to take the card from him, but Lyle pulled it back.

"My mistake." Lyle pocketed his card.

The guard raised his arm and pointed to the building's identification near the roof. "See, this is E-7. Why didn't you know your card wouldn't work?"

"Slow learner."

"Uh-huh. You're in maintenance. You should know."

"This is a big place."

"I don't like your attitude."

"That's what my ex-wife used to say."

"Where're your tools?"

"My drill shorted out. Damn near killed me. It's being repaired."

The man rested a hand on the butt of his gun and continued to glare.

"Relax," Lyle said, "I'm new. Just going through orientation. I'm trying to get *oriented*."

The man's stare lost some of its menace.

"So," Lyle said, "is this your job? Guarding this door?"

# CHAPTER 65

K ate stared at the windshield for a split second, then jerked backward. She stumbled along the side of the truck, grabbed the edge of the bed, and worked her way behind it. The shooting rehearsal continued as the actors ducked behind chairs and overturned tables.

When Moody yelled "cut" the actors relaxed and crew members moved about, some rearranging the patio furniture. Kate still held on to a corner of the truck's bed and frantically scanned the crowded movie set. A middle-aged woman in the crowd glanced at Kate, saw the windshield bullet hole, and screamed.

A uniformed, unarmed security officer walked toward Kate until he got close to the pickup's cab. Then he ducked and covered the next three yards in a crouch. He reached Kate and shouted into his radio. Moments later, a second security officer appeared. He pulled out a pistol and moved to the patio. "Drop your weapons," he shouted at the actors. One of them looked at the armed officer and dropped his gun on the pavement. The other actor-gunmen plopped their pistols on tables with sharp metal-on-metal sounds. The officer spoke into his radio as he held his gun on the actors. "Up against the wall," Kate heard him bark.

Another officer joined the one next to Kate. He examined the bullet hole as the other man yelled for everyone in the crowd to move back, off the parking lot and around the corner. The tourists didn't need encouragement. "Someone got shot," a tourist shouted as he ran. People dashed across the parking lot, parents dragging their children, the elderly helping each other move as fast as they could.

Crew members dashed around the corner of the bowling alley or ducked behind a service truck and storage containers. An NC security car screeched to a halt and two armed officers got out. One joined the officer on the patio, the other entered the bowling alley. Another officer arrived on an electric cart. He jumped out and started looking around the movie camera, cables, and other equipment.

Stephanie joined a handful of people who crowded around Kate.

"I'm fine," Kate said. "Just a little shaky, that's all."

"I'll call an ambulance," said an officer.

"No, not necessary. I'm not hurt." She walked away from the truck and held her arms out to show she had not been hit.

"What's going on? What happened?" Wyatt Lewis pushed his way through the crowd.

Kate heard the noise of another car arriving. She glanced over people's heads and saw Howard get out of an unmarked vintage car with flashing red lights.

"Stephanie, was that an accident with the guns?" Alan Clappison, the associate producer, joined the gathering. "Someone could have been hurt. Are you okay, Ms. Sorensen?"

Clappison looked at the bullet hole surrounded by spider-web fractures. "This is horrible. Where's Wes?"

Soon a siren's wail preceded two San Navarro County Sheriff's cars pulling into the parking lot. Deputies jumped out. Three deputies and security officers walked into the bowling alley and out through the café. Others roamed the set, searching. Movie crew members, sensing the danger was over, moved out of their hiding places.

Hours later Kate would ask, "Was anyone detained, arrested?"

# CHAPTER 66

The instructor with overbite began the afternoon orientation session by telling the new hires how many thousands of CCTV cameras were in the park. Was this to reassure them about park security or warn them not to pull any hanky-panky? Lyle perked up when she moved on to prox cards and security zones. A slide showed the different access priority levels. Lyle eased his prox card up from his shirt pocket. The letter B signified he had more access than the average employee. So why didn't his card work on Building E-7?

He tried to soak up everything that would help him reconnoiter the tech side of the park, but much of the information he would never need. The instructor told the new hires to stay current on daily events by consulting the employee-only pages of the park's website.

Class broke up before five o'clock. Lyle wanted to go back and check out the buildings identified with letters and numbers. Avoiding the Wizard of Oz forest, he found Building E-7 with the guarded corner door. He passed the door without seeing the guard and continued to the other end of the building, slightly less than a half-marathon distance away. Floor to ceiling glass windows wrapped around this corner of the structure and double glass doors invited Lyle to enter. He waved his card at the access pad and walked in.

Four desks clustered in one corner of the room. Each featured a computer screen and a person pecking away at a keyboard. Lyle couldn't tell if they were clerical or technical staff. A couch, a dozen chairs, and low tables filled the rest of the room. No signs indicated the function of the building or who the reception person might be. Across the room, he saw double metal doors and another access pad.

"Help you?" A young man stopped typing and acknowledged Lyle's presence.

"Someone called with an electrical problem," Lyle said.

"Which office?"

"I was hoping you could tell me. Programming?"

"For operations, systems, development?"

"I'll find it." He pulled out his phone and pretended to consult it as he moved to the metal doors. With a wave of his card, he was through. Now what? He saw an empty meeting room ahead, and a corridor extended to the left and right. He turned left.

A wide window on one side of the hall revealed a room with two rows of cubicles in blues and browns with people working at computers, others standing and talking over the low walls. Lyle could see no signs to indicate what the mass of people might be working on. They looked like tech types, although it could have been a call center for all Lyle knew. Millennials and younger were in the majority and casual dress the preferred uniform.

Down the hall, a series of numbered doors led who knows where. He turned right at a connecting hallway and found himself heading upstream against a flow of people. Their demeanor and bits of conversations told Lyle they were leaving for the day.

The last guy to pass him wore a dress shirt and tie. A boss? He turned around. "Can I help you find something?"

*Damn, I need to look like I know where I'm going.* "Report of an electrical problem in... component engineering," Lyle said. *If there's such a place.*

The man wrinkled his forehead. "Component engineering?" he said slowly, looking at Lyle. "Isn't that in E-4?"

"Oh, thanks. I'll call and check. Did they send me on a wild goose chase again?" He nodded thanks and kept moving, hoping the man would go home. He did.

Around the next corner, Lyle entered an open area with eight cubicles in the center and private, glassed-in offices along two walls. Only a few of the cubes were occupied. He walked slowly along, glancing at computer screens. He saw diagrams, charts, calculations, drawings, text.

Not knowing exactly what he was looking for meant every office or desk could lead him in the right direction. But which one? His maintenance uniform helped. Most people ignored him. An unoccupied private office contained a desk, chairs, and a work table with three computer screens all lit up. He meandered in, looking at papers on the desk and scanning diagrams on the screens. As he turned to go, something in one corner of a screen grabbed his attention. Inside a small orange rectangle he saw blue letters P-D-E. This couldn't be a coincidence. Lyle pulled out his phone and switched it to camera mode.

"Can I help you?"

In one continuous motion, Lyle silently pressed the shutter and looked up. A security officer stood in the doorway, his arms folded across his chest. Multiple stripes on his sleeve signified some high rank. He looked at Lyle with an expression Lyle had seen on wanted posters.

"What's going on?"

"Looking for an outage. Someone called about an electrical problem. I was just about to call and check." Lyle let his arm holding the phone drop casually to his side.

The man didn't move. "Who requested this?"

"I dunno." *Did the guy see me take the picture?* "They just told me to get over here. No one tells me nothin'. Looks like the power's steady here."

The officer uncrossed his arms. A tall Asian man in a suit stopped at the door. "What's happening?"

"Hey, Sam. Someone called in an electrical problem," the security officer said. He looked at Lyle. "An outage?"

Lyle shrugged and started moving away from the computer screens.

"He doesn't know who called about it," the officer said.

About forty, Sam wore a dark suit, his black hair short and parted on the side. He walked to the desk. The officer now stood away from the door. Lyle saw an escape path. "I'll call my office and see if I can straighten this out," he said.

He walked to the door and noticed Sam step from his desk and stare at the screen he'd just photographed. "Wait a minute," Sam said. He took two steps toward Lyle and looked at his name badge, then his face. "Where're your tools? How can you repair anything?" The man's voice was soft and modulated.

*Tools again. I'm going to have to find a tool kit.* "I'm a supervisor here to check the problem, see. Then I tell 'em what resources we need. No need to send a whole crew if it's nothin'."

Sam maintained eye contact as Lyle backed out the door. He turned and was five steps away when a squat man hurried out of an office looking the other way and almost knocked him down. Lyle glanced at the man, mumbled "excuse me," and moved on. He imagined the man staring at his back, and at the same moment he remembered the same man, the same feeling, weeks before.

He wanted to rush out of the building and check the photo he'd taken, but he took his time. He passed the room that looked like a call center. The rat-faced security officer stood next to a cubicle talking. Lyle tried to make eye contact rather than look away—too suspicious—but he wasn't sure if the officer even saw him. He waved to the guy in the reception area as he went by and was finally outside.

He cut across the park, crowded that afternoon. He back-tracked twice on the way to the parking lot. Probably he wouldn't be followed. His uniform served as good cover and the stumpy

thug wouldn't have remembered him. Who looks at cab drivers?
Soon he found the safety of his car.

He pulled out his phone to check the computer screen photo.
Blank. He could see the office wall and the table, but the computer
screen itself was an empty bright rectangle.

# CHAPTER 67

W hen all the excitement died down, I had to go report this to the executive producer."

"Is he here?" Howard asked.

"No, he's in LA," Clappison said.

"Then you could have called him from the bowling alley parking lot."

Kate hovered outside the door to Howard's office, listening to him question Alan Clappison. The associate producer's manner mixed condescension and irritation.

"Look, I already explained this to the sheriff's detectives. I needed to file a written report at the same time. This is a multi-million dollar production. An incident like this could affect publicity and then, most importantly, our investors. When I finished the report, I came back to the set."

"Someone could have been killed," Howard said. "Leaving the scene of a crime is a serious matter."

"The sheriff knows all this."

"Okay, Mr. Clappison. I have a report to make as well." He sounded exasperated. "We need to ensure that everyone is safe while your studio is filming here."

"The studio, yes," he said.

Kate heard his chair move on the floor, so she ducked around a corner until he'd gone.

"Hi Kate," Howard said when she walked into his office. "Did you hear any of that?"

"The last part." She sat in a chair opposite Howard's desk—not the chair Clappison had occupied. "He's supposed to be watching company expenditures."

"Yeah? Well, he doesn't have a record, but his actions were suspicious." He set his pen down and met Kate's eyes. "How are *you* doing?"

"I'm okay. They missed me, right?" She chuckled and didn't like the nervous tone in her voice. She felt better having changed into casual clothes. She'd work out tonight and be back to normal, or closer to it.

"Before Clappison, I talked to Wyatt Lewis, Sievers's agent. He said he's a friend of yours, and you can vouch for him."

"That's pretty funny. Not true of course."

"He claimed he saw a shadowy figure inside the café when the guns went off, but his description was so vague it was useless."

"That's the kind of answers I've been getting talking to people about Julian Russo's death. I have suspects, but motivation to kill is scarce."

"People have been killed for a few dollars in change. How about an old grudge?"

"Possibly."

"You think the person who took a shot at you is the one who killed Russo?"

"Seems obvious, right? I've thought about this. Maybe thought too much. But there could be more than one person involved. Tori Malcomb, the movie publicist, might be the strongest suspect, but I don't think she was at the bowling alley this morning. Maybe I should ask Rey. Or her."

"Was this just a warning for you to stop nosing around?"

She swept her long hair off her shoulders and gathered it on one side of her neck. "Killing me would have been a more persuasive argument."

"You're tougher than you look, Ms. Sorensen."

*So are you, Howard.* With hours still left in the day, he looked like he'd interrogated every witness himself. Maybe he had. She stopped twisting her hair and put her hands in her lap. "I'm grateful you got there so soon. I relaxed just a little when I saw you. You got everyone working together."

"Separating the actors and crew from the tourists and park employees took time. Rey and the sheriff are obviously handling the investigation. I'm helping out and trying to check some boxes so we'll have our own comprehensive report." He glanced at his computer screen. "Max will want details."

"Did the sheriff do any gunshot residue tests?"

"Good observation. Rey hasn't shared that with me."

"Could any of the movie guns have fired the shot?"

"Deputies collected the weapons," Howard said, "but it's extremely unlikely."

"I didn't think it was an accident, at least after I got over the initial shock."

"The videos didn't show any actors pointing their guns in your direction."

"The CCTV, how could I forget?"

"Not much help." He leaned back in his chair. "We eliminated some people who were in camera range, but you can't see the shooter. At least from the quick views I saw this afternoon. One of Rey's detectives is working with our video experts going over the film with some new software, but I'm not optimistic."

"We have an amazing system. I know."

"Yes, but it's only as good as the placement of the cameras. The movie equipment, storage boxes, and a supply truck blocked cameras and created big holes in what we can see. Even the patio umbrellas blocked a partial camera view. All in all, only about two minutes of video is the critical time. Maybe they'll find something."

"The slug that missed me?"

He raised a hand and pointed a finger in the air. "There's another issue. The shot hit the pickup truck at an angle. It went through the windshield and out the open side window. There was an open path for the bullet to cut across the parking lot. They're looking for it."

*If I only knew who and why.*

"You need to take precautions."

She nodded. *Just what I was thinking.*

"You live in the Timeless Village high rise, right? I'd like to put someone on your floor—or in the building."

"It would be stupid of me to say no. But you know I have my own firearm."

"I'll put someone in the lobby. Call security and he or she will be at your apartment in seconds."

"Thanks."

"What are you going to do now, hunker down? I doubt that."

"Oh, listen." She put a hand on the edge of his desk. "Before I answer that, please promise me not to tell Lyle about this?"

"He's in California tracking down Tom Wyrick."

"I know, and I don't want this to get in his way." *He doesn't need to rush home to protect me.* She believed that you don't share a life with someone because you *need* them, because *he* can make you happy and complete. *It would be nice to work with Lyle on this, but he has his own struggles.*

"It might be in the news."

"If so, okay, otherwise I'll tell him in my own way."

# CHAPTER 68

L yle dialed Rob Napier. "I think I found it."

"You're at Premier Studios Backstage."

"Right." Lyle glanced around. The parking lot was half full. "I was nosing around in a bunch of secure offices and I saw a computer screen with PDE on it. I took a picture, but I had a problem and the computer screen came out bright white. It's way overexposed."

"What did it look like?"

"It was a diagram or something, but what got my attention was the PDE in the corner. It looked like a logo. The letters were angled or slanted, like italics. But I only saw it for a second."

"Sounds like ours."

"Yeah?"

"One of our designers created a new font for it."

"Something else makes me think these guys have our programs. It's a long story, but before Wyrick disappeared, I think he rode in my cab with two other guys. I just saw one of them here."

"No sign of Tom?"

"Not yet." *If he's still around.* Lyle wondered if Rob had the same thought. "I suppose there's no reason he would be here if they already have all our files."

"That depends on whether he's finished everything. If not, he'd probably be working with their programmers or engineers using their computer systems. I don't have even a concept of how long it would take him. Depends on how he tweaks it. He's very inventive."

"I know. He stole our secrets."

"That is true."

"I wish I could be sure about the PDE logo. Maybe I'll go back and see if I can find another PDE on someone's screen."

"You might not need to. Send me the photo. Tomorrow I can get someone to work on the image with Photoshop and see if we can bring up anything. I can call you in the morning."

As he was sending the photo to Rob, Lyle realized this was the first time he'd acknowledged to anyone what he'd been thinking. That Tom Wyrick was the bearded man in his cab that night.

Five thirty. Time to quit for the day. Lyle wondered if he could find a good seafood place close by. He fired up the Mustang, then realized he was still in uniform and his street clothes were in his locker. He preferred wearing his street clothes off duty, so he turned off the car and walked back to the costume locker area. He hadn't jogged in several days, but he got his miles in just criss-crossing Premier Backstage.

In the locker room a few employees dressed or undressed, a ride attendant, a tour guide, a celebrity lookalike. Lyle slipped off his shoes and had his uniform blouse half unbuttoned before he opened his locker. Lying on his neatly folded, button-down collar shirt was a human finger.

# CHAPTER 69

"Have you found Wyrick?" Kate asked.

"Not quite, but I think I picked up his trail. I'm pretty sure Premier Backstage is behind the theft."

"Wow. That's good news." She sipped her pinot gris. A strenuous workout, a shower, and wine helped ease the tension and soften the memory of being shot at. She felt restored to the point she could manage without sharing it with Lyle right now.

"I'm a maintenance man so moving around the park and sticking my nose in offices here and there is easy. People glance at you once and go back to work—while I'm looking over their shoulders." He explained seeing the PDE logo on a computer screen and mentioned the tough-looking character he remembered from a Nostalgia City cab ride.

"What's your next step?"

"I want to confirm this tomorrow, collect *some* kind of evidence —maybe even a hint that Wyrick is or was here—then I have to call the feds. But I want to be sure, first."

"It's not dangerous, is it?" *Says the person who almost took a bullet today.*

"I'll be careful."

*I hope he's not going to drag up what I said about being more careful than in Orlando.*

"I miss you, Kate."

"Yeah, me too."

"What's happening with *your* investigation?"

"It's clear as mud." She leaned back on her couch and clicked her phone to speaker mode. "My suspects list is still just a bunch of wild guesses with weak motives."

"What about Tori, the publicist?"

"Yeah, I should probably talk to her again. But I figured out why the director, Wes Moody, threatened me and told me to stop talking to people. It has nothing to do with Julian. He doesn't want me poking into his personal life because I think he's having an affair with Jana Osbourn."

"Is he—?"

"Married? Yes, many years. I saw him outside Jana's room in the hotel the other day, and then I remembered when she got stung by the scorpion Wes looked very upset. More than just concern for a leading star. He insisted on riding to the infirmary with her and left the rest of the cast and crew standing around. It looks like I'm identifying all the people who *didn't* do it."

"How about OJ?"

"No, he's on the golf course looking for the real killer."

"Still?"

*I can't be too bad off if I can share a dumb joke like that.* "Seriously, everyone who had a connection to Julian either has an alibi or little reason to kill him."

"A random killing?"

"Like road rage? I'll keep scribbling on the yellow pad until something makes sense."

# CHAPTER 70

"But you're sure you're okay?" Drenda said. "Last night you sounded a little shaky."

"It was close, but I'm okay."

They sat opposite each other at the PR Department's small conference table.

"And they don't know who shot at you?"

"Not yet, but it was probably someone who wanted me to stop investigating."

"Which means, of course, you're unequivocally committed to solving this."

"That's why I need your help again. I've got a strange feeling we can find out who killed Julian, and the answer's right in front of us."

Drenda pointed to the papers and photos spread out on the table.

"Maybe not literally, but it could be. I'm getting antsy." Kate shuffled through the video stills of the cars leaving the park the morning Julian was killed. "I've been trying to find a connection—"

"To the PAD disappearance and secret plans," Drenda said. "I've been considering this myself."

*Right on cue.* "You know about this?"

"It's not a well-kept secret. And Tom Wyrick is—or was—our resident theme-park savant."

Drenda wore a period-authentic outfit, as usual, accentuated by large, squared-off glasses—also period-authentic. The glasses contributed to her professorial appearance. She picked up a newspaper story about Julian's death.

"You've eliminated obvious suspects," she said, "including the odious psycho actor and others. We need to widen the category of suspect—and look for disparate motives."

"That's exactly my assumption," Kate said. "If this *is* related to PAD, why would someone kill an aging actor who has nothing to do with theme park rides and to my knowledge has never been to Nostalgia City before?" She flipped to an empty page in her yellow pad.

Kate explained security's confiscating his drone. "Did someone from PAD *think* he was spying and kill him?"

"And remain mute?" Drenda said. "We could talk to PAD employees."

"Howard and Rey have already done that and they're still puzzled."

"Let's back up and look at the crime analytically," Drenda said, "like the sheriff might do—or did. This news article gives a few details."

Kate knew the article almost by heart. "I know. They found the body. Used his IDs to identify him. Did an autopsy and interviewed the witnesses to help pin down the time of death. All that's mentioned."

"I wonder what they found in his hotel room," Drenda said. "He was staying here, correct?"

"I never thought of that. They would certainly have searched his room."

"Presumably they didn't find signs of violence, and that reinforced their hypothesis that Mr. Russo committed suicide."

"Funny," Kate said, "Rey never mentioned Julian's room. He did say there was no suicide note. Julian was staying in one of the garden rooms in the Traveler's Court Hotel." She found her phone on the table under several of the photos, picked it up, and dialed. "I'll ask Rey."

After a moment, she put the phone down. "Went straight to voicemail. I'll call back."

"I wonder *when* they looked at his room," Drenda said.

"That's a good question, too."

"Did you investigate Mr. Russo's background? Did he have a record? Was he in need of money?"

"I don't think he needed money. His agent said he had two other film projects pending. And I'm sure Rey would have told me if he had a criminal record."

"Maybe when you talk to Rey about searching his room, you can ask him," Drenda said.

"I know how we can find out about the search of his room at least—even if I can't get a hold of Rey."

"Right. And discover what else we might see?"

"You and I are on the same tack today," Kate said. "And since Julian had a garden room, we might have a nice clear shot from a camera."

. . .

Krystol Robinson wasn't on duty in the Control Center, but Kate saw Howard as soon as she and Drenda walked in. In a tie and white shirt with rolled-up sleeves, he talked to a uniformed security officer.

"Good plan," Howard said to the officer. He turned to Kate and Drenda. "Hey Kate, you're looking *oh-kay*."

"That good?"

"I mean—"

"It's fine. Thanks."

"Can't you use video to find out who nearly shot Kate?" Drenda asked without preface.

Howard described the problems with their limited camera views. "Deputies are working on it. I am too."

"I understand," Kate said, "but what we'd like to do today is look at some tapes from the day Julian was killed." She explained exactly what they wanted, and Howard asked an officer to set them up.

In the viewing room, Kate adjusted the tabletop screen so they could both see it.

"I wonder if sheriff's deputies looked at this tape," Drenda said.

"We should also be able to see when Julian left his room that morning."

The CCTV picture provided a close look at Julian's ground-floor room in a two-story hotel wing overlooking a desertscape garden.

Drenda clicked the mouse and moved the video ahead as they watched the time stamp. At 8:24 a.m. Julian appeared. He carried a dark drone that looked like the one Kate had retrieved for him after security confiscated it. They watched him walk around a corner toward the parking lot.

"So if we speed up through the morning and afternoon," Drenda said, "we should see deputies going in."

They fast-forwarded several hours seeing other guests come and go at lightning speed, no one stopping at Julian's. When Kate saw an unusual blur, she asked Drenda to stop. A maid pushed a cart up the walkway and stopped at Julian's door. She unlocked the door with a card and went in.

"That's funny," Kate said. "Wouldn't you think deputies would have called the hotel and asked them to leave Julian's room untouched?"

"They thought it was suicide, but they'd still want the room in the condition it was in when Mr. Russo left."

"Would you place the maid in her mid-twenties?"

Drenda nodded and they watched the time stamp click off the minutes.

Drenda sped up the video. "She's in there a long time."

Finally, the maid came out and started rolling the cart down the aisle. She didn't stop at any other rooms.

"Wait, back up," Kate said. "Does she look like a maid to you? Her outfit is okay but look at her hair. She didn't just brush it out like that herself."

"It's styled," Drenda said. "Expensive? Let's enlarge the picture. Very attractive and that's rather elegant makeup too, for someone cleaning toilets."

"She didn't clean the toilet. She just walked in with no cleaning tools and stayed there for fifteen minutes. Then she walked away without going in any other rooms."

"We shall print a picture of this *maid*."

"She was looking for something."

# CHAPTER 71

The finger was supposed to persuade him to back off, stay away, but it only convinced Lyle that Premier Studios Backstage was behind the theft of PDE.

When he had found the loose digit in his locker he wrapped it in a paper towel, got dressed, and screeched out of the park in his Mustang. In the morning he would get one more piece of evidence—even something small—then turn the whole mess over to the feds. Rey had been unable to trace the first severed digit, so Lyle wanted to substantiate his case with something other than a finger. It wouldn't be useful evidence unless the feds happened to find and interrogate three-finger Jack. The finger now rested in his hotel room's fridge.

He ate dinner in the hotel restaurant, talked to Kate on the phone without mentioning the finger, and slept with his 9mm.

In the morning, he picked up his phone to look for ideas. Another place to start. He clicked to the Premier Backstage employee's website. The first thing he saw was the events calendar. At noon the Chinese American Cooperative Trade Institute luncheon, hosted by Mrs. Lian Zhang, was meeting in the James Cagney Room. That was Mrs. Z. He couldn't resist. Would he find evidence there? Maybe. But he really wanted to get a load of what

Mrs. Z had to say. Maybe he could ask her a few questions after the meeting, like did she sell secrets to Beijing, and did she mislay a finger.

Lyle found the James Cagney Room after a few wrong turns. It was one of many meeting rooms in a convention complex styled to look like a 1930's Hollywood Boulevard theatre. How appropriate for Mrs. Z's meeting. He carried a tool bag he'd found in a janitor's closet. Two Chinese women sat at a table outside the meeting room checking off names and handing out name stickers. Lyle bypassed the women but was stopped at the door.

"Premier security," said a man whose dark suit and earpiece made him look like a secret service agent. "This is restricted. Only authorized staff. Are you approved here?"

"Beats me. They told me to get over here and make sure the sound system works."

The security officer looked confused. "You need to wait until I can get authorization."

Lyle looked at his watch. "Okay. If the meeting starts and Mrs. Z's mic doesn't work, she won't be complaining to me."

A man dressed as a server addressed the plainclothes officer. "Food service is having a problem with deliveries."

"Damn it," the officer said. He pressed a button on his lapel and started talking, presumably into his radio. All Lyle heard was, "a Code 26 meeting."

The officer waited, holding a hand to his ear. Lyle made a show of looking at his watch again.

"Hey, go ahead," the officer said.

The room held ten tables of eight with a head table and lectern. As the seats filled up, Lyle loitered in a corner and opened an electrical box on the wall. He looked inside and nodded as if everything looked in order. When he glanced back at the room, he saw a familiar face, and his brain kicked into overdrive. He looked back at the electrical box so he could think. He hadn't planned to hang around for the whole luncheon, but now he needed to be there at the end. In the meantime, he needed to find a quiet place for a talk.

He closed the electrical panel and carried his tool case to the first service door along the wall. A corridor to the left led to the kitchen. He turned right and followed the hall past a storage room lined with stacks of dining chairs and pushed through a door that locked behind him. He was in a public corridor. With plenty of time on his hands, he found a quiet corner of the building he could use after the meeting then made himself scarce for about ninety minutes.

He walked back into the James Cagney Room as Mrs. Z made her final remarks. A good-looking woman in her early fifties, she wore a gray suit and silver blouse with a Chinese pattern. She thanked everyone for coming and finished with words in Chinese. She could have been reciting from Mao's Little Red Book for all Lyle knew. He tried to look busy near the exit as the room emptied out. One of the last people to pass was FBI Agent Lisa Peng.

Lyle caught up with her outside the banquet room. He matched her stride but didn't stay too close.

"What are you doing here?" she said in an angry whisper.

"Probably the same as you are." He didn't look at her.

"You're interfering. You need to leave. I'm going to have you arrested." She managed to smile through clenched teeth.

"I need to tell you what I found out. Then it's all yours." The crowd had thinned out, and no one else was close enough to hear him. "Turn left up ahead and go all the way to the end. There's a hallway on the right with no cameras. I'll meet you."

Lyle stopped and went into an empty meeting room. He waited four minutes then walked back into the hallway. The meeting space he'd scoped out was a deserted alcove that used to hold a row of public telephones. A shelf along the wall and tell-tale outlines showed where the phones had been.

He walked into the alcove. No Agent Peng.

Doors at the end of the passage were labeled Men and Women.

Lyle chose Women. Agent Peng stood in the middle of the floor with a hand on one hip. Her dark suit and dark stare pounded a tune inside Lyle's head.

"You can't be here. You're jeopardizing a bureau operation."

Instinctively Lyle glanced at the three stalls.

"It's empty. Now, why are you here?"

"Looks like you were right about the Chinese connection. Is Mrs. Z going to use our ride secrets or sell them?"

"While you were chasing around in Florida, we were building a case here. Now if you have anything relevant, tell me, then leave."

*Ouch.* "You know why I'm here. I'm looking for Wyrick and our secrets. I know they're working on PDE here. I saw it on a computer monitor. I sent a photo of it to an engineer at Nostalgia City and he confirmed this morning it was one of ours. I haven't seen Tom Wyrick."

"We believe he was killed. He was living in a house here in the Valley, but he hasn't been seen recently."

"So the Chinese industrial spies killed him."

"Unlikely. They try to avoid violence."

*They smile when they pick your pocket rather than hit you over the head?* "What about the finger they left in my locker here yesterday? That's two now." He held up two fingers not realizing the irony until he looked at his hand.

"We believe Mrs. Z's husband is working behind the scenes with members of a Mexican gang. They're the ones with the fingers."

"They hand them out like a new father hands out cigars."

"I think you should take this seriously Mr. Deming. The Segura Cartel is ruthless. Whatever their involvement in this is, they kill indiscriminately."

"I figured that out with the second finger. You're a little late in telling me, Agent Peng."

"Don't call me that." She crossed her arms on her chest. "Is that all the information you have?"

"There's a Chinese guy named Sam. I met him when I was pretending to check out a power failure. He gave me the once over. He has PDE on his computer. And there's a short, stocky guy I saw in Nostalgia City before Wyrick disappeared."

"We know about Sam. He's Mrs. Z's cousin."

"So are you here to buy the PDE?"

"You need to leave, *now*. Leave the park. Are you actually working here or did you steal the uniform?"

"I'm an official, card-carrying maintenance man. But I'm free to leave and no one will miss me." He pulled out his prox card. "Here, this might come in handy. It gives you access to all but the most secure areas of the park. But I'd use it carefully. I have a feeling someone is tracking me with it. And of course, there are cameras everywhere."

She looked at him as if he'd just warned her that criminals were bad people. "Call the local Bureau office when you leave," she said. "Ask for Agent Futrell. He's at our command center. They'll want you to come in and tell your whole story."

"Should I give 'em the finger?"

# CHAPTER 72

S tephanie obviously doesn't understand.

"This is a picture of someone who pretended to be a maid and went through Julian's room right after he was killed," Kate said. "You don't recognize her?"

"No, who is it?"

"I don't know. That's why I'm asking. She must have been trying to find something."

Stephanie looked more wrung out than Kate felt. "You've got to stop this," she said. "You almost got killed."

The thermostat in Stephanie's suite must have been turned way down to keep the air chilly. Kate wished she'd brought a sweater. Filming had paused for lunch and Steph had come back to her room for a break. She made coffee in her kitchenette.

"This is my fault. I begged you to find who killed Julian, but now it's gone too far. Way too dangerous."

"I'm being careful. But we're very close. Whoever took a shot at me"—*and tried to run me into a ditch*—"has to be the person who killed Julian, or knows who did. We just need a break. You're sure this photo isn't anyone from Appropriate Brand Pictures?"

"I have to know like almost everyone. She's not one of ours."

"Then maybe she works at the park." Kate put the photo down on the table and stared at it. She heard the coffee pot give off a last wheeze. When she stepped toward the kitchenette something on a nearby closet shelf caught her attention.

"Steph, what's that?" She pointed to the closet.

"Oh, that belonged to Julian. I didn't know what to do with it so I just stuck it up there. It looks kind of expensive."

Kate reached up and pulled out a drone. "So this is what they look like folded up."

"He left it here one day."

"But this isn't the one you had before, the one I picked up from Howard."

"I guess he switched them or something. Every time I see him —saw him—he had a drone."

Kate set the drone down on the table and found the controller on the closet shelf. "Do you know how to work these things? Why don't we see what video he recorded with this."

"I've never flown one, but he connected it to my computer to show me videos."

Kate studied the body of the drone looking for connection outlets while Steph set up her laptop on the table. "It plugs in with a USB." Steph took the drone from Kate and inserted a plug in a tiny hole in the drone's body.

After a false start, she had the drone video on her screen. As the picture came to life, she and Kate saw an aerial view of a road cutting across open desert. The drone descended to circle cactus plants close to the ground then ascended, expanding a view of the desert, an intersection, and utility poles.

"I know where this is," Kate said. "It's not far outside the park."

As they watched, the drone descended and followed the street. Two cars parked by the side of the road came into view. The drone moved closer and Kate saw Alan Clappison and the mystery-maid woman remove a large boxy object out of the back of a light-colored SUV and carry it to another SUV. A shiny new black one. Before the couple pushed their load into the other vehicle, they suddenly looked up. Clappison said something. The drone didn't capture sound, but Clappison's scowl told Kate what she needed to know. Then she read his lips. "What the fuck?"

"That's Alan," Stephanie said. "What's he doing?" She paused the video and they studied the screen.

"This looks like our stolen ride model," Kate said. She pointed at the screen. "See the little cars going through the entrance? Julian caught them off guard. Probably by accident. She's giving Clappison the stolen model."

"He killed Julian," Stephanie shouted.

*Julian caught them stealing.* Kate looked away from the screen, then stood and walked to the coffee maker without seeing it. *The woman must have stolen the model. They're putting it into Clappison's car. This is the video the woman looked for in Julian's room. This is why he was killed.*

"This woman must have helped steal the secret ride programs, too," Kate said. "But what's Clappison's connection?"

"I don't know. He joined us just before we started shooting."

"Didn't you tell me your company leases sound stage space at some big Hollywood movie studio?"

"Premier Studios in Chatsworth." She clenched her fists. "I think that's where he's from. Maybe he also works for the Premier theme park."

"That's where Lyle is right now. At *their* theme park."

Kate looked back at the laptop screen and the expression on Clappison's face. *He's mad and he's scared. He and that woman stole the model—and our secret programs."*

"Julian caught him," Stephanie said, "and Alan had to destroy this video." She lowered her voice and her mouth barely moved. "He's going to pay."

"Before I came over here I got a text from Lyle. I didn't have time to call him back." She read Lyle's text again.

I'M DONE. THIS IS THE FED'S PROBLEM NOW. I
FOUND A CHILIDOG STAND (YUM!) SO I'M GOING TO
EAT THEN BAIL OUT. I'LL CALL YOU AFTER LUNCH
AND EXPLAIN.

# CHAPTER 73

Lyle walked across the park heading for the employee parking lot. Handing the mess over to the FBI would set him free. He could visualize himself back in his Nostalgia City cab, regaling tourists from Peoria with 1970s lore. But two items fogged his daydream. First, he wondered if the FBI's interest in safeguarding Nostalgia City's proprietary property might be secondary to catching Mrs. Z and rounding up everyone involved. Second, he was starving. He hadn't bothered to eat when he waited for Mrs. Z's luncheon to finish.

He wasn't sure what to do with the first concern, but he knew how to satisfy the second. He found what he was looking for at a remote corner of the park. A food stand in the shape of a colossal hot dog sat in the middle of a circle of tables and chairs. Lyle looked up at the menu painted on a broad squiggle of faux yellow mustard. Two chili dogs should be enough. He joined the queue to order and texted Kate. After he ordered he looked around at the people eating to see what the food looked like. Would there be enough chili on the dogs?

A young bearded man at the edge of the dining area was just finishing. He didn't have any food left in front of him, but he caught Lyle's eye. He was the same person he'd seen in his taxi that night in Nostalgia City. The same person whose photo still took up space in Lyle's cell phone. The person the FBI agent just told him was probably dead.

Tom Wyrick picked up his paper plate and cup, dropped them in a nearby trash can, and strolled away.

Lyle waited a few moments then followed. He still carried his tool kit. He'd planned to abandon it after lunch, but now it helped him look like a busy park employee.

Wyrick wandered toward a fake-front old-west building bordered by trees and bushes. He walked around the side of the building, through the bushes, and disappeared. Lyle followed and came to a wooden gate labeled "employees only." Damn, he'd given his prox card to Lisa Peng. Fortunately, the gate swung open with a push.

Through the gate, Lyle saw a row of rickety western store-fronts on one side of a paved drive and nondescript stucco build-ings on the other. One building stretched for hundreds of yards and bore G-3 near the roof. A wide, roll-up door was closed. Lyle watched Wyrick walk through a standard-size metal door next to it. It banged shut behind him. Lyle stood at the locked door, powerless to get inside—again.

Two employees sped by in an electric cart, and a few others, some dressed in various uniforms, walked down the sidewalk that separated G-3 from the adjoining building. A custodian fifty feet away walked in his direction. Lyle ducked around the corner near the door. He set down his tool bag and grabbed a hammer, screwdriver, and crescent wrench. Then just before the man walked by, he stood up with the tools in one hand and the tool bag in the other.

"Excuse me," he said to the custodian, "could you help?" He raised the hand that held the tools. "I can't get at my prox card. Could you get the door for me?"

"Sure," said the man with a smile. His prox card dangled from a tiny retractable spool pinned to his chest. He waved the card at a sensor and held the door for Lyle.

A corridor led straight ahead, and to the right, closed double doors. Lyle stashed his tools back in the bag and opened the double doors. He saw a ceiling rising twenty feet or more to metal roof supports. The wide room contained broken down electric carts, tractors like the kind used to pull luggage wagons at airports, tool benches, and other equipment. No sign of Wyrick, or anyone else.

He went back to the corridor and took a set of stairs to his right. It took him to a closed door on the mezzanine level. He turned the handle and pushed the door open, but it stopped half-way. Lyle stuck his head in and saw a loft area filled with stacks of dusty storage crates and boxes. One box kept the door from opening fully. Obviously, he wouldn't find Wyrick here, either.

He turned to go, then heard voices. He slipped sideways through the door then ducked. Open to the floor below, the loft was enclosed by a railing wall with periodic narrow openings. He peered at an angle through one of the gaps.

Below and twenty-five feet along the lower floor from him, two men sat at a casually arranged office area with tables and chairs. One of the men, a guy in his early 40s with thinning blond hair, sat on a tabletop and spoke to the other man. He paused when Sam—the guy Agent Peng told him was Mrs. Z's cousin—walked in.

"Hey Al. I was at a meeting in LA. When did you get in?"

"Last night. Sounds like we're getting close." Al sat with his back to Lyle, but his voice carried.

"Where's Wyrick?"

"He's way back in the lab," said a third man. Lyle recognized him as the short, bulky thug he'd seen the day before. From above, he looked even squatter.

"Go check on him," Al said. "And shut the door."

Lyle saw the man with no neck get up and walk below the loft then heard a door close. "I haven't had a chance to talk with you much," Al said. "Lian told me everything was going smoothly. That right?"

"The sale will be completed this afternoon." Sam sat in a chair where Lyle could see him. "Offshore bank transfers in the agreed-upon increments. The PRC developers—tech people—think this could have far-reaching applications. Civilian control, even military."

"Maybe Lian should have raised the price."

"Your wife knows what to do. We're going to make ten times more than from any other sale."

"I'm ready."

"Are you sure you're in the clear? Killing that actor was foolish, reckless."

"I didn't have a fucking choice. He caught us with his video drone transferring Wyrick's damn ride model."

"So you had to kill him?"

Al eased himself off the table and took a chair closer to Sam. Lyle moved over a foot to keep him in sight.

"Listen, that drone showed up out of nowhere. Then I saw Julian Russo down the road with a controller. Obviously, he knew who I was. I talked to him later and gave him a bullshit story about buying art from a local artist. I don't think he believed me, but he didn't know what to make of it. I tailed him for a while trying to decide what to do.

"Then the next morning I saw a news story about ride technology being stolen from the park and the disappearance of an employee. Someone who programmed rides. The story was out there. Julian would eventually figure it out. I mean the model looks just like a theme park ride with little cars and tracks. It would've jeopardized everything."

"But—"

"I saw him that morning getting in his car with his drone, so I followed him. He stopped at this canyon lookout."

"Are you so sure no one saw you?"

"There was no one else around," Al said. "I pulled into some bushes away from the parking area. I got out and watched him. He walked to the edge of the canyon with his drone and controller. Then he just set them down and stood there looking out, over the edge. He was a little guy. It wasn't hard to come up behind him and give him a shove."

Al paused and looked up in Lyle's direction.

Lyle stopped breathing. Sunlight flooded through a high window lighting up the office below while Lyle remained in shadow. Al squinted in the sun.

"It was a mistake," Sam said, "for Lian to get you that position with the film company." He folded his hands on his lap.

"I needed to keep an eye on everything. It was a good cover story. I didn't know Wyrick would be gone by the time I got there. Besides, I got the ride model, didn't I?"

"So, did you get the actor's drone?"

"Yeah, but the only thing on it was buildings and sky. We searched his room. The bastard had another drone, but that memory card was blank."

"So you *didn't* get the video?"

"No, but nothing's shown up in more than a week. We're good. The local sheriff said it was suicide, and I'm pretty sure I scared off that bitch who's been saying Julian *didn't* kill himself."

Lyle's head spun a variety of scenarios. *Kate didn't say anything about being scared off. Maybe he's lying to cover his ass. This guy killed Julian Russo. He must have helped Wyrick steal the plans. And he's Mrs. Z's husband!*

He needed to call Kate right away. But getting to Wyrick was also a priority. His best choice was to get the hell out and call the Feds.

His rapid thoughts were interrupted when he felt cold metal pressed against his neck.

# CHAPTER 74

What he lacked in stature, no-neck made up in girth and the Ruger semi-auto he pointed at Lyle. "You again, huh?" He took a step back keeping the gun pointed at Lyle crouched on the floor.

"Hey Al," he shouted. "You got a visitor up here."

In a minute, Al and Sam came through the door and saw Lyle. Sam spit out several words in Chinese.

Al ordered the captive to stand. He pulled out Lyle's wallet and cell phone. "He's from Polk, Arizona."

"This is not good," Sam said. "He was spying in my office yesterday. This could spoil—"

"It spoils nothing," Al said.

"What are you going to do?"

"You don't need to know. Just go back to your cozy office and forget about this. We won't worry about him until we know the sale is complete."

"If Lian ever found out what you've been doing with these guys," he looked at no-neck, "she'd throw you out. And you'd be lucky if that's *all* she did." Sam stood staring silently at Al for a long time, his thin lips pressed tight. After a moment he looked at the floor, then walked out.

Lyle could tell Al they needed to let him go because the FBI was ready to strike. But it might jeopardize the sting. And he was more afraid of Agent Peng than he was of no-neck or Al.

"Stick out your hands," Al said to Lyle. Al picked up a half-empty roll of duct tape from one of the stacked cartons and wrapped Lyle's wrists together. Then he looked around the room until his gaze stopped at an open wooden storage crate. The empty crate stood about a yard high and four feet square. "Get in," Al said.

"Why don't we talk about this?" Lyle said. "I'm sure we can work something out with Nostalgia City. Besides your wife's going to kill you if she finds out how you treat visitors."

Al backhanded Lyle across the face. He raised his bound hands to strike back, but no-neck jabbed the gun in his stomach. He stepped into the crate, laid down on his side, and curled his legs up.

Al placed the lid on the box. "We have to bend these tabs down. Look in his tool case for something."

Lyle heard the fasteners being banged down.

"When the deal's all done, you can haul this crate out somewhere," Al said. "Too bad there's not enough room in there for Wyrick."

Lyle heard one of them tightening the clamps and wondered if the crate was airtight.

# CHAPTER 75

Before she left Steph's hotel, Kate tried to call Lyle. No answer. She caught a shuttle bus then dashed to her car. While she drove to her apartment she called Joann.

"I need to fly to Southern California. Call and see if the corporate jet is available. If so, tell the pilot we need to land in the San Fernando Valley. Van Nuys is probably the farthest west. Then call a rental company and get me a car at Van Nuys or whatever airport we're flying to. Make sure it has GPS."

"Problems?"

"I know who killed Julian Russo and probably where our ride secrets are. Lyle's in California. He may know what's going on too, but I can't get hold of him. And call Howard. No wait, I'll call him. I think that's all I need. Thanks."

She called the security chief and found him in his office. "Howard, Alan Clappison killed Julian Russo. He's probably the one who took a shot at me, too. We've got an incriminating video that Julian shot of him loading the stolen ride model into his car. There's also a woman in the video. I think she works here. They had to be involved in stealing our secrets."

"Wait a minute. "How'd you see this video?"

"It was on one of Julian's drones. He left it in Stephanie Tyler's room. Steph didn't think anything about it because Julian always had a drone with him—as you know. We just looked at the video for the first time. Clappison looked crazy. Julian obviously surprised them."

"Where's the video now?"

"Steph has the drone that contains the video card. I told her to hold it for the sheriff. I'm afraid we both touched the drone, but we put it in a bag. It should still have Julian's prints on it, too. Obviously this needs to get to Rey. And Clappison is staying at the Decades Hotel. He may be in his room now."

"Have any idea who the female accomplice is?"

"I don't, but I have a picture of her." She explained the video of the mystery maid searching Julian's room. "Clappison killed him, then this woman searched Julian's room looking for the video. Steph can show you her picture, too."

"What are *you* going to do?"

"This Clappison guy is connected to Premier Studios Backstage. I'm pretty sure that's where our stolen programs are. Lyle's already there. I'm flying over this afternoon."

"There must be other people involved, too. This could be a shit show."

"Thanks for the colorful description."

"You sure you should fly over there? I'll call Rey and we'll alert the FBI. Rey'll have deputies over here ASAP to detain Clappison. I'll personally see he doesn't leave first. But why don't you leave the rest to the feds?"

"Clappison took a shot at me, so he's probably armed. Be careful."

She reached her apartment building and went over details in her head. Howard would take care of everything here. He'd identify the mystery maid, and the feds would be on the case.

By the time she'd finished throwing a few clothes and other items in a suitcase, Joann called to say the corporate jet was at her disposal. A rental car would be waiting for her at Van Nuys Airport.

"Max knows you're taking the jet," Joann said. "It was unavoidable."

"That's okay."

She tried Lyle's phone again. No response.

# CHAPTER 76

Was he breathing in sawdust or just sawdust smell from the wooden crate? At least it was mixed with oxygen. Lyle had tried curling up so he could push the lid with his back, but there wasn't room to turn over. He gnawed at the duct tape around his wrists. The adhesive coated his tongue. He banged his hip against the lid. The noise didn't alert anyone, nor did it loosen the lid.

His frustration level and exertion made him gulp the air. How long had he been there, an hour, two hours? No way to tell. He couldn't see his watch in the darkness. Relax, conserve energy.

Between breaths, he heard someone walking among the crates, tapping them. The next sound told him someone was prying the metal tabs off the lid. In a moment the cover slid aside. Lyle blinked at the light, but soon saw a face he recognized.

"Tom Wyrick, I presume."

Wyrick helped him stand up. He twisted his torso forward and back, side to side, did a knee bend, then using a trick he learned when he was on the force, Lyle drove his arms down toward his waist as he spread his elbows. The duct tape parted with a crack. Lyle groaned as he moved his arms in all directions.

"I overheard them say you're Lyle Deming and you work for Nostalgia City. Are you here to get PDE back?"

"And *you*." Lyle stretched his shoulders back, felt the tension, and relaxed.

"I'm not going anywhere. But *you* have to get out."

Lyle glanced out the window and saw that it was dark. He pulled the remaining strips of tape off his wrists. "You think your friends are going to be happy you let me go?"

He didn't wait for Wyrick to respond. He found his tool bag and poked into it with a screwdriver. He'd smeared heavy grease over the tools at the bottom to discourage foraging. Apparently, it worked. His 9mm Beretta was where he'd hidden it.

"We have a deal," Wyrick said, eyeing Lyle's pistol. "They owe me money for everything." He looked like Lyle imagined him from his photos. Long face, dark beard, determined eyes. Handsome in a way women would like. He looked trim and fit when he easily lifted the crate cover.

Lyle looked over the railing into the empty office below. "Where is everybody?"

"Some of them left. The rest are in the kitchen at the other end of the building."

"If you gave them the final PDE plans," Lyle said, "they won't want you around. What do you think they were planning to do with me? These guys have already murdered at least one person at Nostalgia City."

Wyrick's eyebrows came together, and he took a breath through his mouth. "Who got killed? Was it—"

"A movie actor who was in the wrong place at the wrong time."

"Hey, I had nothing to do with it. God, they killed somebody? I didn't know." He slammed his fist down on a storage crate, then froze wide-eyed at the noise he'd made. "I got trapped into this. Yeah, I know, I was wrong. I took the PDE. I've been working on it here. But I didn't think anyone would get hurt. I don't want this. Please, please get out of here."

"You're not safe either."

"I'll get out of this, and no one will get the PDE."

"They're selling it to China."

"Hey, I know." He lowered his voice. "But it won't happen."

*How in hell does he know about the FBI?* "What do you mean?"

Wyrick glanced at the railing and the open space above the office below. "We need to move."

. . .

Lyle replaced the lid on his would-be coffin. He carried his tool case and pistol and followed Wyrick across a hallway into an office that looked as if it hadn't been used since The Doors were topping the charts. Old blue metal desks and decrepit swivel chairs furnished the room. Windows on the opposite wall looked down on the empty transportation garage Lyle had peeked into earlier. Wyrick flipped on the lights and closed the door.

Lyle tested one of the chairs and decided it would hold his weight.

Wyrick sat on a desk in front of him. "No one is going to use the PDE. I sabotaged it. Unless you enter a few lines of code, it will self-destruct—and destroy everything. It will look like malware or maybe even a hardware problem. No one will know."

"Like a virus?"

"Something like that." He flipped his hands in the air to simulate an explosion. "It will wreak havoc on any system that runs it."

"Why did you steal PDE in the first place?" *As if I didn't know.*

"Hey, I was in trouble. I owed money. A lot of money."

"Gambling?"

"Yeah, I bet on sports."

Lyle remembered what his accountant friend had told him, how much Wyrick wagered. "Crossroads Casino?"

"Mostly."

"What else?"

"I did some online and used my credit cards. And I lost. Big time. But I found a way out."

"What was it?"

"Someone at work connected me with Al's people. She said they could help. They loaned me money. I just needed a little more. I knew I could win."

Lyle tried to affect a nonjudgmental expression. "And you lost. More than once?"

"I didn't *want* to steal anything from the park. They trapped me. What could I do?"

"So you took money from loan sharks and were surprised they wanted something in return?" *He's a genius? He must be missing parts of his brain that don't involve computers or math.*

"Hey, I couldn't pay them back. They said they just wanted a little information. But after I told them about the PDE, they wanted more. I didn't have a choice. I would have gone to jail."

"So you gave them the whole enchilada."

"They cancelled some of my debts and promised more, a lot more. The PDE project wasn't finished, so I came here to complete the work. But I told you I sabotaged it."

"Yeah, so you said."

Wyrick stared into space. Lyle tapped him on the leg. "Aren't your handlers going to be missing you about now?"

"Huh? No. I wander around all the time. As long as I stay close, they don't bother me."

"How do they know where you are?" Lyle immediately scanned the ceiling, cursing himself for the lapse.

"No. No, there're no cameras in the building." Wyrick lifted a pant leg to reveal an electronic monitor around his ankle."

"You can still get out of here. I have tools and I know how to get these things off. ICE used to use them sometimes on immigrants in Arizona."

Wyrick slid off the desk and wandered to the window. He stared into the garage below. "That's where they said they got it, from ICE."

*Did they steal it or have some other arrangement?* "Uh-huh."

Wyrick turned around. "You don't understand. I have a deal. I need to wait. After the sale, they're supposed to pay me and I'm on my way."

"Where?"

"I don't know."

"What happens when the program self-destructs?"

"It won't happen instantly. I'll have time to get the money and get away."

"You think they're going to pay you off and let you go? Do you know your buddy Al is working with a Mexican drug cartel? The guy with no neck is probably one of them. They're going to bury you in the desert, same place they planned to put me."

"They've threatened me before. The guy you call no-neck handed me a human finger in a Nostalgia City cab." He groaned and his face became an even paler shade of white, but his look said his scientific brain might finally be kicking in. "Damn, shit. I gotta think." He paced up and down the window, then walked back.

Lyle said, "Could you restore the entire PDE concept, plans, and program—everything that's involved—for Nostalgia City?"

A blank gape was all Wyrick offered for seconds. Then he nodded slowly. "I saved everything in the cloud. Encrypted. No one can get at it."

"Okay. I'm working for Max Maxwell. Maybe if you return the entire PDE, it might persuade him not to press charges. You'd still have to answer to law enforcement, but Max has deep pockets. And the sheriff could protect you from the cartel." *Maybe, might, could. Chances of all this happening are slim, but this guy's genuinely trapped, even if it is his own fault. It'd be much better for everyone if I get him out of here walking, rather than carried out in a box. Better for me, too.*

Wyrick looked at his ankle. "You can really take this off?"

"Yes, but the problem is, as soon as the monitor is off, it'll signal whoever's tracking you. We'll have to run like hell."

# CHAPTER 77

Lyle could still leave Wyrick's monitor in place when they bailed out. Of course from what Wyrick told him, that would alert the bad guys because after dark his perimeter to roam included just the building. Removing the monitor would alert them too, but without the monitor, once they were hotfooting it out of the park they couldn't be followed—electronically, anyway.

As eager as Lyle was to leave, he studied the monitor. It was a complicated model, not one of the simple ones held on by a thin rubber strap. He knelt while Wyrick sat on a chair with his feet flat on the floor. Lyle set his tool bag on his left, the Beretta to his right. The job was to examine the anklet carefully and test to see how tight it was without triggering the alarm. Once that happened, Wyrick needed to be ready to run.

"I can't believe how much I screwed everything up," Wyrick said. "My fucking gambling. I thought I could win it back. I always thought that. Damn." He moved his foot.

"Whoa. You want to set off the alarm? It wasn't your gambling addiction that got you into this. It was borrowing money."

"Hey, I know. Funny how when you owe money they always seem to find you, don't they?" Wyrick's voice dropped, and he spoke in a monotone. "I borrowed a lot, and of course I lost it. I just needed a little luck to win it all back. Can I tell you about it?"

"No."

"So, this one weekend my girlfriend was working double shifts. I went out for a drink after work with Allison, someone I work with. I think she really invited *me*. It wasn't a big deal. We got to talking. I had a couple of drinks. I told her I lost a lot of money. I said I could win it all back if I just had a little more. She told me she might know a way I could get money. Then we had sex. It just happened."

Lyle stopped fiddling with the ankle monitor, looked up at Wyrick.

"Hey, it was just like that," he said, his voice still flat. "Of course to *get* the money she said I needed to give her some details of the PDE. But I thought my luck would change. I would win it back."

*Allison Byers recruited Wyrick. He was an easy mark. I wonder if she got recruited herself by Chinese nationals when she was working in Silicon Valley.* "So you had sex with Allison and gave her all our secrets."

"No. It wasn't about that. We didn't do it again. I felt guilty. I loved my girlfriend Sarah. Allison blackmailed me. I told you that. Not only would I go to jail, she said she'd tell Sarah about our weekend sex. I was trapped."

Lyle glanced up again at Wyrick.

No longer reliving his mistakes, Wyrick raised his voice. "Hey, I was jammed up. No choice. But I really tried to stop them. I told one of their guys I needed a model of the ride. It was stupid. Why would I need that? But they didn't know. I wanted them to get caught."

"But they didn't." *Except by Julian Russo, and that cost him his life.*

Wyrick's shoulders slumped, everything sinking in.

Lyle shoved all his tools except one back in his tool bag. He picked up his semi-auto and stuck it in his belt behind his back.

"How many guys in Al's gang—the cartel, or whoever—are here?"

"I've seen four or five together, not counting a security guard who's in on it."

"Well, we're ready. As soon as I take this off, we run."

Wyrick stood and stretched. Lyle bent over his ankle.

"Ready?"

With a dull pop, the ankle monitor hit the floor, and Lyle pushed Wyrick out the door and down the stairs. They dashed out of the building.

"Back to the park," Wyrick said. "We'll blend in."

*A tourist and a maintenance man, sure. At least they're less likely to shoot at us in a crowd. Is the park still open?*

Lyle didn't hear the gun report, but when they pushed open the wooden gate, a corner of the fence exploded in a shower of splinters.

# CHAPTER 78

Kate watched a bearded man tear out around the corner of an old-west building with Lyle right behind him. She stood beside a closed hot dog stand as they dashed by. Immediately, she saw a man running after them carrying a stubby rifle with a long barrel. When the weapon jerked in the man's hands, she saw tiny sparks flying but only heard a loud clicking. It was an assault weapon with a silencer. His shots missed, and the man stopped to take better aim.

He never fired again because a bullet from Kate's SIG Sauer pistol hit him in the chest. He fell over, toppling metal chairs with an echoing crash. *Shoot at Lyle? No you don't.* Two other men armed with pistols appeared around the corner. Kate put two slugs in the wall next to them, and they dived backward.

Given a moment of safety, Kate sprinted after Lyle. She hid her gun in her purse but held onto the grip. She could feel her hand shaking, either from the 9mm recoil or the sight of the gunman crashing to the ground clutching his chest.

Premier Backstage was closing for the evening, and tourists were fortunately scarce in this corner of the park. The old-west storefronts and boardwalks were probably the scene of regular shoot-outs, so maybe guests took the shots in stride. That's what she hoped. But as she rushed out of the frontier town and toward a modern roundabout, the crowds grew. Better for her and Lyle to blend in, not good for bystanders. The guy Lyle followed turned right around the circular street and slowed. Kate caught up. Lyle looked over his shoulder—probably expecting to see gunmen after him. She offered him a wan smile.

"I heard shooting," he said. He grabbed the man in front of him by the back of his shirt and pulled him to a stop.

"A guy with a silencer on an Uzi or something was after you."

"But I heard shots."

Kate opened her purse slightly. Lyle glanced inside. "That guy won't be following us," she said. "But there're others."

"Thanks—we both thank you. Kate, this is Tom Wyrick."

*Very much alive.* "I thought so. We need to keep moving. There were at least two other guys with guns. They can't be far away."

Wyrick stared up at Kate.

"You call the cops?" Lyle asked.

"Of course, and Howard called the FBI."

"They're here already," Lyle said in Kate's direction. "But let's not wait. I know a good place to hide over here."

Kate glanced over her shoulder again. "Lead the way."

She followed Lyle and Wyrick past the entrance to a sci-fi movie ride. Teens and children milled about or stood in line staring at cell phones. The biggest excitement of these kids' lives could be fifty yards away—and gaining. Kate moved forward at a speed-walk pace and looked for signs of law enforcement—and their pursuers. Too many people could get hurt. She remembered the confusion, panic, and blood she'd seen after a ride accident during one of her first days at Nostalgia City. She didn't want to see it again.

"This way," Lyle said. He pushed Wyrick left. A circuitous dirt path through shrubs and brambles led to a stand of trees. They followed the path through a narrow opening, and it became a yellow brick road.

"The Land of Oz," Kate said almost to herself, and they ducked under low boughs and entered the ghostly forest.

"This isn't as simple as it looks," Lyle said. "The brick road winds through a maze. I went through this yesterday."

After a few minutes, Lyle led them to a narrow path that ended in a deserted circle of looming, cartoonish trees.

"How in the hell did you find us?" Lyle asked.

"Your text. You said you were going for chili dogs. That giant hot dog is the only place in the park that sells chili."

"Even still—"

"I found out who killed Julian. His name is Alan Clappison. He works here. I tried calling you for hours and there was no answer—"

"So here you are." He gave her a quick but tight hug.

Wyrick wandered inside the circle of trees, peering out through branches.

"This guy Clappison," Lyle said, "muscular, thinning blond hair, about forty?"

Kate nodded.

"They call him *Al* here."

"He took a shot at me the other day."

"What?!"

"It was at the movie set. The actors were firing blanks, and someone shot out the windshield of the car where I was standing."

Lyle grabbed her by the shoulders. "Kate."

"Obviously I'm okay. By the time I figured out it was Clappison, he had already left to come here."

He clutched her shoulders tighter. "But Kate."

"I know. I didn't want to worry you. You had enough going on. It's over and I'm okay."

They both looked up when a noise from somewhere brought them back to the present. They fell silent but heard nothing more.

Lyle said, "Clappison's married to Mrs. Z."

"Who?"

"Lian Zhang, she's the one who's selling our secrets to the Chinese. In fact, the deal is probably done by now." He lowered his voice. "The FBI is on to them. I was hoping to drag our genius here back to Arizona with the PDE plans. He's a gambler and was in debt to Al and his buddies. That's why he sold out. That and a little extracurricular sex with a hot PAD employee named Allison Byers."

Kate fished in her purse and pulled out a folded photo.

"That's her. How did you—"

"I'll explain later. Don't you think we need to—"

"Wait a sec." Lyle pointed to Kate's purse.

"How in the hell did you get that piece into the park?"

"They should have more women screening visitors. When I was in the security line, I had trouble with the laces on my tennis shoes." She pulled down the zipper of her form-fitting blouse. "I just bent over to fix my shoe and the security guards were so eager to help me. And I was holding up the line, so they got me through quickly. I gave them a big thanks."

She zipped up her blouse and pulled out her phone. "We need to call the police or the FBI."

"The FBI has a command post nearby. I need to call Agent Futrell."

"Unnecessary, Mr. Deming." Agent Lisa Peng stepped into the clearing followed by two other agents. She held a pistol. "The video surveillance is excellent here. Even in the Oz Forest. We saw the guys chasing you. Agents are running them down."

Wyrick withdrew into the trees as the FBI agent spoke. "I think this is the man you're really looking for," Kate said. She nodded toward Wyrick.

One of the other agents holstered his weapon and pulled out handcuffs. Wyrick resisted momentarily, then surrendered his wrists.

As the cuffs clicked closed, machine gun fire shredded the tree branches above the clearing.

# CHAPTER 79

Lyle pulled Kate to the ground. *Where is the machine gun?* Another blast slammed into a tree trunk. Lyle crawled through an opening in the trees and Kate followed. They moved on hands and knees. Although the forest undergrowth felt synthetic, it nonetheless scratched their arms and faces as they moved away from the automatic weapons fire.

After a few minutes, Lyle felt harder ground under his knees. Yellow bricks. He got to his feet but crouched, Kate next to him. Another machine gun blast was followed by sporadic single shots. Then quiet.

He wasn't sure which direction to take on the brick road. He pulled out his gun and looked in one direction, then the other.

"Let's try this way," Kate said.

"Clear." The loud voice boomed from somewhere behind them.

Soon Lyle and Kate reached the edge of the make-believe forest. Ahead, a prehistoric version of a merry-go-round with dinosaurs instead of horses sat motionless. To the left, they saw the entrance to a cartoon-themed dark ride. Small groups of guests hurried past, making their way to the exits.

"Obviously everyone's getting out," Kate said. "But the gunfire has stopped."

"I hope Wyrick is okay. He's got the secrets in his head."

Kate gave him a shove. "And we wouldn't want him to get *hurt* either."

"Right, of course. He's a little messed up. I can see how being a genius doesn't make you smart. I'll tell you all about the poor guy when—"

He looked across the terrazzo and concrete midway and saw a blond man darting along in the shadows, looking over his shoulder as he went. "Kate," he whispered, "That's him."

"Yes."

Lyle looked around. No cops or agents chased him. "Let's get him." He tucked his gun out of sight and they moved after the skulking figure.

Clappison trotted around the edge of the carousel. Lyle and Kate jogged to keep up. When he passed under a streetlight, he turned and looked directly at them. Lyle saw a scowl of anger and self-preservation. Clappison paused for a second and looked in all directions, then he dashed to the entrance of the Twisted Knights Ride, a soaring, fanciful version of a medieval castle. He ran through the empty maze of railings where guests normally queued. Lyle and Kate closed on him. He leaped around the last barrier, passed a ride attendant, and jumped into the front row of a car shaped like an ancient horse cart painted in electric orange and red.

"Why's he going in there?" Kate said as they maneuvered through the railings. "The ride will dump him out at the exit and we'll be waiting."

Lyle watched Clappison's car move through the darkened castle entrance. "Maybe there's a way out inside, and he won't come out the regular exit. I'll go get him." He threw himself over the last railing. "But watch the exit, just in case. Be careful."

Kate nodded and reached in her purse.

Lyle turned back to the ride.

A young man in a bright tunic and faux chain mail looked up at Lyle. "Are you going to ride? The park is closing."

Lyle ignored him and jumped into a car. He felt a safety bar move down and press into his lap. Then he looked up to see steep, twisting tracks extending through the top of the castle. *No, no. This is a roller coaster.*

His car glided forward. Lyle gripped the safety bar with both hands. He ducked—unnecessarily—as he passed under low-hanging portcullis spikes at the castle entry. He didn't need the high-pitched cackles and clanking chains he heard in the passageway to make his stomach contract. His car moved along a murky tunnel, then turned sharply right. A giant suit of armor with a ghastly grin teetered on a ledge above him. As it toppled toward the tracks, Lyle's car scooted just under the noisy metal avalanche.

Another turn brought him into a torture chamber. Low moans alternated with a dull click, click, click. To Lyle's right, a grotesque leather-clad figure pulled the lever of a mechanism attached to the arms and legs of a poor soul tied to the rack. The victim, a grinning purple gremlin from some animated movie, looked more tickled than tortured, but Lyle was in no mood for fun-house humor. Two other cartoon characters hung from chains on the wall, their arms stretched to impossible lengths.

Lyle's car suddenly whooshed down a chute. It slowed as it entered an oak-beamed great hall. Voices filled the room. On one side of the tracks, men and women of all sizes and shapes talked and ate at a ridiculously long banquet table that stretched almost to infinity. At the end of the hall, Lyle saw the tracks tilting upward—probably leading to the *twisted* part of the Twisted Knights Ride. Lyle hung on.

On the other side of the great hall, a king, who looked like a cartoon mascot for a breakfast cereal, held court. The moving figures of knights, jesters, and ladies in iridescent gowns appeared to be a mixture of robots and projections. Some moved with erratic motions, others walked and gestured smoothly—like the man in modern clothes who walked across the king's court toward a stone doorway. Clappison looked over his shoulder, then ducked into the passageway. Somehow, he had climbed out of his car.

# CHAPTER 80

Kate didn't know where to find the ride's exit. Typically, the exit was *somewhere* near the entrance. She walked to the left of the entry queue, around a fanciful castle turret, and saw the jutting framework of roller coaster tracks. The tracks extended beyond the top of the castle, then plummeted into a series of spiral turns and dips. An empty car flew through a curve and disappeared around a corner. Her visceral reaction was probably nothing like what Lyle's would be.

Nothing she could do now—except find the exit and be ready for anything. Two teenagers and an older couple hustled past her, otherwise the park looked empty. She reversed course, passed the ride entrance, and walked around the castle wall. *The exit has to be around here somewhere.*

"Ma'am? Excuse me, but the park is closed. The exit gate is this way."

The uniformed security officer pointed in the opposite direction to which she was headed.

"I'm waiting for my friend. He's on this ride."

The security man stood four or five inches shorter than Kate. He knitted his eyebrows as he looked up at her. "The ride is closed."

She debated about what to tell him and decided on the truth. "I know what's going on at the park. We talked to the FBI. We're witnesses—victims, really. My friend is in there with one of the gunmen. Can you call for help?"

"Sorry, my radio's not working." He tapped the black rectangle on his belt. On the other side of his belt he wore a holstered semi-auto. "Law enforcement is locking everything down. That's why you have to leave. It's dangerous."

"I'm not leaving until he comes out." She walked past him and around the edge of a rampart. The ride's exit ramp lay ahead.

The officer followed. "Okay ma'am. We'll wait here until he comes out."

The ramp led from a stone arch down to pavement level. Kate stood near a rock wall and stared at the exit.

■ ■ ■

Lyle pushed on the safety bar, trying to squeeze out. He struggled to lean sideways but couldn't get his thigh past the bar. Then he pulled his weapon out from behind his back and gained wiggle room. His car moved along the floor of the king's court, but in twenty feet he'd be on the roller coaster up-slope. He set his weapon on the seat and used both hands to pull up on the bar as he worked his legs out. Once one thigh—then the rest of his leg— was free, he had room to pull his other leg out. But as he stood up, he saw the last few feet of open floor space. He leaped, landed on one foot, and held his arms out for balance. He stood up in time to see his car move up the slope—with his Berretta on the seat.

The escape from his car had taken only seconds. He turned to the stone doorway Clappison had ducked into. Dancing around a gyrating jester, he almost fell over a robotic woman kneeling before the king. "Sorry, m'lady."

Did Clappison have a gun? Lyle hadn't seen one when Mrs. Z's young husband ran ahead of them across the midway. Maybe he was unarmed. Lyle stepped into the doorway. Before his eyes could adjust to the darkness, a muzzle flash and gunshot sent him reeling backward. *Okay, he's got a gun.*

If Clappison had a way out through the castle, he'd probably make tracks. He wouldn't have been running if he didn't know the police and FBI were swarming all over. Judging by the distance to the muzzle flash, Lyle figured the dark passageway ahead of him was only about thirty feet long.

The son of a bitch had shot at Kate and locked him in a coffin. He would stop him.

He looked around for a weapon. One of the motionless knights casually held a wicked-looking two-handed sword. *I could slice and dice Clappison with this thing.* He grasped the sword. Too light. He tapped it on the ground. It wasn't metal, probably fiberglass, but heavy enough to inflict injury if he got close enough.

Back at the entryway, he picked up a tin tankard and threw it into the hall. It echoed as it tumbled along the ground, followed by silence. Before he had time to think, Lyle charged through the hallway, the sword in front of him. At the end of the passage, the medieval ambiance gave way to pipes, wires, and rough plaster walls. Floodlights at intervals lit the passageway, and a catwalk above clung to one wall. Clappison walked at a modest clip twenty yards in front of him. After a few steps, it became obvious that chasing him down the narrow passage with a fiberglass sword was a suicide mission.

Ahead, Clappison turned into a doorway. Lyle remained cautious and listened as he crept forward. Before he'd gone halfway to where he'd last seen his quarry, Clappison stepped back into the main corridor. He looked at Lyle and laughed, then raised his weapon.

The gun blast filled the narrow passageway. Clappison doubled over, dropping his pistol. On the catwalk above, Lyle saw Sam holding a shiny revolver.

Sam motioned with the gun down the corridor. "You can get out that way."

As Lyle passed by, Sam remained motionless. So did Clappison. Blood flowed below his neck.

Once outside, Lyle looked up and saw the rollercoaster scaffolding. He knew Kate would be waiting at the ride exit, so he hoofed it around the perimeter of the make-believe castle. When he rounded a rampart, he saw Kate standing off to his left at the end of the exit ramp. A security officer stood a few steps behind her, his eyes trained on the exit door. As Lyle got closer, he recognized the officer—the rat-faced guard who'd hassled him before. Was he the security officer who Wyrick said was in league with Clappison?

He slowed his pace and crept up behind the officer. When he was a half-dozen strides away, the ride stopped, the jangling of the rollercoaster replaced by silence. The officer casually unsnapped the strap over his semi-auto and pulled out the gun. Lyle moved forward. Kate must have sensed something because she turned, and the officer pointed his weapon at her. At the same time, Lyle reached for the guard, seized his right arm, and slammed it into the rock wall. The gun fired a wild shot then fell to the ground.

Kate jumped back from the report, then picked up the pistol. Lyle pinned the officer's arm behind him and thrust him, chest first, against the wall.

"You bastard," the guard said. "You should have stayed in your box."

# CHAPTER 81

I s this a celebration lunch, or what?" asked Rey Martinez as he slid into a booth at the NC executive dining room. "Pretty fancy."

Lyle leaned over and nudged Kate. "I only get to come in with *her*."

"I wore a suit today special. I see you're dressed up too, Lyle."

"He is," Kate said. "He's wearing something other than jeans."

She finally started to feel relaxed and herself again a week after shooting a man and after days of talking with prosecutors, private attorneys, cops, and federal agents. She hoped Lyle was shedding his stress, too.

"This lunch is just for the three of us," Lyle said. "Max is throwing a big employee blow-out at the end of the week to celebrate getting our ride secrets back. But no one is supposed to know the reason for the party."

A server appeared with menus and took their drink orders.

"One of the reasons we invited you today," Kate said when the server left, "was because Lyle—"

"Was because I wanted to apologize again," he said. "I put you in jeopardy when I was stressed. I made a bad decision—I hate that phrase—but I did it because it was the easiest thing for me at the time."

"As it turned out, we didn't need the evidence at Wyrick's condo, anyway."

"I'm grateful for that but more grateful for a friend like you."

Kate looked at Lyle out of the corner of her eye. She wondered if this was hard for him to say. Maybe not.

"You're an original Lyle." Rey looked at him and nodded. "And still a friend."

"I've been thinking about taking a meditation class," Lyle said. "It helps you focus on the present moment even better than this." He held up his right wrist, displaying his rubber band. "I've actually tried meditating once or twice. You just relax and be calm."

"*You* seem calm, Kate," Rey said. "You alright?"

"I'm getting there. Not working much this week. Been getting a lot of sleep."

"I always give my officers time off when they're involved in a shooting. Are you going to be in the clear?"

"Yes she is," Lyle said. "Self-defense. The guy she shot was firing a submachine gun."

"He's recovering, thank goodness," Kate said. "That makes it easier."

"I know Howard is also glad things are relatively back to normal," Rey said. "He was stressed over the theft, too."

"And it wasn't his fault," Lyle said. "He took it hard. But now he's got the perimeter fence, more cameras, and everyone is much more security conscious."

Kate nodded in agreement. *This week, at least.*

The drinks arrived and Lyle asked the server to give them time to decide.

Rey lifted his drink. "So everyone's doing better."

"Except Al Clappison," Lyle said. "He blackmailed Wyrick, murdered Julian Russo, and was running with the Mexican mob.

Mrs. Z would have been humiliated and would have wanted to kill him."

"So Sam did it for her," Kate said. "I wonder if they'll ever find him."

"The arrest of Mrs. Z and her associates seems to have tarnished the good name of her organization," Lyle said. "Agent Peng told me the FBI had been watching the Chinese American Cooperative Trade Institute for some time. They should nickname this the saguaro case." He looked at Rey. "Its acronym?"

"You mean CACTI?"

"Or they could have just called it the prickly pear."

"There ya go," Rey said. He looked at Kate. "Is the filming going ahead okay at the park?"

"Yes, Stephanie is seeing to that. There will be more unpleasant publicity out of all this, but it will no doubt generate interest in *Murder for No Reason*. Tori, the film's publicist, will be happy."

"Max won't be," Lyle said.

"But people are still flocking to see Psycho Sievers, so Max can't complain about the bottom line."

"What about Carlos?" Kate asked. "You didn't tell me if Pamela Quarrie was going to give him his job back."

Rey looked from Kate to Lyle and back.

"The guy helped me out," Lyle said. He explained how the former NC employee had phonied up a job application so Lyle could snoop as a maintenance man. "After Mrs. Z had her fall from grace, somehow the word got out that Carlos had helped. But instead of getting sacked, he got a promotion. The park's president was eager to show he knew nothing of his exec VP's machinations, so he gave Carlos the job he wanted. I talked to Pamela anyway and she's going to offer Carlos a job. So he'll have a choice."

"A happy ending," Kate said.

Rey looked up from his menu. "You can't say the same for Mr. Wyrick and Ms. Byers."

"What's the latest?" Lyle asked.

"Allison Byers is up to her neck in everything, but she *still* claims she didn't know Russo's death was a murder until much later. We'll see. As for Wyrick, since he restored the park's closely guarded secrets—"

"Not *too* closely guarded," Lyle said.

"Right." Rey frowned. "As I was saying, he's going to testify against CACTI and everyone else involved in the espionage, so it will be up to federal prosecutors. I doubt he'll *walk*, but I've been surprised before."

"His former girlfriend might wait for him," Lyle said.

Rey gave him a puzzled look.

"The redhead who didn't really swallow the finger."

"Oh yeah." Rey smiled and sipped his drink.

"He never told me about the finger," Kate said. She smirked and shot a quick glance at Lyle. "He says he didn't want to worry me."

"You don't mean the finger in his cab, do you?"

"No," Lyle said, "there was another one."

"So tell him," Kate urged.

Lyle explained finding the severed finger in his locker at Premier Studios Backstage. "It was a warning like they'd given Tom Wyrick. That's what this particular mob does."

"If we'd only known then."

Kate elbowed Lyle. "Go on."

"Well, okay. After the gun battle at Premier Backstage, after Sam killed Clappison, we obviously went through the questioning routine with the police and FBI. As a result, we didn't get back to the hotel until about nine or ten in the morning. The hotel staff was waiting for me. They called the police. Officers knocked on the door just as I was getting undressed."

"Are you still talking about the finger?" Rey said.

"I'm getting there. So they come charging in the room and want to know what I was doing with a dead finger. Could you have a *live* finger? That'd be something to see."

Kate looked at him. "*Lyle.*"

"Yes, yes. Apparently, when the maid cleaned my room, she checked the fridge. Are they supposed to look in there before you check out? Anyway, she picked up the finger. I don't know what she thought it was, a sausage? When she realized it wasn't from a restaurant doggie bag, she started yelling. Someone called the manager."

"So what did the local cops do?"

"They asked me where I got the finger. How could I explain all that? Before I told them the story, I peeked in the fridge and the finger was still there. The hotel manager wanted the cops to catch me red-handed.

"I had a great time telling the LAPD officers the story. Of course they thought I was certifiably nuts. But I encouraged them to check with their superiors."

"That sounds like you." Rey set his menu down. "Okay, I'm hungry. What looks good?"

Lyle looked at Kate. "Finger sandwiches?"

# NOTE FROM THE AUTHOR

Writing is a solitary occupation; that's why messages from readers are so special. I have some on the wall in my office. Hope you enjoyed reading this book. If so, please consider writing a short review on your favorite book site. It helps.

If you'd like to contact me or would like more information on my other books, please visit my website at https://baconsmysteries.com.

# ACKNOWLEDGMENTS

Many people helped make the book a reality. I'm indebted to critique group members and beta readers: Mike Klapheke, Faith Cartier, Mary Adler, Rene Averett, Nicole Frens, Russell Jones, Brian Cave, David Hagerty, Ruth Myers, Evelyn Nettleship, Marsha Oest, Katie Markofski, and Andrea Lenz.

For technical areas covered in the book I thank Washoe County Medical Examiner Dr. Laura Knight, with whom I had an interesting talk about severed fingers, and long-time Hollywood actor turned writer Clive Rosengren. Conversations with Jim Francis, a corporate security expert with a five-star CV, were immensely valuable. His expert advice helped me improve Lyle's corporate undercover work. Of course any errors belong to me, not the experts I consulted.

Thanks to my editor Christel Hall for her diligent work on my manuscript and to my daughters, my friends and my fellow writers for their encouragement and support during the dark days of the pandemic.

As always, I thank my wife for her love and for putting up with me.

# ABOUT THE AUTHOR

Mark S. Bacon began his career as a Southern California newspaper police reporter, one of his crime stories becoming key evidence in a murder case that spanned decades. After working for two newspapers, he moved to advertising and marketing when he became a copywriter for Knott's Berry Farm, the theme park down the road from Disneyland. Experience working at Knott's formed part of the inspiration for his creation of Nostalgia City theme park.

Before turning to fiction, Bacon wrote business books including one that was printed in three editions, four languages, named best business book of the year by *Library Journal*, and selected by the Book of the Month Club and two other book clubs. His articles have appeared in the *Washington Post, Cleveland Plain Dealer, San Antonio Express News, The Denver Post, Orange Coast*, and many other publications. Most recently he was a correspondent for the *San Francisco Chronicle*.

*Death in Nostalgia City* is the first book in the Nostalgia City mystery series. It was recommended for book clubs in 2019 by the American Library Association. Second book in the series, *Desert Kill Switch*, was the top fiction entry in the 2018 Great Southwest Book Festival. Bacon is working on mystery #5

Bacon is the author of flash fiction mystery books including, *Cops, Crooks and Other Stories in 100 Words - Revised Edition*. He taught journalism as a member of the adjunct faculty at Cal Poly University – Pomona, the University of Nevada – Reno, and the University of Redlands. He earned an MA in mass media from

UNLV and a BA in journalism from Fresno State. He lives in Reno with his wife, Anne, and their golden retriever.

# THE NOSTALGIA CITY MYSTERY SERIES

Made in the USA
Columbia, SC
25 January 2024

30974589R00212